Janice Camerson. Known
ter of a late professor of L
Hawaiian customs. Janice has returned to Hawaii to act as the advisor for a movie based on a novel she wrote about her own failed romance.

Lily Wu. A lovely young woman who is skilled in many areas—from detection to mah-jongg—and whose family adopted the adult Janice and keeps a room for her in New York's Chinatown.

Luther Avery. An architect, he offers to put up Janice. He has allowed some native Hawaiians to build a village around the ruins of an ancient temple on his land.

Julia Avery. Luther's wife, she has recently become gravely ill.

Walter Benson. Luther's brother-in-law.

Maude Benson. His wife and Julia's sister. She came to the Averys for a short visit and stayed on to run the household during Julia's illness. She thinks the Islands need more churches, more sobriety and fewer pagan idols.

Ellen Benson. Their awkward 18-year-old daughter.

Faye Clark. The Averys' neighbor. She was kicked out of college—indirectly because of Janice's actions—when she was discovered carrying marijuana cigarettes and contraceptives.

Malia. A beautiful Hawaiian girl who hopes that her sensual skill at the hula will get her a job in a New York City nightclub. She is the Averys' maid and once worked for Faye Clark.

John Atherton. Julia's doctor.

Henry Mahea. The Averys' late gardener, who claims to have seen a kahuna.

David Kimi. A close childhood friend, David surprises Janice when he tells her she is no longer welcome in the village.

Tony Davis. Janice wondered why this "tall, dark and vital" young man was putting the rush on her on board the *Lurline*.

Joe Kalani. A cowboy. Benson fired him for drinking but allows him to live in a cave on the property.

Stephanie "Steve" Dugan. A reporter.

Captain Kamakua. A policeman who speaks many languages

Makaleha. A seller of leis who taught Janice to do the hula as a child and who was one of the original squatters on the Averys' land.

Dr. Ethel Chun. Lily's cousin, whose son **Richard**, his Great Dane **Dynamite**, and various friends make up Lily's island irregulars.

Plus assorted islanders and servants.

Books by Juanita Sheridan

The Lily Wu Quartet

The Chinese Chop (1949)
Reprinted in 2001 by
The Rue Morgue Press

The Kahuna Killer (1951)
Reprinted in 2002 by
The Rue Morgue Press

Forthcoming from
The Rue Morgue Press

The Mano Murders (1952)
The Waikiki Widow (1953

with
Dorothy Dudley
What Dark Secret? (1943)

THE KAHUNA KILLER
by Juanita Sheridan

The Rue Morgue Press
Boulder, Colorado

FOR LYN

Laughing companion on a six-thousand-mile adventure.
Me ke aloha pau ole.

ISBN: 0-915230-47-X

Reprinted with the permission of Ross Hart,
the author's son and literary executor

The Rue Morgue Press
P.O. Box 4119
Boulder, Colorado 80306
Tel: 800-699-6214
Fax: 303-443-4010

Printed by
Johnson Printing

PRINTED IN THE UNITED STATES OF AMERICA

About Juanita Sheridan

Juanita Sheridan's life was as colorful as her mysteries. Born Juanita Lorraine Light in Oklahoma on November 15, 1906, Sheridan claimed in a lengthy letter to her editor at the Doubleday, Doran Crime Club that she came by her knack for murder naturally since her maternal grandfather was killed by Pancho Villa in a holdup while her own father may possibly have been poisoned by a political rival.

After her father's death, Sheridan and her mother hit the road, touring the American West. When she was on vacation from boarding school, Sheridan was often put by her mother on a train "with a tag around my neck which told my name and destination. I was never afraid, and never lost."

That self-reliance came in handy years later when at the height of the Depression (ca. 1930) Sheridan, with an infant son in arms, found herself dropped off at the corner of 7th and Broadway in Los Angeles with only two suitcases and five cents to her name. She used the nickel to telephone a friend, who loaned her five dollars, and went out and got a job as a script girl for $20 a week. Her son Ross went to live with a rich Beverly Hills foster family and at about the age of six was legally adopted by his maternal grandmother. After the adoption, Sheridan, who had by then sold a couple of original screenplays, headed for Hawaii to begin her writing career. Life wasn't all that easy in Hawaii and once again she hit the pawnshops, although, as usual, "the typewriter was the last to go."

To those people, editors included, who thought her plots contained more than a touch of melodrama, Sheridan said she was only writing from life, having been clubbed by a gun, choked into unconsciousness by a man she never saw, and on two occasions "awakened from a sound sleep to find a pair of strange hands reaching for me through the dark. . ."

Sheridan, who married as many as eight times, never used much of the material she gleaned from real life, figuring that no one would believe it: "One of my most interesting friends in Hawaii was the madame of a 'house.' She looked like a schoolteacher, wore glasses and spoke New England. She had a record collection and a library. She was 26 and her annual net was higher than that of many high-voltage executives. I visited her place occasionally, and after the girls learned to trust me I heard some biographies which can't be printed—no one would believe them."

While in Hawaii, Sheridan began selling short stories. She also married architect Fritz Elliott, at which time she asked that Ross be allowed to join her in Honolulu. When the boy's grandmother—and legal guardian—refused, Sheridan came to the mainland, snatched the boy while the older woman was out for a walk and sneaked the two of them on board the *President Hoover* with the steerage passengers, "down where they eat with chopsticks at one big table, the toilets are without doors, and there is no promenade deck." Ross remembers that they embarked on the ship the very day his mother "kidnapped" him, but Sheridan claimed that she and the boy hid out in San Francisco for a week while the FBI hunted for them.

Sheridan sold several stories, including two mysteries with Asian characters, which won $500 prizes. Ross left Hawaii in May 1941 and went back to live with his grandmother. Sheridan, with the manuscript to *What Dark Secret* in her hands, left Hawaii in November of the same year, just a couple of weeks before the Japanese attack on Pearl Harbor.

At some point during this period she settled down (for the time being) in a housing cooperative on a 130-acre farm in Rockland County, New York where she and her current husband bathed in a stream and slept in a tent while helping to construct their house.

Sheridan returned to Hollywood briefly when one of her Lily Wu books was sold to television as the basis for the pilot of a mystery series set in Hawaii. She "left after a couple of sessions with the Hollywood movie types," son Ross reported, because "she couldn't stand the hypocrisy."

Eventually Sheridan settled in Guadalajara, Mexico, with her last husband, Hugh Graham, and found work as a Spanish-English translator. A fall from a horse (she learned to ride while working as a polo horse exerciser in Hollywood in the 1930s) left her with a broken hip. The last time Ross saw her she was in extreme pain and would "lock herself in her room and mix painkillers and alcohol to try to ease the pain." She died in 1974.

Her mystery writing career was brief but memorable for its depiction of mid-20th century Hawaii and for creating one of the earliest female Chinese-American sleuths. If Sheridan called Lily "Oriental," rather than today's accepted term, Asian, she was only using the civilized parlance of the day. Her books are a fierce defense of the many cultures that make up Hawaii. Unlike Sayers or Christie or countless other writers from the first half of the century, she was able to rise above the petty prejudices of her time.

For more information on Sheridan see Tom and Enid Schantz' introduction to Rue Morgue Press edition of *The Chinese Chop*.

CHAPTER ONE

THAT last night on board the *Lurline* I didn't go to sleep at all. The aloha party was in full swing at 2 A.M. and so was I, dancing in the arms of the man who had given me a rush since our first night out from San Francisco. By that hour I was participating in last-night festivities through a daze, but the mood which keyed me so high derived from things headier than wine and confetti and the companionship of Tony Davis. All through the evening, as the *Lurline* swished over a tropic sea smooth as purple glass, my heart had pounded hard, in rhythm with the powerful turbines which thrust us toward our destination, and that joyful beat said: "Going home! Going home! Going home!"

Hawaii. Honolulu. We'd disembark at nine in the morning. And we'd make our first landfall at dawn, in less than three hours. Who could sleep?

Tony touched my elbow as the music finished. "It's cooler outside, Janice," he suggested. "Let's find chairs and wait on deck for daybreak. We'll order some champagne and toast that landfall—and the Islands— together."

I looked at him through a mist of withdrawal, already saying good-by. I'd been lucky to have him at our table, and as shipboard playmate he'd been ideal. Tall and dark and vital, he was the sort a romantic girl dreams of meeting on a tropical cruise. There were several such girls here, and I'd caught envious glances as they wondered how I managed to keep the most attractive man on board ship constantly at my side for several days. Certainly I wasn't as pretty as some of them—or as young—and in odd moments I also wondered why Tony sought me out. I had decided it would be silly to worry over the length of this gift horse's teeth—whatever Tony's reasons, it had been marvelous fun. But, said I to myself, now it's over.

What the romantic girl on a cruise seldom learns until too late, I already knew from experience. There was no future in it. Tony was on vacation from a job which he mentioned vaguely as having to do with statistics, and I was going home. He might give me a rush in Honolulu; we'd surf at

Waikiki, dance at the Royal, see each other daily—until his vacation was over. Then he'd sail for the mainland, back to his normal background and friends, and if I let myself succumb to his undeniable appeal, there would be loneliness after he left.

Besides, I couldn't plan on playtime in Hawaii for a while; I had a job to do. I had left Honolulu less than a year ago with a large check in my pocket, advance on a romance of the tropics which my publishers hoped would be to the islands what *Gone With the Wind* had been to the South. Before publication the novel became a book club selection; each time I received a bank statement I did a double-take at my balance. A publicity campaign was about to be launched, and to complete my bewilderment at the rapidity with which one's life may change, my agent had leased the story to Hollywood and I was hired as technical adviser. I hadn't wanted that job, but I did feel strongly about seeing at least one Hawaiian picture filmed without cellophane *hula* skirts. My father's hobby had been Hawaiiana; his library, his volumes of notes, and the little Hawaiian village where I played as a child had given me authentic background which I wanted re-created for this picture. Now I hoped to persuade the Avery family, on whose property my Hawaiian friends lived, to permit intrusion of a film company on their cherished privacy.

No one on board the *Lurline* knew the real reason for my return to the islands except the girl I was traveling with. I have observed that men, especially in holiday mood, seldom consider the details of a woman's job a fascinating topic of conversation. Even if I hadn't been cautioned about secrecy until publicity releases were ready, I should never have discussed it with Tony.

I looked up at him and managed a yawn. "I'm sorry, Tony, but I must say good night. I haven't finished packing yet, and I need some sleep. Tomorrow—or rather, today—will be a busy day."

"You have family meeting you?"

"No, just friends. I'm staying with the Averys."

He was trailing me down the corridor. "Is that Luther Avery, the architect?"

"Yes. Do you know him?"

"Read about him in a book called *Men of Hawaii*. Hello—whose stateroom is that?"

He nodded toward a door we were passing, from which came sounds of clinking glass, laughter, and one particularly loud voice.

"That's the senator's suite," I told Tony. "There'll undoubtedly be a welcoming committee for him in Honolulu. If our honorable statesman keeps this up all night again, he'll have to be decanted for the governor's reception. Here we are. In case I don't see you during the rush tomorrow, thanks again for making the crossing so enjoyable."

Tony ignored the dismissal. He looked over my shoulder and saw that the room was empty. I had half expected a tussle with him—I'd been winner so far in our brief wrestling matches—but I didn't expect him to enter without an invitation. He strode past me, across the pale green carpet of our *lanai* suite, to the sun deck filled with tropical plants, and stood for a moment watching dark waters slide past the ship. Then he turned with the air of one making a decision.

"Janice," he said, "I've been trying for days to get you to talk about your real reason for going to Honolulu. You've avoided discussing it. I think we ought to get together on this because—well, come and sit down and I'll tell you—"

There was a terrific crash from the adjoining bedroom. Then the shout of an angry voice. Another crash followed. In two steps Tony was beside me, had shoved me behind the protection of his shoulders as he faced the room from where the noise had come. The door burst open and a Chinese boy in a steward's white coat emerged, his face contorted with rage and frustration, bumped into us without apology, and rushed into the corridor.

"What on earth—" Tony began, then broke off as my traveling companion appeared in the doorway. Lily Wu was wearing pajamas of pale rose satin and a mandarin coat of ink blue embroidered with golden dragons. Her black hair was loose on her shoulders, her red mouth curved in a smile. She looked beautiful, untouchable, and not the least disturbed.

I was beginning to understand. "Did you throw something?" I asked.

The dimple in her cheek deepened. "Unfortunately, yes. It was necessary."

"Wasn't that George Leung who left in such a hurry?"

"It was. I ordered sandwiches and coffee. He bribed the steward for the loan of his jacket and a chance to deliver the tray in person. It was the only way he could contrive to get into the bedroom."

She turned to Tony. "George is very naive. He believes that because his father has a million dollars no woman can refuse him her favors. He looked rather droll, I think, with mayonnaise on his eyebrows!" And she giggled softly.

I burst into laughter, my amusement intensified by the look of bewilderment on the face of Tony Davis. He had met Lily on deck with me a few times, but apparently it had not occurred to him that we might be traveling together. When he questioned me obliquely about our friendship, I had taken pleasure in telling him we were more than friends—we were foster sisters. Tony had thought I was joking; now his face reflected surprise—and disappointment. The tête-à-tête he wanted wouldn't be possible.

It may seem strange to some that one whose ancestors were Scottish and Irish should be foster sister to a Chinese girl, but that is more common than many are aware. Usually it is the Chinese who is taken under the wing of a Caucasian family, often of missionary background. In my case the reverse was true. Lily Wu had adopted me as her foster sister in New York, after we spent a weird and dangerous interval there which found us strangers at its onset and culminated in a friendship as close as any I shall ever know. I have a room in the Wu family home in New York's Chinatown. Whether I occupy it for an hour or a decade, that room is always ready, always mine. There are few things I know of in life which offer greater comfort than knowledge that somewhere, unalterable and forever, there is sanctuary waiting. Such good fortune is mine.

I did not speak of these things to Tony or any other person on the *Lurline*. When he had asked me—that oblique approach again—whether my people were missionaries, I told him the truth: I was an orphan, my father had been professor of English at the University of Hawaii, and the Wu family had adopted me. I suppose that was when he thought I was joking.

He was quick to admit it. "I didn't really believe you, you know. If you two girls are traveling together," he said to Lily Wu, "where have you been keeping yourself? I haven't seen you more than three times since we came aboard."

Lily reached for a cigarette and nodded thanks for the light he gave her. "I've been playing mah-jongg."

"Day and night?" he asked.

"Tony," I explained, "mah-jongg addicts are the most passionate gamblers in the world. I've seen sessions which lasted a week, with minimum time out for sleeping, and meals eaten at the game table."

He grinned. "And I thought I'd been in some navy poker games. Any luck?"

She shrugged slightly. "I lost at first. Then I managed to come out ahead."

"How much did you win?"

"About two thousand."

"Dollars?"

"Yes." She turned to me. "Janice, I have phoned for the steward. Send him into me when he comes. Now, if you'll excuse me, I'll finish packing."

When we were alone again I looked at Tony. I will say with out modesty that what I wanted at that moment was to be in his arms. Tony's witty conversation, his expert rhumba, those adroit passes, hadn't left a dent in my resistance. But his behavior tonight—that automatic gesture of protection he had made—crumbled my defenses. When he put his arm around me my heart began to beat a little faster and I was ready to raise my mouth for that long-postponed kiss. He tipped my chin with one hand—and surely

I must have swayed toward him in my eagerness!—then he patted my cheek lightly and said, "Good night, Janice. See you in Honolulu. Happy dreams." As I stared at the closing door I could have throttled him.

The steward knocked an instant later, and I sent him into the bedroom. I followed in time to hear Lily saying: " . . . told me that he gave you a hundred dollars for the use of your jacket so that he could get into this room."

The steward was red-haired and young, with that cynical, aged look that bellhops, waiters, and other public servants often wear. His face turned sulky, and he didn't answer.

Lily stood up, and her tiny figure seemed to gain in height. She held out a hand. "Give me the money."

Fury narrowed his pale eyes; he looked as if he wanted to hit her. Lily went on. "Otherwise I shall report what you have done."

He reached reluctantly into his pocket and handed her a folded paper bill. She looked at it, put it into an envelope on which she wrote a few words. "This money," she told him, "will go to the Seamen's Institute, a place where I am sure you will not spend your declining years. And one more thing," she added as he finished picking up broken dishes and piling them on his tray, "if there is the slightest difficulty with our luggage, if anything whatever is misplaced or damaged, I will see that you never board this ship or any other again."

He stood with his loaded tray and glared hatred at her. She went close to him and hissed, "Have you ever heard of a Chinese *tong*?"

With that he went completely white. He turned on his heel and practically ran out of the room.

After he was gone I said, "Lily, sometimes you are incredibly ruthless."

"Am I?" she asked. "For a bribe that steward betrayed his trust, the well-being of a passenger under his care."

She added, with the half-smile I knew so well, "Suppose my unwelcome visitor had raped me? What if George Leung had even been homicidal?"

I protested, "But that's impossible! Such things don't—"

"Janice," she said softly, "they do. They happen every day."

I had no answer for that. I sat down and held out a hand for the coffee she was pouring. As she handed me a cup she asked, "How's the shipboard romance progressing?"

Her question surprised me. It was not in character for Lily to ask a personal question; that was one of her attributes which I found most agreeable. I answered briefly.

"He doesn't seem to think so, but it's over. You know I have other things to do in Honolulu."

She gave me an appraising look. "You may have wondered why I decided suddenly to make this trip. I do want to visit my cousins, of course, but there was another reason—curiosity. After you left New York, Tony Davis was at your agent's office trying to obtain your California address. She phoned to tell me about it. When I checked with the Matson Line I found his name on the passenger list. That was when I decided to sail with you."

"And changed my reservation from a modest A-deck cabin to a *lanai* suite," I added. "Go on, this is very interesting."

"His cabin is next to the one you originally reserved," she said. "You may have thought it good luck that Tony was at our table. It was arranged."

She took a bite of chicken sandwich, reached into a sleeve of her mandarin coat, and produced a piece of yellow copy paper which she handed to me. I unfolded it and saw that it contained typewritten notes. "What is this?" I asked.

She said, "I found it in a pocket of the topcoat he left on his deck chair our first night out. Read it."

It said: *"J.C. Blond with brown eyes about five feet four, under thirty. Wrote novel with Hawaiian b.g. scheduled publication Dec. Big promotion. Book leased Hollywood J.C. technical adviser since her father Hawaiiana expert and she got b.g. details from native village located Avery property Honolulu. Now en route islands obtain permission for use of village in film. Approach carefully. Sailing* Lurline *in June, check date."*

I sat on my bed and read the notes through twice. The information was accurate, but why was it important to Tony? And why had he not mentioned it to me? Because of that "approach carefully"? I had been told of my publisher's promotion plans, of course, and my agent had educated me to the value of well-timed publicity. Honolulu is just as movie-crazy as any small town, and it would be inadvisable to let anyone know of my reason for being there until releases were ready. Even with *Kapu* signs on the Avery land which were ordinarily respected by the public, we might be overrun by gawkers, a form of pestilence which the Averys had always avoided. None of this seemed to pertain to a man who was not an islander, who could have no interest that I could see either in me or the filming of my story.

I shrugged and handed the paper to Lily. "I don't understand. Unless he's a salesman—insurance, bonds—I've heard from several of those lately."

"This is copy paper," Lily said. "He may be a writer who wants to do a feature story about you."

"About me? I doubt it." Suddenly I was glad I hadn't melted into his arms. "So much for my fatal allure," I said, managing a laugh. "He's spent a lot of time and energy for nothing. At least I can make certain I won't see him in Honolulu." I shrugged away a sting of mortification and started removing clothes from their hangers.

By the time I had finished packing, the sky was turning faintly mauve. I closed the last bag and asked Lily if she would like to go on deck, to which she muttered from beneath covers that she wished I'd keep quiet and let her sleep. I turned out the lights, relieved to be alone at this moment, and rushed outside for my first glimpse of the islands.

Out to the bow I went, from where I could see in all directions. The great ship thrust her nose into purple waters, and a spray of white rushed along her sides with a gigantic purr. Wind blew my hair back, and I grasped the rail and bent into it with delight, trying to absorb that fragrance—faint and tantalizing—the smell of tropical land drawing near.

Phantom perfume of jasmine, wild guavas, of dark green forests rich with ferns and ginger, blended with the salty tang of the Pacific. I breathed deeply and gave myself to the moment. Finally the eastern edge of the world turned amethyst, then pearl, then coral streaked with orange, until the sky flamed and the sea was incandescent with the light of a tropic dawn. Flying fish skimmed past the bow, dolphins rolloped in the distance. After a long hushed while there was a shadowy mass of land—*Hawaii Nei*—rising like illusion from the sea. Molokai. Then Lanai. I couldn't see Maui or Hawaii. At last our destination loomed at the edge of the horizon.

The island of Oahu. Home. My heart leaped and I uttered an involuntary exclamation.

"Having a good nap?"

I turned. Leaning with an elbow on the railing, one long leg crossed over the other, was Tony Davis. He wasn't looking at the island. He was watching me. He grinned as he came nearer, ready to begin conversation. I glared at him before I turned and fled down the deck to the seclusion of my own quarters.

Several hundred people came offshore in the tug to meet the *Lurline*, and among them were what seemed to be dozens of Chinese by the name of Chun, Lily's Hawaii-born cousins. They swarmed into our rooms chattering and laughing, laden with *leis*, and when Lily introduced us they greeted me with flowers, friendliness, and invitations which I promised to accept as soon as time permitted. I told Lily to phone me at the Avery house when she returned from her visit to Kauai, and started for the deck. Luther Avery's cabled invitation to stay at his home had arrived before we sailed; someone from that family would surely meet me.

I had one foot on the stairs when a wiry little bald-headed man in a wrinkled blue seersucker suit stopped in the middle of his descent and looked inquiringly at me.

"You're not by any chance Miss Janice Cameron?" he asked.

"Yes, I am."

He sighed with relief and wiped his brow with a handkerchief as he continued his descent. "This is fortunate! I was wondering how I'd ever find you. I'm Walter Benson, Luther's brother-in-law. He had to meet the senatorial party and asked me to substitute for him." He draped gardenia and ginger *leis* around my neck. "Welcome to Honolulu."

"Thank you. I'm delighted to be home again."

"We're supposed to see Luther in the lounge," he said. "Are you ready to go ashore, packing all done and so forth?"

I told him yes, and we started up the stairs, moving over from time to time to make room for perspiring stewards carrying luggage. He had not mentioned Julia Avery, and I decided that she must also be with the senatorial party. This was unusual, since the Averys as I remembered them had lived very quietly, having little to do with island hullabaloo over prominent visitors.

The lounge was jammed with people being met by friends or relatives who had come offshore in the tug. Many were weeping with joy or letting out little yips of greeting, and the air was thick with the sweet scent of flowers. Some passengers were draped in *leis* to their chins and carried those they couldn't wear on both arms. Near a doorway leading to the deck we saw the senator and his party, standing in a circle with the governor and several of Honolulu's important citizens. Luther Avery was on the fringe of this group, just stepping forward to give the senator a *lei*.

A news photographer in front of them screwed a flashbulb into place, saying, "Now, gentlemen, if you'll step out on deck, we'd like one of the senator looking at Aloha Tower. Hold that *lei*, Mr. Avery; we want a shot of the governor draping one around the senator's neck."

They started toward the deck and my escort stepped forward. "Luther! Here's Miss Cameron."

Luther Avery turned, and his normally serious expression changed into a smile of recognition. He came to me. "Janice! *Aloha nui loa!* Welcome back to your own islands!" He kissed me on the cheek, then draped around my neck one of the wonderful *leis* he carried, the expensive kind which are given to important people. A rope of bright pink carnations, it hung to my ankles, and its spiciness overwhelmed every other fragrance.

One of the reporters turned. "Are you Janice Cameron?"

"Yes, she is," Walter Benson said. "And she's written a book about Hawaii and—"

Luther made a quick gesture and the other man stopped. But the newsman was alert. "When's your book going to be published, Miss Cameron? Will you give us an interview? How about some pics for the Sunday—"

"Take it easy, Bill," Luther said. "Don't neglect our important visitor." He indicated the senator, who by now was standing with his little coterie on the sun-flooded deck, looking around for the camera man. The reporter grinned, nodded, and started toward the prominent gentleman who mustn't have his feelings hurt.

Luther said, "That's one way to get rid of them. I knew you'd hate that sort of thing." He patted my shoulder. "I'm sorrier than I can tell you, but I can't drive you home. This is an unusually crowded day for me. Walter will take good care of you, and I'll see you at the house this evening. We're delighted you're staying with us, Janice—we'll have a good long talk later."

I watched his tall, thin figure hurrying toward the senatorial party which had moved down the deck to get Aloha Tower into the background. The sun shone on his lean head with its grizzled crop of hair; I noticed that Luther now wore a crew cut, and wondered whether it was for coolness or to get rid of white at the temples. He was changed, thinner and older somehow, and the stoop of his narrow shoulders was more pronounced. The scholar's stoop, my father called it. Luther's came from years over a drafting board. I gazed after him with gratitude that he had made me feel so welcome. Maybe it wouldn't be difficult after all to persuade him; maybe he felt as I did that it would be a good thing to have one honest movie made about the islands.

Walter Benson was fidgeting at my side. "We'd better start toward the gangplank," he urged. "We'll be a long time getting off of here." I followed as he began to work through the crowd along the deck.

The *Lurline* was berthed now, and as movement of the ship stopped the heat became apparent. I gazed over the bright city before us toward Nuuanu in the background not twenty minutes away, where a misty cloud floated under the arch of a rainbow, drenching the valley with moisture. My house was there, left to me when my father died six years before. It was rented now to a naval officer. I'd drive out to see it as soon as I could.

The Royal Hawaiian Band was playing "Aloha Oe," and a singer's sweet soprano rang out in the haunting, heart stirring words. As we inched along the deck my escort turned to me with an involuntary, "Beautiful, isn't it?" and I murmured agreement over the lump in my throat. We started down the gangplank and I said, still wondering about my hostess's nonappearance, "How is Mrs. Avery?"

"She's somewhat better," he said. "Although the doctor says her recovery is unusually slow. She asked to be excused for not meeting you, but of course a crowd like this is too much for her."

I felt a slight shock at his words, and my bright mood was dimmed by a formless unease. I hadn't been told of any illness. I started to say so when I found myself stepping onto the concrete of the shed, moving with the crowd toward the street. Walter Benson told me to wait just outside the building while he claimed my luggage, and I stood there, backed against the wall to permit others to pass.

Lei vendors near me called constantly, people pressed on all sides, and the air was filled with the odor of flowers, pineapple bran, and roasting Kona coffee. It was home, it was wonderfully familiar—and it was very hot. I began to perspire under my wreaths of flowers.

A jolly Hawaiian woman approached me, displaying an armload of flowered wreaths. "You want nice *lei*?" she asked. As I shook my head she moved closer. She held out a plump brown arm and insisted, "*Lei*, sweet ginger *lei*!" With a broad smile she waved fragrant flowers under my nose.

Then she said in an undertone, smiling and waving flowers before me: "*Aloha, Kulolo. Malama pono.* Better you don' go Avery place. Plenty *pilikia.*"

Kulolo. My heart stirred happily at hearing my Hawaiian pet name, given me by my father and known only to intimate island friends. The shock came later, with tardy comprehension of the rest of her words. This woman was giving me a warning.

I stared at her. Before I could utter a word of question she was gone into the crowd. I took a step in that direction, and was stopped by a hand on my arm.

"This way," Walter Benson said. "The car's across the street."

I let myself be guided to the waiting sedan and seated in the tonneau. Walter Benson settled himself at my side as the Japanese chauffeur finished stowing bags in the luggage compartment, then slipped behind the wheel and headed the big car toward Bishop Street. During our journey out Ala Moana toward Waikiki we spoke of commonplaces, I answered remarks which I do not remember. All the while my mind was uneasily engaged in wondering what the *lei* woman had tried to tell me.

Malama pono. Watch out, be careful. *Pilikia.* That word means trouble.

CHAPTER TWO

THE car turned right and down the steep driveway marked "Private Road— *Kapu,*" and I saw the Pacific sparkling through coco palms which tilted seaward, motionless in the hot air. The big sprawling house was as I re-membered, its faded pink stucco and lapis tiled roof beautifully set against the ocean's lighter blue and multicolored greens of the garden. A tall hibis-cus hedge on the *ewa* or west side of the vast lawn separated it from the next estate, while a rocky hill studded with shrubbery rose in the distance on the east or *waikiki* boundary. Beyond that hill was Wainiha, the place where the Hawaiians lived.

We stepped into a dim and quiet entry where torch ginger flamed in a tall floor vase, the red blossoms reflected in a mirror over the hall table. A Japanese maid in dark kimono bowed as we entered.

"Show Miss Cameron to her room, Suka," my host's brother-in-law directed, then said to me, "Julia is resting; she'll see you soon. I'm sorry my own family isn't here to greet you, but the dressmaker must have kept them. Our daughter Ellen is leaving for college this fall; she and her mother are shopping for a wardrobe."

He wiped his brow with a damp handkerchief and glanced past me; I felt that he wished I would go so that he could attend to more important affairs. I murmured thanks for his meeting me and followed the plump little maid up the stairs to a room at the end of the *waikiki* wing of the house. It was large, with windows on two sides, furnished with blond mahogany and rattan, a big *lauhala* mat on the floor.

The room had a feeling of impersonality; there were no flowers or books, not even an ashtray. With my reaction of surprise came another impression: I felt unwelcome, I was reluctant to stay in this house. Ill or not, I thought, my hostess could at least have sent me a note. Then I remembered the warmth of Luther Avery's greeting. I touched the pink carnations around my neck and decided I'd better not be overimaginative.

Watch out. Be careful. Trouble. Warning words which came from a smiling Hawaiian mouth. Those words had not been imagined.

My eyes had been fixed on the frail ninon curtains which hung limp at the open windows. I came out of my abstraction as the little Japanese woman spoke. "Hot today," she said, smiling and showing gold teeth. "Mebbe Kona weather come."

It was breathlessly hot. Most islanders, accustomed to a perfect climate, make a big fuss about the Kona season, when the trades stop blowing and a hot wind comes from the Kona coast. Fever wind, the natives call it. But there was no wind. Such ominous stillness could mean earthquake weather, I thought, and hoped that it did not.

"You want to wash?" Suka opened a door which led to a bath tiled in pale blue. I began removing *leis* and draping them over the arm of a chair. My neck and shoulders were wet from their perfumed weight. "Yes, thank you," I said, "that shower looks good." She gave me a cotton house kimono and grass slippers. "Koji bring suitcase soon," she said, and bowed herself out with a toothy grin.

I decided I would relax and take whatever came next. I was tense from the heat, keyed up by anticipation of this homecoming and from lack of sleep. Soon, I hoped, the good old island spirit of *mahope*, or worry-tomorrow, would possess me again. I hummed "Imi Au" as I stood in the shower, grateful for the rush of water and cool tiles under my feet. I was toweling myself when I heard movement in my room. I reached for the kimono and called, "Who is it?" as someone opened the door.

A Hawaiian girl stood there looking at me. She was very young, with luminous dark eyes and a round face. There was a red hibiscus pinned in the black hair which fell to her shoulders. She wore a faded cotton dress and Japanese grass sandals, and apparently nothing else. Full curves of her body under the thin fabric belied the babyish look on her face.

I hung up the towel and took my kimono from the bathroom stool. "Who are you?"

"I am Malia." She had the true Hawaiian mouth, wide and exquisitely carved, turned up at the corners for laughter. But her mouth was sullen.

"Did you come to help me unpack?" I asked.

She hesitated. "Yes," she said.

I thrust my arms into the kimono and walked into the bedroom. My bags were not there.

"They're in the hall," she told me, then added reluctantly, "You want me to bring them up?"

"I'll help you," I offered, and tied the kimono belt around my waist as we descended to the entrance hall. My bags were standing by the door, and the Hawaiian girl immediately picked up the two lightest ones and started back up the stairs. I reached for my luggage, and as I did so I heard the voice of Walter Benson, lowered to a cautious tone.

"Koji, are you sure you looked carefully?" He was talking to the chauffeur. "You looked along the beach and the path?"

"Yes. I look plenty good. Only one I fin'. No more today. This one I burn."

"That's good, very good. Thank you, Koji." Footsteps started across the room.

I retreated, leaving my luggage on the floor. What was Walter Benson looking for, which must be burned when found?

In my room I opened a dressing case, and the Hawaiian girl immediately began pulling clothes out onto the bed, examining them with interest. Oblivious of my presence, she unfolded a nylon nightgown of cyclamen pink and held it before her at the mirror. Childish vanity showed on her pretty face, mingled with envy of me for being more fortunate than she, for owning the nightgown.

She intercepted my glance and said, "I am going to have a gown like this." There was utter certainty in her words. I sat down and regarded her with interest.

"You are?"

She stroked tiny pleats in the sheer fabric. "I will have much money soon. Then I will buy a gown, and some nylon stockings, and a silk dress."

"Are you saving your wages to buy them?"

"Wages?" She shrugged disdain. "I am going to be a famous dancer in a night club in New York." Another flat statement.

This brought light. Many Hawaiian girls had gone to the mainland with nightclub contracts, and had won some popularity. But their fame was short-lived. The real *hula* is too esoteric for the unenlightened, and the vulgar version of it too common to hold public favor long.

"You are a *hula* dancer?" I asked.

Her head went up proudly. "The best in the school. At graduation the *kumo* said so."

"Who was your *kumo*?"

She mentioned the name of the most revered teacher in the islands, and I regarded her with new respect mingled with curiosity. She didn't seem like the type of girl who could graduate from a temple school, where discipline was as rigorous as that endured by the Ballet Russe or the famous dancers of Bali. Hawaiian temple dancers must be virgins, subject to countless strict taboos, living apart from the community. If this girl was a virgin, I was a very poor judge of my own sex.

Her wide mouth curled as if she read my thoughts. "Now I am going away to be a famous dancer," she told me, tossing dark waves of hair over her shoulders. "And I will have much money."

Money meant a lot to her. I wondered whether she had already received an advance on her contract to pay for passage. I wondered what her family thought of the prospect. "Where do you live?" I asked. "At Wainiha?" I gestured toward the Hawaiian village, and she nodded.

Then I did the sort of thing one does on impulse of the moment and sometimes regrets for a lifetime. I told her about the movie that was going to be made in Hawaii, possibly in the very place where she lived. "If you are the best dancer of your troupe, Malia, perhaps you can work in the picture, and they will pay you more than a nightclub."

Her sullenness vanished, replaced by a smile of delight. She hugged the gown to her and said, "If that is so, then I do not go away. I stay here and dance for the movies. When I am famous from the movies the nightclub will pay more."

Belatedly I remembered my agent's injunction to keep quiet until publicity releases were ready. I explained briefly, and to my relief she nodded immediate comprehension.

"I won't talk." A sly look came over her face. "Some won't like it."

Plenty of competition in the *hula* troupe, I surmised. Then her childishly transparent expression altered again, and her dark eyes glittered with malice. "But I know somebody will be surprised." She's going to torment some infatuated man, I thought, and felt briefly sorry for her victim.

"Malia!" The Japanese maid stood in the doorway, frowning. "Bad girl you! Boss say no mo' stop here. Downstairs go!"

Malia's eyes flashed fury at the little *oba-san*, and she started to utter a retort, then thought better of it. She flung my gown onto a chair and flounced out of the room.

Suka went to the bed and began folding clothes to put into bureau drawers. "No good, that kin'," she muttered half to herself. She picked up the dinner dress I'd worn on board ship "You wear tonight?" When I nodded she said, "I press fo' you." As she left the room she told me, "Missus Avely say *kaukau* in garden. You come down now."

Lunch in the garden sounded inviting, and I was hungry, having been too excited to take more than coffee for breakfast. I dressed in the same frock I'd worn for my arrival, a turquoise shantung which was a nice contrast for the pink carnation *lei* Luther gave me, and looped the strand twice around my neck as I started toward the garden.

"Welcome to Hawaii, Janice," my hostess greeted me. "How charming you look."

She was resting on a white ironwork chaise longue piled with cushions, placed under a magnificent banyan tree which spread an island of shade in the sunlight. "I am sorry that I could not meet you, my dear," she said in a tired voice. "But Walter has explained. Won't you be seated?"

"Thank you, Mrs. Avery. You're very kind to invite me here."

I sank into the seat she indicated, and the smile which had begun on my lips froze half formed. I turned my eyes toward the ground on pretext of maneuvering my chair to better advantage, in order to guard my expression before looking into her face again. I had received a shock.

I had last seen Julia Avery about two years ago, and memory of her appearance on that occasion, a university faculty tea, flashed vividly to me. Stately and gracious, her tall, firm-fleshed body draped in a fashionable afternoon gown, her head proud under a crown of thick brown hair, she had been a vitally handsome woman. Now she was changed almost beyond recognition.

She was emaciated, her flesh was slack, her face looked gaunt and hollowed, and her hair had turned almost white. In spite of effort at self-control, I must have shown my distress in some way—I was on the verge of blurting out that I hadn't known of her illness, and how sorry I was—but she gave me no opportunity.

"I hope you had a good crossing," she said in an artificial voice.

"It was delightful," I said automatically, observing with a mounting sense of shock that she was more than merely ill—she was crippled.

She touched the two canes which leaned against the chaise, as my eyes fixed on them, and said, "I hope you find your room comfortable, and that you will excuse me for not taking you there. Stairs are difficult for me now.

Since my accident I must walk with care until these bones are healed." She indicated the covered tray which was on the table between us. "Would you mind serving us?"

Illness might explain the change in her, the white hair, the wasted look. Even the tragic expression in her deep-set eyes? Perhaps. It might have been a bad collision, someone else horribly injured, or a life lost—possibly mention of it disturbed her. I served melon and salad, and we ate to the accompaniment of perfunctory remarks: the ship's crossing, the weather, social and economic changes in Hawaii during my absence, the governor's reception being given that night for the newly arrived senator.

Coconut palms rattled conversationally in vagrant breezes; water swished in and retreated, leaving foam on the sand; bright tropical flowers surrounded us; the iced papaya into which I slipped my spoon was sweet as nectar. I should have relaxed, absorbed with all senses the beauty and serenity of the place.

But there was no serenity.

Gradually I became aware that tension, as much a part of the atmosphere as the fragrance from the carnations around my neck, was generated by the woman who sat opposite me. She must be very nervous after her accident, I thought, hoping that was the explanation.

She said, "What would you like to do today, Janice? I made no plans, thinking it best to consult you first. Do you wish to invite friends for cocktails, perhaps, or dinner this evening? We must put in an appearance later at the governor's reception, unfortunately. I am sorry we are not very gay, but we have been living quietly; my sister Maude and her family are our only guests. They have a ranch on Maui, but have been staying here since— since my illness. But any of your friends will be welcome, of course."

I had let no one except the Averys know of my arrival, and told her so. "I have a job, you know," I added, giving her an opening to mention my purpose in being there. She ignored it. I ate more fruit salad. Finally I said: "There are two things I should love to do: first, go swimming. I can't tell you how beautiful that ocean looks to me after the beaches of the mainland. Second, I should love to stroll over that hill and spend the afternoon visiting my Hawaiian friends in the— I beg your pardon?"

"Nothing."

"I thought you spoke. Well, to come down to earth, I can't do either. I must see the agent who is handling my property. I must go to the bank. I need to do some shopping. So I'll get duties over today, and tomorrow I'll swim and then spend the afternoon at Wainiha—"

I stopped speaking as her fork rattled on the glass table. She was staring at the linen napkin crushed in her lap, and she seemed about to utter some kind of protest.

"Mrs. Avery," I said, "is there anything wrong?"

She wet her lips. "No, nothing. Nothing at all." She grasped her sticks and prepared to rise. "The doctor orders rest immediately after lunch each day, and I must obey." After she had struggled to her feet she said, "Do you drive? Good. Take the station wagon in the garage; the keys are in it. And have a pleasant day, my dear. There will be cocktails on the *lanai* at six-thirty."

After she had gone, after Suka came and removed the remains of our lunch, I sat there doing a slow burn. Julia Avery didn't want me to talk about the Hawaiian village, probably was outraged at the idea of a film company setting foot on her sacred domain. I had not been given a chance to discuss it with her, to explain how camera and sound trucks might be maneuvered to location with the minimum of disturbance to residents of the Avery estate. Her distaste for the subject was as definite as a slap in the face. Why, then, had I been invited to stay in her house? I couldn't understand it. But I resolved to discuss the village and my hopes for it with one who I knew would be sympathetic—Luther Avery. It was he, more than his wife, who had been my father's friend. I would talk to Luther. With this decision made, I started toward the garage.

It was wonderful to drive again. I hadn't been behind a steering wheel for a long time, since in Manhattan a car is a problem more than a pleasure. I cruised along the Ala Wai, over to Beretania Street, then instead of stopping in the business district, I found myself headed up Nuuanu Avenue, toward that rainbow I'd seen in the valley. I didn't even stop at my own house there, but went on, through shadowy jungle groves of trees, of broad-leafed vines and tall plants which spread away from the rising curves of the road, up to the Pali. There I stopped at the stone wall overlooking the windward side of Oahu and got out of the car. The wind wasn't very strong that day, but it rushed incessantly past, and I sat on the wall in solitude, my eyes drinking in the beauty for which I had hungered during many months of absence. Thousands of feet below the Pali the tranquil valley lay, and beyond it at Kailua the ocean spread sapphire to the horizon.

Looking at a magnificent spectacle of the earth is the best cure I know for self-preoccupation. And doing so at the Pali, where the constant wind pressing against every pore makes one physically a part of the spectacle, never fails to dissolve irritation and pettiness of spirit. I felt rasped nerves smoothing, felt apprehensions blown away, and with this debris gone, the spring of memory began to flow. My thoughts went back over the years to my childhood, before I was bereft of my family, before I let my heart be broken by a man who wasn't worth a second thought, before I sublimated loneliness and frustration in a novel which happened to sell because it was about an unusual background and reached the market at just the right time.

I went back to my happiest days, to the reason why the Hawaiian village meant so much to me.

My mother died when I was nine, and after she was gone my father took on the job of being both parents, with the help of Saito, our devoted Japanese housekeeper. Fortunately for both of us, Father and I were kindred spirits; what would have happened had we not been, I don't care to conjecture. He enjoyed teaching English at the university, and was a well-liked professor, but I think now that one of the chief attractions of his job must have been the leisure time he had, with a not too rigorous schedule of classes and long summer vacations. This freedom gave him opportunity to gratify his chief passion, which was the study of every aspect, past and present, of Polynesian life.

He used to scandalize more dignified faculty associates by scampering around over the beaches in a pair of ragged shorts, rugged as a goat and almost as sure-footed. He was an avid collector; he collected shells and plants and flowers with as much enthusiasm as he collected friends of all races. Especially Hawaiians.

Father used to take me fishing at a favorite place along the coast where there was a fairly good beach and a wonderful deep swimming hole at the edge of a rocky shelf. This was on Avery land, over the hill from their house, and at that time the land was taken over by a Hawaiian family who simply camped on the spot, getting their subsistence from fishing and a little gardening, minding their own business and asking nothing but to be left in peace. Makaleha was that squatter, and my father used to talk to her for hours, absorbing Hawaiian lore and learning the language, while I played with her numerous brood, naked and brown as the rest of them and equally unselfconscious. They taught me to swim, to fish Hawaiian style with spear and net, to love raw *opihis* and *poi*, to play a guitar—and Makaleha, who in her youth had been one of the best in her village, taught me to *hula*. How she used to scold when I relaxed into a belly-wiggle, the *umi-umi*, instead of a disciplined roll of the hips! Always under her loud scolding, Hawaiian style, was the sound of laughter. I loved her.

After we knew them better we used to bring water when we went there for the day, since the one drawback of their camping ground was absence of water for drinking. Bathing, of course, was no problem, with several billion gallons of clean Pacific for their front lawn.

It was through our water carrying that we met the Averys, normally a family who moved in a realm apart from our own. The only easy access to the land where Makaleha had her tent was by the Avery driveway, which bore the big sign, "*Kapu*." Father and I respected the *kapu* and used a steep and rocky trail from the highway. I stumbled one day and fell, inflicting a deep cut on my leg from the glass of the water bottle I was carrying. That was the occasion on which Father carried me to the Avery house, covered with blood and whimpering, and asked one of the servants for a first-aid kit. The Averys heard them talking and came out to help.

After my leg was bandaged we sat on the grass, I leaning against my father's shoulder, while the adults chatted. Luther Avery suggested, hearing of my stumble on the trail, that we use their driveway in future. We were glad to do so, because this made it easier to carry fishing gear and supplies. After that we took many gallons of water to the Hawaiians. And it was my father who gave the Averys the idea of running a pipeline to their camping grounds. We were at their house one Sunday afternoon, drinking iced tea on the lawn, when Father mentioned the land to our host.

"It is generous of you, Luther, to let those people stay there unmolested," he said.

"There is nothing generous about it." Luther looked uncomfortable. "They don't cost us anything, and the land's worthless."

Julia Avery added, "We wouldn't evict them even if it weren't worthless. It isn't generally known—and we certainly don't want it to be—but that land is considered sacred by many Hawaiians. Somewhere on that hillside is the remains of an old *heiau*."

"What's a *heiau*, Father?" I had asked.

He explained that it was an ancient temple altar, where religious rites were performed many years ago. There were many such ruins scattered around the islands, and they were left strictly alone even by modern Hawaiians, while the land on which they were found was seldom disturbed.

"Perhaps," my father said, "a hundred years ago the place where Julia's father built this house was a thriving native village.

"Their *kahuna*, the priest, probably secluded himself in the little valley beyond the beach, and they erected their temple on that ridge overlooking the water. The altar is all that is left."

"There have been many stories," Julia added, "of people who destroyed old *heiaus* and brought disaster on themselves and their families." She spoke with gravity, and I shivered in delighted terror.

My highly developed imagination caught the picture and retained it; later when I went to the village I looked for the *heiau* but found nothing but a pile of black stones. Makaleha frowned when I asked her about it, and diverted my attention. Since the subject made her uneasy, I never questioned her again.

It was as a result of our conversation that the Averys decided to make life easier for their Hawaiian neighbors by giving them water. They ran a pipe from their main line to the little valley, and installed it in the side of the hill under a rock so realistically that it looked like a natural spring. Water followed the face of the rock into a natural depression at its base, then trickled on down into the ocean.

Makaleha didn't say *mahalo*—thank you—she just made stronger tent pegs and anchored her tribe more firmly to the land. Months later a little Hawaiian boy appeared at our house and delivered a package for Father and me. Makaleha had made hat *leis* for us, exquisite bands of blue peacock feathers. Such *leis* are prized the islands over, for they are difficult to make and correspondingly fabulous in price. That was Makaleha's *mahalo*. The Averys received a similar gift.

After a while another family drifted in and camped alongside Makaleha. There was plenty land, plenty water, plenty fish in ocean—why not? They built a few simple shacks, and another family came. That was the start of the little village.

Father was pleased to see that they kept to themselves, and some un-written law prevented overcrowding of the land. After a few more families had settled there, the village ceased to grow. Perhaps they were the only ones left on Oahu who cared to live in such a primitive manner, without source of income other than native crafts made for curio stores, without electricity or plumbing or refrigeration. Whatever the reason, the village remained small and quiet. Tourists never heard of the place. They learned of early Hawaiian life from the commercial village at Waikiki. Most tour-ists weren't really interested, anyhow.

My father became ill when I was in my middle teens. He accepted invalidism cheerfully and devoted his hours of physical inactivity to filling notebooks with the Polynesian lore he had accumulated. Gradually he be-came completely absorbed in his work; we lost all social contacts, includ-ing the Averys. I went through adolescence sharply aware of the mores of my fellow students at Punahou; shyness made me wish to be unobtrusive, and that was achieved by being as much like the herd as possible. Although I swam better than most of them, they didn't know it; the girls weren't aware that I could do *hulas* they had never heard of. What mattered was that I couldn't fox-trot, I didn't have any small talk, and my clothes, chosen by Saito, were unbecoming. Hours when my schoolmates were yelling at foot-ball games I helped Father by typing his scribbled notes. But after he died I didn't go to Makaleha's village again.

Now I would go. I would visit Makaleha—I remembered suddenly that her name meant Naughty Eyes—and would find her fatter and jollier than ever, lolling on the sand surrounded by laughing babies as she had always been. I would take my shoes off and sit with her and we would laugh and sing and eat. Then I would go swimming in the special pool I remembered, which the Hawaiians had shown me, where the floor of the ocean was car-peted with white sand, where bright jewels of fishes swam in the undersea coral garden.

A car drew alongside the Avery station wagon, and music from its radio jolted me back into the present. I looked at my watch and found that I had been dreaming there for more than two hours. The bank would soon be closed—the real-estate agent might already have gone home . . . it was hot on the streets of Honolulu, where I should be doing my shopping . . . *Mahope* . . . Tomorrow was soon enough. I got into the car and turned its nose down the Pali road for a solitary trip around the island.

On the way back to Honolulu, I encountered a funeral procession, making its way slowly toward a nearby cemetery. It was crossing the road in front of me, and traffic had halted on both sides of the intersection to permit the cortege to pass. I stopped the motor and leaned on the wheel, watching the faces of people who followed the coffin. Most of them were Hawaiians, with a few Orientals and whites, and they were poorly dressed, riding in battered cars of ancient vintage. Except one car toward the rear; at sight of it I sat upright and stared. The sedan was the one which had so recently carried me as passenger, and riding in it, her haggard face pressed against the window with a look of terrible sadness, was Julia Avery.

CHAPTER TWO

BY THE time I returned to the house I was tired to the point of numbness. A shower revived me a little, but as I sat at the dressing table I knew I couldn't postpone much longer the sleep which was settling over me as pervasively as twilight now settled over the island. I put on the lemon-yellow chiffon dinner dress which Suka had pressed for me and stepped into the hall, where I met Luther Avery.

"Janice. I was just coming for you." He stopped and regarded my appearance with a fond but puzzled expression. "How you have changed! I can hardly believe you're the same little tousle-haired girl who used to visit here."

"I hope this is an improvement."

"I don't know. You *wahines* that stay on the mainland awhile come home with something added—maybe it's sophistication. Perhaps I'm old-fashioned, but I miss that sweetness, that—" He shrugged his lack of words.

"Do you mean docility?" I asked.

Luther smiled and shook his head. "I don't know what I mean. But it's the opposite of sophistication."

He wore the trappings of sophistication himself: tropical dinner jacket, white shirt, pearl studs. But on Luther's tall boniness even the best-cut garments somehow lost their shape, looked droopy or wrinkled; he could never wear clothes with an air, as Tony Davis did, for instance. Luther's appearance was like the houses he designed, comfortable but without distinction; it made him seem rather pathetic.

Voices rose from the lower part of the house and he said, "Let's go down and have a drink; the rest of the family wants to meet you." He took my arm as we started down the stairs together.

"Julia probably told you that her sister Maude and her family are with us for an indefinite visit," Luther was saying. "They came over from Maui originally to stay a month. But Julia went to the hospital a week after they arrived, and she isn't strong yet. Maude has helped a great deal by taking over domestic management for us."

So Mrs. Benson was the one responsible for the lack of hospitality I had felt on my arrival. Remembering the soap dish which I had inducted into odd service, I wondered whether she was the type who disapproved of smoking and underlined that disapproval by failing to provide ashtrays for others. Julia did not smoke but she would never have been so inconsiderate of a guest.

At the foot of the stairs I turned to Luther. "What happened to Julia? She mentioned an accident, but she seems rather nervous and I didn't question her about it."

His naturally sober expression became more grave. "Julia suffered a very bad fall. It's a wonder she wasn't killed." His mouth tightened, he looked angry at the recollection, and I dropped the subject as we approached the *lanai*.

Walter Benson rose at our arrival, and Luther introduced me to the girl sitting near him. Ellen Benson, the daughter who was preparing to go to college, was eighteen, brown-haired and gray-eyed, dressed in modest white pique. She smiled shyly at me, and regarded my yellow frock and green sandals with interest.

The Hawaiian girl I had previously met wheeled a mobile bar across the flagstoned floor and asked, "You wish a cocktail?" She was dressed in uniform now, her beautiful hair constricted in a net, shoes on her feet, and her face a sullen mask.

Luther picked up the silver shaker. "Run along, Malia, I'll serve the drinks." As she turned away he asked, "Will Mrs. Avery be down?"

"Yes. She is dressing now."

"I hope she had a good rest today."

"Yes, sir. A good long rest."

I looked at her in astonishment. The girl was lying. Julia Avery had not been resting; the domestic staff must know that. Perhaps Malia hadn't been here during the afternoon; possibly she didn't know of Julia's unhappy excursion. Then, as she passed me on her way into the house, I saw by the quirk of her mouth and the malicious glitter in her eyes that she did know, she derived some sort of spiteful satisfaction from telling her lie.

"I'm going to give you a daiquiri, Janice," Luther told me. "Is that all right?"

"Delightful."

I settled into a chair and reached for a cigarette in the box beside me. It was empty. Walter Benson jumped to his feet and offered me a crumpled package. When he inquired whether I'd had a pleasant afternoon I told him about my trip around the island. Ellen Benson watched me quietly, sipping Coke and lemon. I tasted my drink, hoping it would be sufficient stimulant to keep me awake through what promised to be a very dull evening. It was too weak.

The *lanai* was a pleasant place, furnished with stick reed and rattan, much used in the tropics because it is termite-proof and cool. Flame bougainvillea and yellow cup-of-gold climbed stone pillars which supported the upstairs terrace; there were bamboo tubs of tree ferns, shell ginger, and waxy red anthurium, while butterfly orchids swung from moss-filled baskets against the faded pink wall of the house. I turned my eyes toward the ocean, framed in coco palms, glimmering in evening light. At the water's edge moved a thick figure, with head bent in an attitude of search. I started to ask who the searcher was and noticed that Walter Benson was also watching, sitting on the edge of his chair. When the figure began to approach the house he settled back into his seat and regarded his wrinkled socks with attention.

"Hello, Maude," Luther called. "Come and join the party. Did you have a nice walk?"

"You know perfectly well, Luther," she said in a loud, flat voice, "that I was not walking for pleasure. I was looking to see whether any more of those—"

Her husband shifted his weight and made a gesture in my direction; she shut her mouth like a trap when she saw me. I was disappointed; I wanted to know what she had been looking for. Could it be the same thing Walter Benson had been worried about earlier in the day? Luther seemed oblivious of any awkwardness as he said, "This is Janice Cameron, Maude."

She nodded at me, then went through a routine which I soon learned was habitual, before she seated herself in the chair nearest mine. She tilted it and looked on the legs and arms, removed cushions and turned them to inspect them closely. Her husband explained with a brief laugh, "Maude is afraid of scorpions and centipedes. She was badly bitten last year."

She paid no attention to him except for a sound which was a cross between a snort and a grunt. When the chair finally passed inspection she shoved the pillows back into it; rattan creaked futile protest as she sat down.

"So you're Professor Cameron's daughter," she said to me, as if that were accusation. "We have some books of his at home. Walter has read them. Your father was interested in the aborigines, wasn't he?"

I had never thought of my Hawaiian friends as aborigines. I stiffened, and murmured something to the effect that the Bishop Museum also had some of Father's books, but that information seemed to mean nothing to her.

"And Luther tells me you've written a novel about the natives." She settled more solidly into the protesting chair and waved a pudgy hand toward Luther. "Nothing for me, thanks." Then: "Ellen! What are you drinking?"

The girl's answer was toneless. "Coke, Mama."

Mrs. Benson resumed her interrogation. "And have you produced another of those libelous books claiming that the missionaries handed the natives Bibles in exchange for their land?" she demanded, and without waiting for an answer, declaimed, "Those writers are enemies of Christian society! What these islands need is more churches, more sobriety, and less idealizing of a group of ignorant, debased pagans!"

Well! If this was a sample of Julia Avery's family, no wonder I had never met them here before. The Averys probably saw as little of this woman as possible. It was difficult to believe that she and Julia were sisters. And no wonder the husband and daughter were such nonentities. They had probably become so in self-protection from the hysteria latent in every note of her belligerent voice.

She was a big, tallowy woman with gray-streaked hair under a net and deep-set eyes so brown that they looked black—dark torches to light her fanaticism. Her dinner dress was of ecru crepe with clumsy lines, the product of some underpaid and talentless village dressmaker. She wore its graceless folds like armor.

I was saved from further conversation with her by the arrival of a guest who appeared suddenly in the open doorway to the living room. Luther greeted him warmly, introduced him to me as Dr. Atherton, and asked whether I remembered him.

I said with some embarrassment that I didn't, and the doctor, a big, deep-voiced man with a leonine head of white hair, laughed good-naturedly. "No reason why she should, Luther; we've never met. But"—he smiled at me—"I am one of many who had a high regard for your father."

I relaxed like a stroked kitten and regarded him with approval. He accepted a cocktail from Luther and asked as he seated himself, "How's my patient today? Is Julia feeling well enough to go to the reception with us?"

She appeared in time to answer his question in person. "I feel perfectly fit, John," she said. "I intend to go."

Julia didn't look fit. Her dress was lovely, made of fragile lace in a soft rose shade, but it sagged on her wasted body. Her eyes were sunk into her skull, and makeup couldn't cover the ravages in her face. Diamonds glittered in her ears and on thin fingers which clutched the two canes at her side. Luther hastened to help her into a chair, and she smiled her thanks and pressed his hand affectionately.

"Faye just called," she said to him, "inviting us to a party she's giving tomorrow night. I accepted."

Maude Benson said sharply, "Not for us, I hope."

Her daughter protested, "Oh, Mama, if Mrs. Clarke is giving a party, it ought to be something special."

Her mother scowled. "I have no doubt that it will be. But we are most certainly not—"

Walter Benson said in a voice carefully devoid of emphasis, "She is entertaining in honor of the senator."

His wife turned to him quickly. "How do you know?"

"I saw her out there this afternoon"—he waved toward the ocean—"and walked out to watch her swimming. She's marvelously good, you know. Some friend was with her, who just arrived today, and she introduced me to him and said then that she was giving a *luau* tomorrow. The senator was a neighbor of hers in Washington."

I said, surprised, "I didn't know anyone could swim here. The beach is full of coral, isn't it?"

Julia answered. "Not now. She is having it cleaned out. It costs a fortune."

Ellen Benson added, "And she's even dredging in front of Aunt Julia's. I think that's generous of her."

"If she didn't, the work would be wasted," Luther explained. He turned to me. "You know how coral grows, Janice."

At mention of the name Faye, some memory had stirred, and now I asked, "Has Mrs. Clarke lived here long?"

Julia answered. "Not recently. She was born in the islands and went to school here some years ago. Then she married a naval officer and they moved to Washington. He was many years older than she, and he died just at the end of the war. Mrs. Clarke came back here to live, and has taken the Harper place next door. Luther is doing some work for her at present."

She smiled at her husband. "It's rather elaborate, isn't it, dear?"

Luther agreed, then added with a wry smile, "I'll admit some of the ideas she has are pretty startling to an old conservative like me. I wondered at first why she didn't choose one of the younger, more radical architects, but Faye says she has enough radical ideas of her own, she needs someone who knows good construction to keep her from making mistakes."

"Perhaps you know her, Janice," Julia said. "She'd be older than you, possibly, but she went to the University of Hawaii. Her maiden name was Miller."

"I knew her years ago," Dr. Atherton said. "And from what I hear of her now, she is just the same, only more so." He chuckled and got up to pour himself another drink. "I wouldn't miss one of her parties for anything. Besides, this is for our political bigshot; it's our civic duty to go." He glanced at Maude Benson and then winked at her daughter.

Mrs. Benson capitulated at that. "Perhaps we should go," she said grudgingly, "as a courtesy to the senator."

Ellen Benson's face lighted; she started to exclaim with pleasure, then sobered and looked down at her glass with a little frown. Her father was also dissembling. He rose abruptly and walked out toward the water. I noticed then that he was bowlegged and walked with the rolling gait of a horseman who considers putting his feet on solid ground an unnecessary nuisance. I watched him with half attention, while I began to recall Faye Miller as I had known her a long time ago.

The prospect of our meeting left me with mixed emotions. It meant nothing to me, but might be unpleasant to Faye, for I had been the innocent cause of her being dismissed from the university in a scandal which would have torn the place apart if it had ever been made public. So far as I knew, not a whisper had leaked out, and I had almost forgotten the episode. Until today I had forgotten the central figure in it. Now I began to remember.

In every school there is a girl who is set apart from the others by beauty or personality, and quite often she is the kind of girl the rest would like to be if they only dared. But they seldom dare. All through my school days it had been Faye who filled that role, who added spice to campus gossip, who was a problem to teachers, the envy of other girls, and the delight or torment of every boy who knew her. From the time we were in Punahou, Faye had moved in a spotlight. When her classmates were still wearing saddle oxfords and socks, Faye wore heels and sheer stockings; while they were at home on weeknights doing lessons, Faye was out on a date, never worrying about geometry or history, since there was always some infatuated boy to do her assignments.

Her clothes were different too, or perhaps it was the way she wore them, for from the time she was thirteen Faye walked in an aura of sheer femaleness which made every male within fifty feet conscious of her. In high school she came to class wearing orchids, murmuring of a champagne hangover and a "heavy date" the night before. In the university she proclaimed that school sports were childish and college students infantile bores. By that time she had found the tourists at Waikiki more entertaining than her classmates, who had small allowances and whose ideas of diversion were a tea dance on the Young Hotel roof, a swimming party at Kailua, or a little necking in a parked car at the Pali. Faye declared that she had outgrown such unsophisticated things; she hinted at parties in suites at the Royal Hawaiian or on board the yacht of some visiting millionaire. Her mother, who owned a second-rate hat shop on Fort Street, worked hard to see that Faye finished college. But, thanks to me, she never did.

It happened in our junior year. I was called out of class one afternoon to go home to my father, and when I rushed into the house in a panic, fearing he'd had another heart attack, I found him sitting in his study looking sterner than I had ever known he could be. He said to me in a strange voice: "Sit down, Janice. I want to ask you some questions. Where did you get this?"

He reached under the pillows propped behind him and took out a black silk envelope, the sort designed for a woman's purse, which carries powder, comb, lipstick, and other personal accessories. I could not identify it at first. Then I answered, "Oh, that's not mine. I found it on my chair in Professor King's room this morning. Some girl in the class ahead of me left it there."

I looked at his grave face. He waited. "I stuck it in my bag," I went on, "and intended to turn it in. But Grace Ariyoshi offered me a ride at noon and I was in such a hurry to get home that I forgot. Where did you find it?"

"On the floor of the living room." His expression softened. "Did you toss your bag on a chair as usual, when you came in?"

I nodded. "I guess so, when I dumped my books. I know you and Saito are always reminding me, but—"

My father continued, touching the black silk envelope as he spoke: "When I found it, the contents were scattered on the floor. I retrieved them. Do you know whom it belongs to?"

I unsnapped the envelope and spilled out the contents. Lipstick, eye makeup, loose-powder compact, cigarettes, odd little boxes—I recognized the compact from having had it shown to me the week before. It was of gold, with initials in pearls—F.M.

"It's Faye Miller's!" I said. "What funny cigarettes!" I picked one up, and my father slapped it out of my hand. I looked at him in amazement.

"I'm sorry, Kulolo," he said. "I apologize for even questioning you. But I was so horrified, so frightened for a moment—"

The funny cigarettes were marihuana. And among other articles in the very feminine little envelope was a box containing what I realized some years later were contraceptives. I went back to classes knowing nothing other than that. But the university campus saw no more of Faye. I never knew what was said to her or what happened, nor did anyone else. She sailed for the mainland two days later, and since that time I had not seen her again or even thought about her. Now I was to meet her in a new status, as rich widow and neighbor of my father's old friends, and I wondered. Did they know anything of Faye's history? Probably not. The conservative Averys would be horrified. And was Faye aware that I had been the one who inadvertently caused her expulsion not only from college but from the islands? I hoped fervently that she was not.

"Who is Walter talking to out there?" Dr. Atherton asked, and his question caused us to look toward the water's edge where Walter stood with another man. They were too far away for us to hear their conversation, and their figures were merely silhouetted against moving waters with a backdrop of rosy sunset light. At sight of that tall man standing by Walter, I sat up and stared hard. His profile was familiar, and the quickened beat of my heart revealed that my announced disinterest in seeing him again had been pretense. When he struck a pose I had seen a hundred times, crossing one long leg over the other as he stood, with knee bent and toes out almost in ballet position, recognition was certain.

The friend whom Faye had invited to swim with her was Tony Davis.

As I watched, he handed Walter an object which the other took from him with reluctance and held gingerly, as if its touch was unpleasant. Then a woman's figure appeared, dressed in white, and slipped an arm through Tony's, while Walter Benson turned and started back toward the house. Tony and Faye Clarke stood watching him for a moment before they disappeared behind the hibiscus hedge which divided the two properties.

As Walter came near enough to be aware of our observation his steps lagged, he looked dismayed. Finally he made an abrupt detour toward the side of the house. He was stopped by the voice of his wife. "Walter, come here!"

He turned reluctantly.

"What did that man give you? Let me see it!" she demanded.

He hesitated, but as she started to rise with the attitude of preparing to give chase, he held out a small dark mass which was sodden with sea water. Maude Benson took it and laid it on the arm of her chair while we all craned to look.

"Hullo!" Dr. Atherton said. "Who's renouncing Christianity around here?"

No one answered. What Tony had given Walter Benson was the object of the latter's worried inquiry of the morning, about which the Japanese chauffeur had reassured him. It was the object of Maude Benson's angry search of a short while ago. And as I looked at the little leather book with its binding broken and gilt worn from its paper, unforgettable words leaped from the printed page: *". . . Behold, I will bring evil upon this place, and upon the inhabitants thereof . . ."*

The thing which Tony had found was a Bible.

For a moment there was silence. Then Maude Benson read aloud in a harsh voice: *". . . Because they have forsaken me, and have burned incense unto other gods, that they might provoke me to anger with all the works of their hands; therefore my wrath shall be poured out upon this place, and shall not be quenched."*

She laid one hand heavily on the open book and raised dark fanatic eyes. "Luther, I told you!" she cried. "You wouldn't believe me! How much longer are you going to tolerate—"

"Maude, be quiet!"

Julia's voice, iron-stern and not to be disregarded.

"Give the book to me, please," Julia said, and Maude handed it to her. She wrapped a lace handkerchief around it and picked up her two canes. Holding the damp little package carefully, she pulled herself to her feet and started into the house in a slow, dragging walk.

"Luther," she called over her shoulder, "will you tell Suka she can serve dinner? Go in, all of you. I shall join you presently."

* * * *

I didn't go to the governor's reception. In spite of multitudinous questions in my mind, in spite of tensions of conflicting personalities which had made my psychic antennae jerk like Dr. Jaggar's seismograph during a Kilauea quake, even despite the excitement of seeing Tony again and my curiosity—and yes, jealousy—at seeing him with Faye Clarke, my abused nervous system couldn't maintain consciousness any longer. As we pushed our chairs back from the table, I knew that I must have sleep. I apologized to Julia and Luther, explaining that I hadn't been to bed the night before, and they said my absence didn't matter in the least.

After they all departed I went up to my room, feeling relief at being in a completely quiet house, longing just to put myself into a horizontal position. I closed my door and kicked off high heels as I looked around to see where Suka had set my dressing case. I located it on a chair at the side of the room, near which were standing my other three—no, only two—bags. What had happened to the fourth bag? It was the heaviest, because it contained papers: a carbon of my novel manuscript, several notebooks filled with memoranda, recent correspondence with my agent, and a few newly published books which I had intended to read on board ship but which, thanks to Tony's diverting companionship, I had never opened.

I sat on the edge of the bed and stared stupidly at the row of luggage. Did the chauffeur put that bag into the Avery car? Had I seen it with other luggage in the lower hall? I couldn't remember. Suddenly it assumed major importance, as a lost article so often does to one who has taken its possession for granted. It was important. I could never duplicate the notebooks or manuscript carbon, and I needed the correspondence for reference. I began to try to remember, and in my heavy fatigue could produce only hazy impressions. Maybe I had forgotten it and Lily brought it ashore with her hand luggage when she left our suite; she had been the last one out. I longed for sleep, yet even my sleep would be troubled if I didn't try to find that missing piece of luggage. Wearily I slipped my feet into the green sandals again and went down to the lower hall. Nothing there. I found a telephone in the library and sat down to put in a call to Kauai.

Lily's response came to me over a background of staccato Chinese voices punctuated by frequent laughter. The Chuns were having an *aloha* party. We had difficulty in establishing contact until she hushed some of them. "What is it, Janice?" she said.

I told her about the missing bag and asked whether she had it. In the back of my mind was the episode with the cabin steward and fear of his possible reprisal. I disliked the prospect of causing trouble for the fellow, but if he knew something about my luggage it was imperative to take action immediately; the *Lurline* was in port for a very short time.

"I haven't unpacked yet," Lily told me. "I've been too busy. The bags are at my cousin's house, and she lives several miles from here. I'll make a check and let you know in the morning."

"Good! That makes me feel better." I sighed deeply. Over the wire Lily's voice came on a sharper tone: "Janice, what is wrong? You seem distressed. Has anything happened?"

At her question I realized that too much had happened, that I had been resisting assimilation of variegated disturbing things through a long and trying day. As I began to relate them to her in sequence, they developed some sort of pattern, still nebulous in my tired mind, yet beginning to take form with an ugly outline.

I finished talking and felt relieved to hear her say, "You sound as if you've been having a bad dream. That is what happens to frivolous girls who dance and drink and go without sleep for thirty-six hours. Why don't you get some rest and forget it? Call me in the morning and I'll let you know about the bag—it's probably here with my luggage."

Somebody at the Chun house let off a string of firecrackers, and at that moment I disliked very much the Chinese idea that noise is essential at a celebration. Lily laughed and murmured indistinct words and then we said good night.

I went back to my room and turned out the lights, glanced briefly at the pale radiance of a rising moon, and fell across my bed completely dressed, into a sound sleep.

I awakened some time later with moonlight shining directly on my face. I opened my eyes reluctantly and moved my head out of the light, then lay there across the bed listening to night sounds: the rattle of palm fronds, the distant hissing of waves on sand, the odd stirrings of an empty house. Far away I could hear a booming surf. Boom-boom-boom. I gave myself to the rhythm of it, still in that floating state which borders on unconsciousness. Boom-booma-boom. Boom-boom. Boom-booma-boom. Boom-boom.

No surf sounded like that.

I turned so that the ear next the bed was free, and as hearing sharpened I became aware of what the sound meant. Drums. Boom-booma-boom. Boom-boom. Boom-booma-boom. Boom-boom. Temple drums. I had heard them many times before. I raised my head, trying to catch the chanting which accompanied them. Hawaiian *oliolis*, their cadence rising on a minor note, are always clear above the drumbeat which provides a background rhythm. I could hear no chant. Just the drums. Boom-booma-boom. Boom-boom. Boom-booma-boom. Boom-boom. The beating continued, now loud, now very soft. I went to the window and looked out toward the Hawaiian village, from where the sound of the drums came. All I could see in the moonlight was the rocky hill which hid the village from sight. The drums beat on. Maybe they were having a party. Maybe Malia was dancing. Suddenly I had a strong desire to go there.

I looked for shoes, discarded the thought of high heels, and found the grass slippers Suka had provided for me. I should have preferred going barefoot, but no longer had the tough soles of my childhood, when I could walk unconcerned over sharp lava rock. I peeled off stockings and girdle and slipped my feet into the cross straps of the grass sandals. No time for changing clothes. It was important to get to Wainiha before the musicians lost their mood and the party ended. I almost ran out of the house, across the lawn toward the path I remembered so well. I climbed hurriedly to the top of the hill, holding my full skirts tight around me to prevent catching on shrubbery and rocks. The drums were louder now; they seemed to echo from the hills behind the village.

As I reached the top of the rise, they stopped.

I stood and looked at a black and silent place. There were the little houses I remembered, the outlines of the village were the same—yet changed. In brooding darkness the place held its breath, no vegetation stirred, nothing moved, there was not a sign of human life. Suddenly the moon emerged from behind a somber cloud, and I saw the *heiau*, the pile of black stones which I had seen as a child. They were more than a pile now; they were arranged in a manner which indicated that their ancient function had been restored. Walking toward them, I perceived that they glistened in the moonlight.

As I neared the glistening black stones my flesh began to shrink, my heartbeat quickened into a deafening thud of alarm, some atavistic sense caused invisible hairs along my spine to rise stiffly. I felt as if a hundred hostile eyes watched me; I wanted to cringe from horror almost unleashed, from the blow that was coming, the spear hurtling through blackness into my flesh. I whirled around and saw nothing, heard nothing, yet that feeling of primitive terror grew unbearably strong. I retreated from the stones, found the path, and fled.

When I was once more in the house, sitting in a chair and gasping for breath, waiting for my pounding heart to slow its beat, I looked dully at the folds of my long skirt.

The yellow chiffon was stained with blood.

CHAPTER FOUR

I HAD put on a nightgown and thin silk robe when the sound of a car in the driveway told me that the family had returned. I held my door open a crack and watched the Bensons straggle down the hall in silence and disappear behind closed doors. Presently Julia and Luther appeared.

They climbed stairs slowly together, Luther's arm around his wife's shoulders; they were murmuring to each other. When they reached the upper level I called cautiously and beckoned them to my room. At sight of me they stopped, and Julia looked as if she would prefer to retreat. But Luther said, "Let's go and have a chat with Janice, dear." Then, more firmly, "It is time we did so."

Julia braced herself visibly as she answered, "You are right."

Inside my room she glanced around her in surprise and dismay. "Janice," she exclaimed, "forgive me for being such an inattentive hostess! I took for granted—" She lowered herself into a chair and said to Luther, "Please bring an ashtray. There should be some in the library."

I wasn't thinking of ashtrays at that moment. When Luther returned I thanked him and said directly, "Forgive me for keeping you up at this late hour, but I must talk with you. Something is wrong here, and you're trying to conceal it from me."

Luther and Julia looked quickly at each other and then away. I went on. "I'm almost afraid to know what it is you're covering up. But I think it concerns me, or at least some plans I've made, so please explain what's going on."

Julia started to speak, but Luther laid an admonitory hand over hers and said, "You're right, Janice. We knew we couldn't keep it from you indefinitely, although I think Julia was hoping we could. But we thought, since this was your first day home—" He sighed and stalled for time by lighting a cigarette which he held in thin, nicotine-stained fingers.

"I hardly know where to begin," he continued reluctantly, "just as I do not know exactly what to say. So much of this is conjecture, it might sound improbable. I'm afraid—"

"Tell it to me, please, conjecture and all." Then, as he still hesitated, and as Julia huddled mutely in her chair, I added, "I went to the village tonight. The drums woke me."

Julia exclaimed softly, and Luther's eyes as they met mine were sick with worry. "The drums!" he repeated in a tired voice.

"So you heard them too. Go on, Janice."

"I followed the sound of the drums to Wainiha. And I saw no one there—not a living soul. But something was there. Something was beating the drums. And the old *heiau*—Luther, the *heiau* was sprinkled with blood!"

Julia made a sound like a moan and clutched the arms of her chair.

Luther dropped his cigarette, picked it up again, and stared at it as if he hardly knew what he was doing. "Blood. A sacrifice," he muttered. "I was afraid, very much afraid, of that."

I leaned toward him. "What has happened? What is going on over there?"

I feared that I knew. But I wanted to hear it from the Averys before I put a single dread surmise into words.

Luther said, as if speech were wrenched from him: "We are not certain. But from things which are happening—Bibles, for instance, thrown into the sea as symbolic repudiation of Christianity—we are afraid that the Hawaiians have reverted. They've gone back to temple rites, sacrifices, secret practices which we thought long forgotten."

He sighed heavily, as if overcome by the weight of his apprehensions. Then his voice hardened. "But you and Julia were born here and I've lived here twenty-five years. We know that these things are never forgotten. They're under the surface, under the smiling, lying surface of every—" He stopped as Julia made a pained exclamation. Then he asked, in a more normal voice, "Janice, do you remember your father telling us, years ago, about the old *heiau*?"

"I remember. Wainiha means 'wild water,' and several men have drowned in the waters near the village. The *heiau* was built to propitiate the Shark God and prevent him from claiming any more sacrifices. Fishermen made tribute there. But it was in ruins when I saw it last. When was it rebuilt—and by whom?"

"We don't know. You are aware that Julia and I have never interfered with the village; we've left them unmolested just as they respected our privacy by staying on their side of the hill. We have never been like your father, able to mingle with them on an equal basis; neither Julia nor I wanted to, and it would have been silly to pretend."

"They didn't expect it of us, Luther," his wife interpolated, "just as they didn't wish to enter our world. But they knew we would not interfere with them."

She explained to me, "When my father died he left the ranch to Maude and this property to me. He requested in his will that I should never sell Wainiha so long as any vestige of the *heiau* remained or any natives lived peacefully on the land."

I remembered Maude's bitter resentment over the claim of certain historians that the missionaries gave the natives Bibles in exchange for their land. Julia's and Maude's forebears were missionary stock. Perhaps their father had tried to palliate some feeling of guilt by such a token gesture to these dispossessed people who had lived on the islands centuries before the white man ever came.

Luther was talking, and I heard, ". . . people might think it a quixotic request, but Julia prefers to abide by her father's wishes. Her sister doesn't agree."

Julia nodded. "Maude, I regret to say, dislikes the natives and would like to see them evicted. I'm afraid that she handles the Hawaiian employees on the ranch rather harshly."

"It just happened," Luther added, "that we were visiting the Bensons on Maui at the time these things began. When we came home we found that all our servants had left except Suka, and old Henry Mahea, our gardener. Do you remember him?"

"I think I do, vaguely. A lame old fellow with white hair?"

"That was Henry. He had a broken hip as a child and it never healed properly. We sent him to Dr. Larsen for treatment, but nothing could be done. Well, when we returned from Maui and found Suka hysterical with fright, with every door and window in the house locked, and Henry hiding in the garage, we were bewildered. Henry came to us then and said that a *kahuna* had appeared in the village."

"A *kahuna*! A witch doctor! But they don't—" I had started to say that they don't practice their secret arts any more, but I knew that was not so. They do, in Hawaii today. Some know about them, but they are not willing to talk. And none will admit knowledge of where they stay or how to find one.

In the days of the *alii*, the great chiefs, there were many *kahunas*. These were trained from early childhood by their elders, who subjected acolytes to severe disciplines, then passed on to them by word of mouth their incantations and their esoteric knowledge. Many were revered for their healing powers derived from therapeutic use of herbs, plants, and certain Hawaiian clays. Others were respected as *kaulas*, foretellers of coming events. And some were greatly feared as *kahuna anaanas*, those who dealt death.

I did not ask Luther what kind of *kahuna* lived at Wainiha now.

In spite of the hot night, I felt the flesh on my arms rising, and I shivered. For an instant, under the spell of my own imagination, I had almost succumbed to that fear again. Then I looked at the grave faces of the Averys, watching me, their eyes haunted with worry they had tried to conceal. I shook my head in angry rejection.

"Have you seen this supposed *kahuna*?" I asked.

Julia started to speak, and Luther answered hastily, "Nobody has. All we know is what Henry told us, that he's living in the village among the Hawaiians. You know the belief, that a *kahuna* can take any form, that of a child, or an animal—Madame Pele is a thousand years old, but she is supposed to appear often as a beautiful young girl." The scorn in Luther's voice showed how much credence he gave to such stories.

I brought him back to the point. "If nobody has seen the *kahuna*, then why did the servants leave?"

Luther lit another cigarette and put the match down very carefully. His eyes avoided mine as he said, "They heard the drums. And some of them saw a procession."

A procession. Spirits of the dead, marching back to the *heiau* for ghostly celebration of some long-forgotten rite. To stand and look on a procession is supposed to bring death. The unfortunate who encounters one, as he throws his net from the reef at twilight or walks home from the taro patch with the makings of the family's *poi*, must drop to the ground and hide his eyes until the spirits have passed. My father's notebooks contained descriptions of processions reported to him by others who had seen them; they were part of the mystery and lure of Hawaii which enthralled him.

"Never scoff at anything in these islands," he used to remind me. "Such stories have been told for too many years, by too many people, to be laughed at. I do not believe, neither do I disbelieve. I continue to ask questions and make notes. Maybe someday I shall find out."

Two pairs of eyes were watching me intently. I forced myself to laugh. "Really, Luther," I said, "that is simply ridicu—"

Luther's expression stopped me. "We felt exactly the same way. I—I still do. But we found Henry's body in the garden early in the morning, two days ago. He had died sometime during the night. The doctor said death resulted from heart failure which might have been caused by shock. From the look on his face—" He made a gesture as if to brush something from before his eyes.

Julia's voice was a whisper. "Malia told us there had been another procession that night."

"Did she see it?"

"She says so."

Luther gave his wife a look of reproach. "But Malia is an overemotional girl, an incorrigible liar, inclined to dramatize everything. She came to work for us after Mrs. Clarke discharged her for stealing. I don't like to have her in the house, but Julia is kindhearted, and besides, we're under-staffed. It's difficult for us to keep servants now. Maude's doing her best, but—" He shrugged again.

I turned to Julia then, with concern. "You shouldn't have taken on the burden of another guest," I said. "You should have let me go to a hotel, since my house isn't available."

Julia smiled faintly. "We are glad you are here."

Luther added with reassuring warmth, "Having you with us will lighten the atmosphere considerably; I can see that Julia feels better already. And Ellen needs younger companionship; the poor girl is perishing of boredom."

He rose and said, throwing back his shoulders as if shifting a heavy load, "I haven't once mentioned your movie plans for the village, but that doesn't mean they're forgotten for a minute. We know what it means to you, and I'm sure we'll be able to work something out. After all, we do own the land. But I should strongly prefer to keep things as quiet as possible until the senator leaves—that's only a week. Do you think you can agree to that? Or is there a particular hurry?"

"No hurry," I said.

I reflected wryly that we *kamaainas*—islanders—were now putting the very barrier between ourselves and mainlanders which we proclaimed fervently should not exist. But I also remembered that some years ago a mainland newspaper had once cited a lengthy Hawaiian name as conclusive argument against statehood for our islands. What, they asked (ignoring many other prominent American names which had been shortened or changed), would happen to the pages of the Congressional Record if we should ever elect to political office a man with a name like David Kekoalauliionapali-hauliokekoolau Kaapuawaokamehameha?

The senator must be protected from hearing the slightest rattle of any Hawaiian skeleton. I was in full accord with Julia and Luther on that, and I reiterated my refusal to give credence to stories of specters and witch doctors and ghosts who beat an ominous rhythm on invisible sharkskin drums.

After we said good night I went to bed thinking of old Henry Mahea, found dead in the garden where he had worked for so many years. Dead from seeing a procession of ghosts? Never. Henry had been aged, illiterate, and filled with primitive folklore he'd heard from childhood. Many of the older Hawaiians, unable to assimilate an alien culture which reached them late in life, had withdrawn from Caucasian influences or sought the protection of a *haole*—white—family in a job which did not require active participation in the life of the community. It had undoubtedly been Henry's funeral Julia went to this afternoon, and she hadn't wished to sadden my homecoming by talking about it. Let the poor old man's superstitions be buried with him.

I turned out the light. Then I lay in my bed for a long time, my nerves taut in spite of myself. Waiting. Listening for the sound of drums booming their ghostly summons under hands which could not be seen.

CHAPTER FIVE

WHEN I came down for breakfast I found Ellen Benson in the living room thumbing a magazine. From her relieved smile at my arrival, I knew she had been waiting for me.

"Hello," I said. "Had breakfast yet?"

"Not yet. I was wondering—is that yours?" She indicated something behind the half-opened door. My missing piece of luggage.

"Yes, it is. I wondered what had happened to it. When I missed it last night, I thought at first—" I stopped in time. I had been about to tell her about the cabin steward and my worry over damage to my luggage, which is more common on steamship lines than most passengers are aware. Then I realized that telling the story would include the episode of George Leung's attempt to seduce Lily, and decided it was not for this sheltered girl's ears.

Was she also protected from knowledge of witch doctors and Polynesian temple rites, or did she know what was happening such a short distance from where she stood? Probably not. Her father had tried to prevent her mother from finding another Bible on the beach. Was he protecting his wife from knowledge of the paganism which she abhorred—or trying to prevent a vituperative public outburst?

"You were saying . . ." the girl prompted, and looked puzzled.

"Excuse me for daydreaming," I said. "I was about to say I thought I had left my bag on the *Lurline*. A good thing I didn't—it has my notebooks in it. How about some breakfast?"

"Let's go in." We started side by side.

She was a head taller than I, and she held herself ungracefully, trying to minimize that height. I knew how she felt, for although I'm of average size, standing by the diminutive Lily Wu when she's wearing flat Chinese slippers makes me feel tall. Better clothes would help her a lot, I thought as we chattered superficialities on the way into the dining room.

Walter Benson was there, scowling into a cup of coffee. His face cleared at our appearance, and when I mentioned his solitariness he said that Maude had eaten and Julia generally breakfasted in bed. Luther had already gone to his office, since it was past eight. I had forgotten how early the business day begins in the islands.

The dining room had French windows which were flung open to the morning, and from the table we looked out on a garden bathed in sunlight, moisture from an early watering still glittering on tropical foliage. Mynah birds stalked across the lawn, commenting querulously on affairs of the day, and palms crackled occasionally as if to remind us that this would be another interval of heat without the relief of cooling trade winds.

After Walter Benson excused himself, his daughter began to question me about my plans for the day, and I soon found that what she wanted was to go with me when I went shopping. Her mother had chosen a dress for her which was too large, and she wanted my help in returning it. If it was anything like the sad white number she had worn last night, the poor girl needed help—and not from her mother.

I explained that I had several errands in town but would be glad to take her with me that afternoon, and we arranged to leave after lunch. As soon as I could excuse myself gracefully, I went to my room on pretense of letters which must catch the outgoing *Lurline*.

I took my heavy bag upstairs and left it, then put on some crepe-soled brogues and a kick-pleated cotton dress which would enable me to walk freely. Going softly to avoid interception, I slipped out of the house by the front door and headed up the drive to the highway. I would go to Wainiha by the old trail which Father and I used years ago.

When I reached the little village the pounding of my pulse was caused by more than the exertion of walking in a hot sun. I was afraid to see it in daylight, afraid of what I might find. Scrambling down the path and emerging near the little spring, I almost gasped with relief as I entered a place both familiar and loved and found it much the same as I had remembered.

Wainiha hadn't grown during the years. The few small shacks straggled in a rough V pattern into the narrow valley which ended in a dense green thicket overhung by boulders of lava rock. Trumpet vines clambered over the houses, camouflaging rough carpentry; lantana flaunted little orange flowers on rocky hillsides. Palms leaned like slim coquettes over roofs of corrugated tin, and *kiawe* trees cast lacy shadows on the warm red earth. A big croton with pointed leaves of variegated red, yellow, and green served for drying a purple *mumu* (Hawaiian-style Mother Hubbard), some tattered shorts, and a net in which a few silver scales shone.

Beneath the largest tree two women sat, weaving *lauhala*, bare brown feet showing under the edge of their cotton dresses. They looked at me steadily, without smiling.

"Hello," I said.

"Hello," one woman answered, without enthusiasm, but with unfailing Hawaiian courtesy. "You want to see somebody?"

"I came to visit Makaleha. Is she here?"

The two women looked at each other, my interrogator asking a silent question, the other answering with a shrug. Then:

"Makaleha don' live here now."

"She has moved?" Thinking of Henry Mahea's death, I felt a chill of dread.

"She went Puunui to stay wit' her sister."

"How long ago?"

A shrug was my answer.

"Whereabouts in Puunui? Do you know her sister's name, or the name of the street?"

They didn't know anything.

I thanked them and walked on, past the house where Makaleha used to live. I stared frankly at the interior of the shack, glimpsing dried squid and fishes hanging from exposed rafters, calabashes of food suspended in nets, an oilcloth-covered table piled with mangoes and pineapple. The sight of it gave me a stronger nostalgia than I had ever felt. I moved lagging feet past the door.

Just before the sea, on a rocky promontory at the right of the settlement, was the *heiau*. I approached it remembering how black and fearful it had looked the night before. Conscious of eyes watching me steadily, I dared not stop to examine it closer, and I could not see whether there were bloodstains on it.

The *heiau* was covered with flowers.

At the beach I turned left and followed a flat rocky ledge around the point beyond which was the swimming hole I knew. Long years ago it had been a canoe anchorage for some Hawaiian chieftain, where his huge outrigger could be hidden safe from storms and human enemies. Coral grew near the shore and it was not safe to walk there; those who knew the place swam or floated past the coral to where the cove deepened into a smooth, sandy undersea basin. It was a good place for catching squid and eels which hid in the few huge rocks on the ocean's floor, and beyond it was a good place for spearing the big fish which followed little *kihikihis* in toward their marine grotto. I had caught my share there when I was a twelve-year-old. When I reached the spot I found someone ahead of me, in the act of poising a spear. I stopped and caught my breath, for I had forgotten that man can be so magnificent.

He was naked except for the red *malo* around his loins, and along his perfect body the long muscles of the swimmer rippled with each movement. His skin was bronze, and sea water dripped from black curls on his head. When he became aware of me he turned, and I saw with joy that I knew him. Many years ago David Kimu had been my playmate. We had swum together often in this very place where we stood.

"David!" I called eagerly. "Aloha!"

He let the spear down to his side and looked directly at me without speaking.

"David Kimu!" I called again. "Don't you remember me? We used to—" I faltered at the expression in his eyes, for they burned with enmity.

Then he said, "You *haole wahine*. Nobody wants you here. Get out!"

Before I could answer, he had slipped into the water without causing even a splash and disappeared.

I started back to the Averys', walking along the beach this time, going slowly and digesting the heavy feeling inside me—sick disappointment overlaid with a fear which I would not name. I tried to reason with myself. I had been childish to expect the little community to remain unchanged for years until I decided to visit it again. I myself had changed, as Luther reminded me, had in fact undergone almost complete metamorphosis since I last saw Wainiha. Why should not its people change also? I had expected everything to remain static for five—no, seven—years until the day I chose to go back and find my old friends. That was not realistic.

What was real, what sickened me, was the hostility of my old playmate. I had so long thought of Wainiha as the one place where *aloha* really meant what it said. But David hadn't recognized me, I consoled myself. He probably thought I was some nosy tourist, come to gawk and to laugh at the simple natives. I looked like one; my hair was upswept, instead of hanging to my shoulders as it used to be, and my fair skin was bleached by a winter in an eastern city. I would try again, I decided, when I wasn't coiffed like a *malihini*—a tourist—when I wasn't wearing clothes from Lord & Taylor and shoes made in London.

Yes, I would go back and try again. But under my rationalization was something which I dreaded to acknowledge, spawned of events of the night before, of the bloody *heiau* and the stories I had been told of native regression. I was afraid. Not in the blind terror of mysterious darkness, but in daylight and facing something incomprehensible but nevertheless a fact. I was more afraid now than I had been before. I quickened my steps into the house, trying to put out of my mind the memory of hostile eyes and the picture of a bloodstained pagan altar covered with flowers.

CHAPTER SIX

IN THE saffron light of a Hawaiian sunset the setting for that memorable party of Faye Clarke's was most impressive. Her place was larger than the Averys' and more modern, set in several acres of lawn over which spread many trees: royal poinciana, covered with blossoms like flames, golden shower and ancient banyan, plus the usual tropical flowers and plants. As we approached the flat-roofed white house, its grounds dotted with chairs and umbrellas, the broad *lanai* accommodating garden furniture, more chairs and tables, there was a feeling of expectancy in the air. This was an event even in party-minded Honolulu. Faye was giving the senator a *luau*, a Hawaiian feast, in lavish style.

Ellen Benson and I arrived early by tacit agreement; I because of tense curiosity about several things, Ellen because she admittedly didn't want to miss a moment of such a gala evening. We walked along the beach from Avery land and across the lawn to the edge of the *lanai*, where we halted until we were oriented, then chose chairs and moved toward them.

Ellen was wearing the new dress I had helped her choose, and to my amusement her mother had not dared protest because, although she knew she didn't like what it did for her daughter, she couldn't find out why. It was of blue nylon net, disarmingly simple but superbly fitted to Ellen's very nice figure. The neck was plain and it had sleeves, but the material curved around her young breasts gently and the waist outlined but did not restrict her own, while the skirt was long enough to be quite modest indeed. Ellen was speechless with pleasure at wearing something which became her so well, and as she modeled it for her family

I had contented myself with glances first at the radiant girl, then at Maude Benson, who surveyed her daughter very much as the hen must have watched the duckling when it headed for the pond and began to swim.

The Bensons, the Averys, and Dr. Atherton drove over because of Julia's lameness, arriving soon after we did. Dr. Atherton helped Julia to be seated comfortably while Maude chose a metal-and-canvas chair which could offer no hiding place for insects. Walter settled near his wife with a bored expression, while Luther excused himself immediately and began greeting the few early guests en route to where the senator sat near the bar, flanked by sycophants and alcohol. The senator was a big man; he carried the strained expression and distended belly which accompany the last stages of pregnancy, with the difference that he brought forth not life but vacuities.

"Faye, my dear," he called to our hostess, who was approaching behind us, "when are we going to see some of those famous *hula-hulas*?" And he waved his glass and sang off-key that appalling thing which goes "Yakshula Hiky-dula." I turned, as much to avoid watching him as to get a close look at Faye Clarke.

I don't remember what I noticed first about Faye: her face, her figure, or the clothes she wore. Each was spectacular.

She was small-boned, slightly under average height, and her tiny waist made curved hips and full, round breasts seem voluptuous by contrast—or was it the way in which she was aware of them? Her skin was a golden tan;

her hair was black, brushed back from her face and swirled into an enormous roll behind her left ear. For most women such an *outré* coiffure might be ridiculous; on Faye Clarke it was perfect. Her eyes were deep blue, framed by long straight lashes, and the faint shadows under them might have come from fatigue, art—or debauchery. She wore a full-skirted dress of violet taffeta slit to the knee, the flaring hem of which was faced with scarlet satin which matched her slippers.

She went directly to a love seat which was next to Maude Benson's chair and said as she sat down. "You'll see some *hulas*, Senator, you'll see dozens. Be patient; we're going to eat first. In the meantime let's have a drink. Mrs. Benson, what would you like? Bourbon, gin, or rum?"

Maude Benson managed to say in a choking voice that she didn't want anything. She leaned back in her chair, endeavoring to exude her usual air of sour sanctity, but failing signally, since her dark eyes when they rested on Faye were so filled with the fires of hell. In the meantime a pretty Japanese girl in kimono and spotless white *tabes* offered a tray from which Faye took a glass.

Whether Faye sat close to Maude by accident or intent, the result was startling. Here, within clawing distance of each other, were two women equally to be disliked, but for opposite reasons. The one who was beautiful seemed completely unaware of what propinquity did for both of them; the other was rigid with awareness. Faye's golden skin, the perfection of her grooming, made Maude Benson look like a leprous old log and accentuated by contrast that quality in herself which produced the effect, somehow, of a perfect fruit just overripe, on point of rottenness. Looking at Faye, one could perceive no slightest flaw, but the impression of imminent decay remained. I don't have premonitions. Perhaps it was that I knew what she was like underneath. Perhaps it was just the perfume which surrounded her, the heavy sweetness of *pikake*, tiny carved ivory blossoms which were pinned in a circle around the swirl of her black hair.

She was the kind of woman who makes other women feel awkward and homely. The apple-green organza which had so appealed to me at McInerny's that afternoon seemed silly and girlish. I pushed my backbone against my chair and held stomach muscles tight to keep my middle flat as it should be. Beside me, Ellen Benson was staring almost hungrily, her gray eyes mirrors of fascination. Across from us Ellen's father, too, was looking at Faye like a man in an aviary hypnotized by a bird whose plumage is so fantastic that he can't believe it is real. From his seat near Julia, Dr. Atherton eyed the round bosom which swelled from Faye's strapless gown with frank and unabashed appreciation. Only Luther seemed uneasy, as if apprehensive that the mysteriously upheld taffeta bodice might slip its moorings and cause embarrassment to everyone. Except, I was certain, its wearer.

The object of this concerted regard seemed sublimely indifferent to all of it. She took banana chips from the proffered tray and her white teeth crunched with enjoyment. She drank a good dollop of her highball before she exhaled with satisfaction.

"I'm dry," she announced. "I've been talking to real-estate agents all afternoon."

Luther reproved her gently. "You ought to let me talk to them for you, Faye; they'll take advantage of a *malihini*."

She turned her lazy smile on him. "I'm not a *malihini*, Luther, remember? I was born here. But I've been away long enough to get rid of your Hawaiian habit of procrastination. When I see what I want I'll get it."

Her tone changed; she added in silky voice, "And it'll be a long day in the morning before a real-estate agent—or any other man—takes advantage of me."

I leaned toward Ellen. "What does she mean?"

Ellen's answer was also whispered. "She's going to build an apartment house at Waikiki, and Uncle Luther is drawing the plans. But so far she hasn't found the right property."

Julia's association with Faye became more comprehensible to me then. Even if she didn't know the lady's past history, Faye's demeanor might have made her company distasteful to Luther's straitlaced wife. But this was business, the great American godhead because of which so many social and ethical breaches must be overlooked. It took a lot of money to finance an establishment like this, and a hundred times more for apartment construction on an island where building costs can conservatively be called fantastic.

Faye's ears had caught the sibilance of our whispers. She turned her head, seeing me for the first time. In spite of the years since we had met, recognition was instantaneous.

"Why, Janice Cameron!" she drawled. "Julia told me you were here, and for the moment I had forgotten. Welcome to Honolulu, and congratulations on your intellectual achievements!"

Red lips curled in a tigress smile, blue eyes widened for an instant, before black lashes swept down and hid what was, revealed in them.

Yes, Faye remembered.

I looked at her with what I hoped was a bland expression, something I've tried to learn from Lily Wu. I answered in a voice as honeyed as her own, "Thank you, Faye. It's wonderful to be home, and to see old friends again."

"Speaking of old friends," she said, "I think you know one of mine"— she glanced over our group in search of someone—"around here somewhere. He arrived on the *Lurline* yesterday. I tried to get him to stay here, but he insists on putting up at Menopause Manor."

She was referring to a conservative and charming little hotel near the Royal Hawaiian, which received its local nickname from predominance of a certain type of feminine clientele.

Maude Benson gasped, but Faye did not seem to hear that sound of outrage. She said, as a figure emerged from the living room of her house, "Here he comes now. *Wikiwiki*, darling, we're miles ahead of you."

The man was Tony, of course. He strolled toward us, a sophisticated figure in the tropical mess jacket and red cummerbund which is the most stunning uniform a young man can wear, and gave Faye a casual salute before he said to me, "Hello, Janice. Told you we'd meet again soon." Then he helped himself to food and a drink and sat down near Faye.

Guests began arriving simultaneously. Well-dressed people greeted each other with enthusiasm, although many of the men had been in business offices together a few short hours ago, while the women met on the street, played bridge frequently, and telephoned each other daily for details of local gossip. Drinks were passed, a Hawaiian orchestra set up instruments and began to play that rollicking island song, "Kilo Kilo o Haleakala," voices murmured and there was laughter from amicable groups as the party took on every semblance of a completely delightful affair.

After a while I rose, ignoring the rather wistful look which Ellen sent me, and walked to the orchestra to request "Liliu E." Tony Davis followed me with two glasses. "Have one?" he said, and I accepted the drink and smiled at him as if I were not the least curious about how he happened to be on "darling" terms with Faye Clarke.

He explained with a grin which showed excellent white teeth beneath his small mustache. "I knew her in Washington; her husband was my commander. She's quite a gal, isn't she?"

"Yes, quite," I agreed.

We strolled across the lawn to where servants were setting places for a *luau*—the famous Hawaiian feast. It was impressively done, and the right touches were there: a long table spread with *lauhala* mats and green leaves, with centerpieces of pineapples, mangoes, and bananas. Table flowers were orchids instead of hibiscus, since the hibiscus closes at night, to the consternation and embarrassment of many a *malihini* hostess giving her first island party. There were *leis* at each place, carnations, roses, ginger—a riot of color and fragrance. There would no doubt be good *luau* food: the essential roast pig, steamed *laulaus* (*ti* leaves filled with butterfish, salt pork, and salmon), coconut pudding, shellfish, *lomi-lomi* salmon with tomatoes and onions—all provided by modern native caterers. The senator was bound to be overwhelmed, for how could he know that the item lacking on this menu was its one essential—the spirit of real *aloha*?

We stood and admired the table for a while and then turned toward the ocean, walking slowly, enjoying the coolness which had come with swift tropical twilight. Out of some obscure spite within me—a desire, I suppose, to belittle Faye in some manner—I said to Tony, "This reminds me of other times, before parties became commercialized. I've been to some real *luaus*, a little farther down this very beach. They had a charm, a spirit of fun that—" I dropped it with a shrug.

Tony said, "Tell me about them, Janice."

"Oh, they didn't look like much," I said, glad of a chance to speak of memories so dear to me, "but they were wonderful. Perhaps because we all participated; we did most of the work ourselves. First we came to the beach early, and got terribly excited over making the *imu*—that's the pit in which the pig is cooked. There was always some Hawaiian man who was the *imu* expert, who gave orders and supervised. Everybody gathered around while he went through his solemn ritual, dropping redhot rocks into a pit of damp sand, laying the pig, all swathed in *ti* leaves and wet burlap, on the hot rocks as tenderly as cradling a baby, spreading yams around him, and other good things, then laying on more rocks and more, and at last a layer of damp sand——" I sighed, remembering.

We stopped near a tree at the edge of the lawn and Tony pulled me down beside him on a marble bench which faced the ocean. The warm air increased the fragrance of the gardenias I wore, while from the sea came a salty, tangy smell and the susurrus of water slipping over sand. We set our glasses down, and it was the most natural thing in the world for me to lean against him, his arm around my waist, as I went on reminiscing.

"Then," I told him, "while you wait for the pig to cook—and that takes hours—you have a *hukilau*. *Huki* means pull, and *lau* is net. It's a long thing weighted at the bottom, and some men row out in a horseshoe route and drop it into the water. A couple of dozen people, or fifty—it doesn't matter—divide into teams, and each group pulls an end of the net toward shore, wading chest-deep into the ocean at first. When it's finally brought in there's terrific excitement, because you never know what you're going to catch: fishes of a hundred kinds, and squid—once we netted an enormous turtle and had the most delicious turtle steaks the next day."

"Do you eat all those fish?" Tony sounded dubious.

"Just the choicest ones. Some of the rest are dried, some thrown back into the water. But catching your dinner fresh at its source and cooking it on the spot is wonderful fun.

"Then the group breaks up and some prepare food and some swim and some set the table, generally just grass mats and leaves and no eating implements at all, and some pick flowers for *leis*, and others make music and some drink liquor and everybody laughs all the time. When the pig is done there's the most terrific excitement as everybody gathers around while the expert dips into a calabash of sea water and removes the hot stones with bare hands, drawing out the suspense until it's almost unbearable. And when the steam begins to rise, when you smell that roast pig, there's a groan of anticipation that goes around the crowd and your mouth waters and you think you can hardly bear to wait!"

Somewhere behind us orange light flared suddenly in the darkness, and we turned to see that torches had been lit around the table, so that it stood spotlighted on Faye's lawn.

"They're about to eat," I said. "We'd better go. I've made myself hungry."

Our heads were very close. "You've made me feel as if I were starving," Tony said, and I shivered as his breath stirred my hair.

"But there's something more urgent than food," he murmured, "which I've wanted for a long time." His mouth bent to mine, and after a while my arms went around him. All I can say about that moment is that it was perfect.

"Hello, Tony." A voice spoke suddenly from the dark, and we started apart. Faye, I thought, she has followed us. But it wasn't Faye.

It was Malia. She was wearing the faded cotton dress, the grass sandals, and her beautiful hair was loose to her shoulders. In the flickering light around us her dark eyes glittered. She ignored my embarrassed greeting.

"I want to talk to you, Tony," she told him, and to my surprise he left me unceremoniously and walked several feet away with her, where they stood for a few minutes talking in such low tones that I couldn't hear a word. Finally he laughed and turned back toward me. I had been so dumfounded that I was still sitting there, gaping.

Tony bent and picked up our glasses, smiling at Malia, who had followed him. "Are you going to dance tonight?" he asked her, pulling me up with his free hand as he spoke. I was far too interested in this diversion to protest, and rose obediently.

Malia walked beside us as we started toward the big table where people were milling around in the light of the torches. "Yes," she said, "I'm gonna dance. Something special, you'll see." She laughed softly as if at a secret she knew.

"I'll be looking forward very much— Now where did she go?" The last was addressed to me, for as he spoke she had disappeared.

"Probably slipped behind the shrubbery," I said, thinking of her shabby dress and my new one, conscious again of that pang of guilt which for some reason she made me feel.

"You told me you'd never been in the islands before," I accused, stopping to speak directly to him. "Where did you know Malia?"

Tony laughed. "In Washington. She was Faye's maid there, and quite a sensation, I can tell you, at a party or two I remember. Faye said she had to fire her recently for stealing; it's a mistake to take a girl like that out of her environment."

"If you can't offer her anything better than a menial life," I said tartly, "it certainly is."

Tony didn't answer this, for we had reached the party and further conversation was impossible. Faye watched us approach the table with a smile I could not understand—why should she feel triumphant because Tony and I had spent some time in the dark together? The gesture with which she summoned him to her side was hardly noticeable, but he obeyed. He took me to my seat between Walter Benson and Luther and then went to sit on her left. Two Hawaiian men wearing *malos*, their bodies glistening with coconut oil, approached the table carrying a *koa* platter with carved feet, on which lay the steaming pig. There were outcries of excitement, proclamations of hunger, congratulations to the cooks, and the feast began.

The senator was on Faye's right, of course, and seated next to him was the pretty blond wife of a vacationing radio star. Farther down the table one of America's most fabulously rich women, well known in Hawaii for her penchant for subsidizing "amusing" local characters, nibbled on *laulau* and presented her long, vacant face to her fellow guests. A woman reporter whom I had known for years sat beside John Atherton. She caught my eye and winked as she stuffed *opakapaka* into her mouth and followed it with a dextrous "two fingers" of *poi*. She was having fun, no doubt laughing to herself at the story she'd pound out tonight before she went to bed, a story which would highlight celebrities and glamour (and omit the scandalous which might have filled two columns). Luther was seated next to the wife of a prominent attorney, eating abstractedly and listening with politeness to nasal chitchat. Julia looked tired, and as I watched her Dr. Atherton bent and said something to which she nodded agreement, closing her eyes wearily as she assented. Maude Benson was talking to a local judge, who reacted, from the expression on his face, as if either her words or the food were giving him gas pains. Walter Benson alternately stared at Faye and glanced toward the periphery of darkness beyond the flaring torches; he seemed to be waiting for someone to appear, possibly the dancers Faye had promised. I was glad to see that Ellen was having a good time. Faye had been kind enough to seat her next to the judge's son, a big agreeable fellow who had recently been graduated from Yale, as is the custom with many sons of *kamaaina* families. They chattered animatedly, calling each other Fred and Ellen, both looking as if they had just discovered something exciting. I hoped it was romance.

I encountered Tony's eyes often, and as we were eating fingers of pine-apple at the end of the meal he pantomimed "See you later," and I nodded, conscious of Faye's observation of this byplay. I might not stand much chance against her kind of competition, but it would be fun to try. Someone had provided Tony with a dossier of me before we sailed together, and I wondered more than ever why. Faye? Not likely, unless she wanted something from me, and I hadn't a thing—except a publishing contract—which she didn't have twice as much of.

After dinner Faye led us to long mats on the grass and we seated ourselves to watch the *hula* troupe. They were very good, and Malia, as she had said, was by far the best. Wearing fresh *ti*-leaf skirts, brief bras, and flowers around neck, wrists, and ankles, the dancers swayed and rippled arms and fingers in the lovely gestures of some old *hulas* whose meaning was lost to most of the audience. When the music quickened to a modern dance, general interest quickened simultaneously. The *hula* troupe was followed by older women in flowered *holokus*, long dresses with ruffled trains, who played their own accompaniment for plaintive songs and wandered around like strolling minstrels, giving guests a chance to stretch themselves, to form conversational groups again, or to head back to the bar.

About eleven o'clock Faye announced, "The moon is coming up. Who wants a swim in the pool? There are bathing suits for everybody who's interested."

"What a hostess!" said the radio star, who was standing near my chair. I agreed with him, looking around meanwhile to locate the swimming pool.

"It's over there in that bamboo grove," someone said, and I walked over with Ellen and her new beau to have a look at it while other guests dispersed toward the house in search of suits and dressing rooms.

The pool was large and very beautiful, with irregularly curved sides, lined with aqua-colored tiles. One look at the clear water made me long to dive into it, and I said to Ellen, "Shall we go home and get our suits?" I had no wish to swim in a borrowed bathing suit, since I had just bought a new one of nylon tricot which fit me like a lover's embrace.

"I'd rather not go home, Janice." Ellen hesitated. She was afraid she might not be permitted to return. "Besides, my suit is pretty old. I'll borrow one from Mrs. Clarke."

"Okay," I said. "I'll be right back."

I found the Averys and Maude Benson getting ready to leave, the latter looking very grim because she could not find the rest of her family. There was some delay while she inquired of various guests whether they knew the whereabouts of Ellen and Walter. I could have told her where Ellen was but didn't. Finally Luther said, "We really must go, Maude; Julia is exhausted. If you want to stay and look for them, you can walk home—it's only a few hundred feet." Maude declined to stay, and I said I'd look for Walter and Ellen when I came back with my suit.

I changed in my room, said good night to Luther and Julia, and walked back along the beach to Faye Clarke's house.

The *waikiki* wing of her house faced the Averys' and did not offer observation to her *luau* guests, unless perhaps they were invited or strayed there by accident as I did. I had to pass it on my way back, and that is how I happened to discover another party going on—a party of a special kind, for a limited number of guests. I heard music as I approached the house, and noticed that light shone from the windows of a room from which the music came. Walking soundlessly on the lawn, I approached a window half hidden by hibiscus and looked into a large room furnished with a Capehart and shelves of record albums, with sofas and chairs pushed back to permit a cleared space in the center of the floor. Several men were there, and a few women, and if I had come equipped with an outboard motor I doubt whether they would have heard me, so intent were they on the figure which occupied the center of the floor and held every eye.

Malia was dancing. Not the old and esoteric *hulas* which had been performed earlier in the evening, nor even the modern humorous dances which had followed that little-appreciated performance. The music to which she moved was something I had never heard: wild music, with a weird melody played on some wind instrument to the beat of jungle drums. Malia's dance interpreted that mood perfectly, in motions which were half savage, half calculatedly obscene, sensual to the point of viciousness. Malia's lovely body thrust and shuddered, twisted in sly sinuosities and quivering invitation, accompanied by ever-moving arms and fingers, shoulders and feet. All the while her facial expression never changed: her big dark eyes stared widely, her mouth was fixed in a smile which held both solicitation and contempt.

Her audience was small, but no great tragedienne, no operatic star, no artist of most superior caliber ever held spectators more rapt. The senator sat glassy-eyed, the drink in his lax hand forgotten in the taste of a stronger intoxicant. The famous radio star watched Malia like a man seeing in flesh incarnate for the first time the substance of his most ecstatic dreams. Walter Benson was there, sitting forward on his chair, both hands pressed hard on his knees. Tony lounged in a rattan chair, his eyes following Malia's every movement. The half dozen other men held poses indicating equal enthrallment. And the few women present—the radio personality's wife, the very rich woman, others whom I didn't know—were as absorbed as the men. Faye sat near the record player, a crystal tumbler in one hand and a cigarette in the other, a half-smile on her mouth.

I looked back at Malia, in time to see her finish her dance in traditional *hula* pose, both arms extended before her, one hand over the other with fingers outstretched, the gesture which says "And thus my dance is finished—I hope it has pleased you." It was only then, when that lovely body was still for a moment, that I became aware of her costume. While she moved it had been one with her, a whirling mass of color. Now I perceived that she was wearing a single sheer garment—my nylon nightgown. I stifled an exclamation as I heard sudden movement beside me. Someone else was hidden there a few feet away, watching through the next window.

There were sounds of applause as Malia stood in the center of the floor, then loud cries for more, more, and Faye, shrugging slightly, went to the record player and turned a switch. Another weird melody began, and Malia's body swayed in the movement with which a dancer gathers the rhythm and prepares to express what the music says to her. There was a sudden crash near me, then a figure moved from behind the protection of a hibiscus bush and burst through the French doors into the house. It was David Kimu, and he strode toward the half-naked girl who had begun a second dance. Ignoring gasps, outcries of protest, he went directly to her and said something in a low voice. Malia didn't stop dancing, but she spit words at him from between her teeth. At that David slapped her with all his strength, so that she reeled on her bare feet, then he picked her up and carried her from the room.

He set her down on the earth a few feet from where I stood, and I heard him say, "Shame on you! I told you, Malia—"

She whirled toward him and let loose an outburst which was half English oaths and half Hawaiian invective. Then she said, "You leave me alone! You mind your business! I know what I'm doing! You thought I was leaving tomorrow, didn't you? Well, I'm not, I'm staying here, and I'm gonna dance in the movies and I'll make plenty money. You can go to hell! You and anybody else that tries to stop me!" She burst into sobs and started running toward the beach, with David following.

I turned away and headed for the swimming pool without looking again at the people in Faye's music room.

CHAPTER SEVEN

FAYE'S swimming pool was a popular place, surrounded by a bamboo grove on two sides, the air drenched with perfume from flowering plants, stephanotis, gardenias, moonflowers; their perfume lay heavy in the hot air of that summer night. Many of Faye's guests had decided to swim, and they frolicked in the water with much splashing and diving, whoops from the men and shriller cries from their feminine playmates.

The Hawaiian boys had arranged themselves near the edge of the pool and played tirelessly, complying with requests for various songs with wonderful good humor. There is nothing a Hawaiian loves more than to see his fellow human beings having fun—love of life pulses so incorrigibly in his own blood stream.

I swam the length of the pool, then tried an underwater stroke which David taught me years ago. The water was too filled with threshing arms and legs for satisfactory navigation, but the feeling of movement was good. Ellen and Fred were racing each other; when she saw me she swam to my side and said, "Is everything all right at home?" I reassured her. Let Maude fret. If she didn't grumble about this, she'd find something else to complain of; Ellen might as well enjoy herself while she could.

Faye had provided bathing suits of the sort which will fit almost any figure, an adjustable halter-and-diaper arrangement. On Ellen it was terrific. She had the Junoesque kind of body which looks better without clothes than covered. She was conscious of this—how could she help being, when Fred's eyes followed her with such open admiration?—in a half-shy, half-proud way which was very charming. When I pulled myself up to the edge of the pool, Ellen followed and sat beside me. She looked sideways at me, then down at her feet, and seemed about to say something.

I decided to help her out. "Ellen, what's on your mind? Are you worried about being here without your family? You needn't feel guilty; you're not doing anything wrong."

She said, watching her ankles, "It's not that, Janice. I just wondered whether I should tell you something, if you'll be annoyed. It's really not my business."

I laid a hand on her wet arm. "Of course I won't be annoyed. Go ahead and tell me."

She said in an embarrassed voice, "It's about Mr. Davis. Do you— Is he—" She couldn't finish.

"Do you mean am I especially interested in him? The answer is no. He's only a tourist on his first trip to Hawaii; we had fun together on the *Lurline*, that's all. Now, what about him?"

Her smile seemed relieved. "Well, I just happen to know that this isn't his first trip to the islands. He was here about a month ago. You know, Mrs. Clarke is clearing the beach in front of these two houses, and I was swimming out there one day, and I saw Mr. Davis sitting on the *lanai* with her, having cocktails. I think they have been—friends, for a long time."

Ellen was so uncomfortable after having made this revelation that I had to lighten the moment for her. I began to laugh with feigned amusement. "The rascal! That's what she meant when she said he was an old friend! Do you think she could be jealous of me, Ellen? I'm flattered."

Ellen giggled. At that moment Fred came up and grabbed her by the ankles. "Come on in, the water's wonderful!" She held to the rim of the pool, letting out little screams of protest, until he pulled her into the water, where they both went down and emerged, laughing. Ellen waved to me as they started off in a race to the other end.

My head felt too warm under the rubber cap and I peeled it off. I was sitting there running my fingers through wet ends of my hair, reflecting on what Ellen had told me, when Tony appeared.

"Hi."

"Hi," I answered. "Got a cigarette?"

"I'll get you one. There's a box here somewhere." He went to a table near by, and I watched him, thinking no wonder he knew his way around Faye's property so well. Had he stayed with her, or had he discreetly registered at a local hotel during his previous visit? And why had he lied to me about it? He was too intelligent to tell such a lie without sufficient reason. The truth would have been easier.

When he sat beside me I said, "Tony, in all the hours we talked aboard ship, you never mentioned knowing anyone in Honolulu. You gave me the impression that you were coming to a completely strange place, you'd be entirely alone here. That was deliberate, wasn't it? Why?"

Tony laughed. "You're a smart little character, Janice. I apologize for the harmless deception. It was in a good cause. I've been in Honolulu before—when I was in the Navy." He paused, smiling into my eyes.

I said nothing while I reflected that here was another lie, a lie by omission. What about his visit here a month ago?

Tony saw disbelief in my face. He moved closer, his tone warmed with affection. "As I explained to you, I knew Faye in Washington." He captured my arm and traced a pattern from wrist to elbow. "I pretended to be a lonely tourist," he said, "because I wanted—I hoped you'd offer to show me around and we could spend a lot of time together. Your life here, the things you told me earlier tonight, for instance, interest me. I want to know you better."

I gave him a long look. "Is that the real reason?"

He met my eyes with an expression of complete candor. "Yes. I find you attractive. Putting it conservatively, I like you. And I want to be something more to you than just a shipboard romance. Do you find that so incredible?"

For a moment I was almost under the spell of the warmness in his voice, the touch of his hand on my arm. Then I remembered a piece of yellow copy paper and the typed information it contained: *"J.C. Blond with brown eyes about five feet four, under thirty. Wrote novel with Hawaiian b.g. sched-*

uled publication Dec. Big promotion . . ." and so forth. He had not once intimated that he knew of my reason for returning to Honolulu. His avoidance of the topic must be significant—probably because that was his chief interest in knowing me. I sighed. It would not be possible to find out anything by direct questions—not tonight, anyhow, with a remembered kiss still dominating our awareness of each other, and a perfume-drenched night around us.

Suddenly I was sick of artificial things, of pools lined with blue tiles and theatrically framed in bamboo and scented flowers; I could smell their fragrance on my own flesh and it was cloyingly sweet.

I turned to Tony. "You say you're interested in the way of life I've known here—let me show you some of it now. There's a wonderful place farther down the beach where I used to swim years ago. There are no gardenias or jasmine, no shining tiles and no hired musicians, but there's clean salt water, there's the music of the ocean, and only the fishes to compete with. I haven't been swimming there for years—"

I stood up. "I want to go there now, Tony. How about it? Would you like to go with me?"

Tony rose and stood irresolute at my side. As he hesitated his eyes followed some movement beyond me, and I turned to see that Faye was coming toward us, talking with two men who trailed at her elbows. Her beautiful dress rustled as she walked, and with each step slim legs and satin-shod feet were revealed. Not an eyelash was disarranged; her poise was superb.

And I stood there dripping, with my wet hair lank around my shoulders. I whirled and said quickly, "So long, Tony. See you around sometime." Then I fled.

Away from the house, the lights, and the noise, I slowed my pace, letting the hot, still night calm my ruffled temper. I had been as silly as a child, I reflected, remembering that I hadn't thanked my hostess for a delightful evening. Once I admitted my bad manners and complete lack of regret for same, I felt better.

There were lights in the Avery house upstairs. Farther along the beach was the Hawaiian village, completely dark and silent. I would have to pass it to reach the swimming hole, unless I climbed the driveway and walked a long distance on the public road and then down a steep thorny path. If I were still twelve I might not be timorous; as a child I had never been afraid of anything on this island. Now I was adult, I knew much more, and there was much more to fear. I didn't go swimming. I turned into the house, like the character who was "docile as a plate," and went to bed . . . .

The next morning I discovered that someone had gone through my luggage. Every bag was unsnapped and the contents had been riffled. The big suitcase which I had brought up the day before stood with its lid half closed, and my notebooks, papers, and correspondence were in disorder, as if they had been thrown back into it by someone who searched in a hurry.

I felt very angry and wanted to complain to the Averys immediately. As I showered I became calmer. I didn't wish to add to Julia's worries by telling her that someone in the house had violated one of the most basic rules of civilized conduct—then with the thought "civilized" I remembered Malia. She must have done this, in hurried search for my nightgown, which she eventually found in the drawer where Suka had put it. With thought of Malia, my anger evaporated and pity took its place.

Malia was probably somewhere in the village now, crying her rebellious heart out, remembering the party and the other women in their lovely dresses, while she had been able to grace her young beauty only with a stolen nightgown. I couldn't condemn her for the kind of dance she did; she offered for sale the one negotiable thing she possessed, and that would not have been marketable had not the demand been so great. Malia wanted money to buy for herself what other women, far less beautiful, demanded as their right. I might make the situation a little easier for her by giving her the gown, as I should have done when I saw how much she coveted it. I could buy another.

I was dressing when Suka knocked on the door. She grinned and bowed when I opened it, and said, "Telephone talk come."

"I'm wanted on the telephone?" Immediately I remembered that I had not told Lily about finding my suitcase.

"Not wanted," Suka said, shaking her head vigorously. "Message come. You boy flen' say he meet you fo' go *au-au* in place you talk him. 'Leven o'clock."

I thanked her and shut the door. Now that Faye was not around and he was alone in his hotel room, Tony had decided to accept my invitation to go swimming. Well, he could just wait there.

Even as I told myself how independent I was, I knew that I would go.

I stepped into the hall, taking my first leisurely look at the upper floor of the house. Stairs rose in the center, around which a rectangular passage ran, railed on the side toward the stair opening, doors in the opposite wall giving access to various rooms. I knew from having watched the Bensons which doors on the *ewa* side led to their bedrooms. The *waikiki* side led down a similar passage; as I stood there a door at the end of it opened, and I caught a quick glimpse of the room. A high drafting table, a *punee*, or couch, covered with pillows, and a telephone on the stand beside it. I could not see the person who opened the door, but apparently I was seen, for it swung shut with a slam.

That wasn't Suka. She would have no reason to conceal her presence there. Luther, probably, since it looked like his workroom. He might be in his underwear and unwilling to be seen. But his and Julia's room was at the other end of the house opposite mine. Then I remembered the telephone—he had probably just made a call.

I went on down the stairs and out to the garden for a stroll. I'm not the kind who can bounce cheerfully from bed to breakfast; I need a little time to adjust to the rhythm of the day. Walking in a garden for a few moments is the most pleasant way I know of to greet the morning.

This day was cooler; the trades had returned. The silent and industrious Koji had already finished watering, and every shrub was jeweled. I walked out toward the garage, where banana trees waved tattered fronds and a sweetheart vine flaunted orange trumpets along the wall, strident color compared to the delicate pink and white of wax begonias. Around the end of the house I found a small pool filled with water hyacinths and fantastic Japanese goldfish. I sat on a stone bench at the edge of the pool to watch them.

The smell of Kona coffee reached me as a stronger breeze swept through the nearby dining room, and I began to grow hungry. I thought of hot coffee, icy papaya sprinkled with lime juice, toast with eggs and bacon—I'd sit there just one more minute and then go in for breakfast.

". . . can't understand you, Walter. I honestly believe you think more of her than you do of your own family." That was Maude's flat voice; the words carried from the dining room, where evidently they were sitting.

Walter's answer came quickly. Only an exceptionally obtuse listener would have failed to detect the ragged note which indicated that he had almost reached the limit of tolerance. "If you must put it so bluntly, I admit that I do. She's given me more pleasure, more actual companionship, than I've ever had from you. Now I'm worried. That's why I'm going—"

"And I say you're not!" Maude was shrill with anger. "You'll stay right here with me where you belong. Don't forget that it's my money, my property, that enables you to—"

"Oh, for Christ's sake shut up!" he exploded. "I'm sick of that old tune of yours. If it weren't for my work—and half of it's trying to make up for your lunkheaded blundering—there wouldn't be any property left. You know that as well as I do. Now you're making the same stupid mistake here. Why can't you mind your own business, leave things alone?"

"This is my business. Julia's my own sister. There is something foul and evil being perpetrated here, and I'm going to find out— Oh, good morning, Ellen. It's time you made your appearance."

"Good morning, Daddy. Good morning, Mama."

"What happened to you last night? I searched everywhere for you when we were ready to leave. You didn't come home until after midnight!" Maude's ill temper was being vented on her daughter now.

"I'm sorry, Mama, I was there all the time. You must have missed me in the crowd. Fred and I were swimming in the pool."

"Fred? Fred who?"

"Fred Coffee. You met him; he's Judge Coffee's son."

"*Judge* Coffee." Maude sounded faintly mollified. "Oh yes."

Suka entered the room then to take Ellen's order, and I rose and made my way quickly around to the front of the house. Koji was there, watering vines along the high retaining wall of the driveway. I called good morning to him and went into the house by the front entrance.

The Bensons were alone at the table, Maude in navy seersucker, Walter wearing freshly laundered white drill in which he looked hot and uncomfortable. He pushed back a half-filled plate and slid his coffee cup in front of him.

"You haven't finished," his wife said.

"That's right." He sent Maude a significant look before he lifted his cup and drank. "I haven't." He greeted me then with such amiability that I regarded him with surprise as I seated myself. Walter had a talent for dissembling which I would not have thought he possessed.

Ellen ate with her eyes on her plate, glancing sideways at me occasionally with a little smile, still remembering the wonderful evening she had spent. What a contrast between her father's source of enjoyment last night and hers. Was it the same hunger, only on a different level? I didn't know.

Neither Luther nor Julia appeared. I asked about them and Walter reminded me that Julia never breakfasted downstairs.

Luther, he said, had left an hour ago for his office. Then it must have been Ellen in Luther's room, I thought, probably using the telephone.

"Walter, there's a scorpion in our shower!" Maude said nervously. "I couldn't finish my bath this morning. I want you to go up and kill it." She shuddered and drank some coffee.

Then she turned to me and said, "Why they call this the Paradise of the Pacific, I can never understand. Poisonous insects, skin rashes, Kona storms, and sneaking natives that hate the sight of us and have to be watched constantly."

I had once heard the desiccated wife of a British colonial governor talk like that. But their station was in a remote and primitive part of the South Pacific, not in modern, civilized Hawaii. I looked at her in astonishment.

"There are no snakes here," I offered. "And we have Kona weather for only a few weeks out of the year."

"And, Mama, you know the insects aren't really poisonous. You just happen to be allergic," Ellen added pacifically.

"Then that makes them poisonous," Maude snapped.

Walter explained that Maude had had the misfortune to be stung by a scorpion and had been deathly sick for weeks afterward. Nobody mentioned the natives. I was wondering why, if she hated Hawaii so much, Maude Benson remained there. Possibly because of the ranch she owned, possibly because she enjoyed complaining. And the "pagan" practices of the Hawaiians might hold the same fascination for her that Malia's dancing held for her husband. I hoped that Ellen was going far away, to a school where she would meet lots of nice, normal people.

After breakfast I telephoned the island of Kauai and was told that Lily had just gone out. I left a message for her to call me when she returned, and went upstairs to look through my luggage and see whether anything was missing. As far as I could tell, everything was there. Malia would not have been interested in my notebooks, anyway. At that, I wondered why she had bothered to scramble them up. Could it have been done by someone else in the house? But that was ridiculous. Luther and Julia would have been welcome to read my notes if they wanted to, and the Bensons could have no possible interest.

At eleven o'clock I put on my bathing suit and the grass slippers and walked toward Wainiha. The same two women were under the same tree, weaving *lauhala* again. Beneath another tree nearby an old man dozed on a mat, his shriveled skin brown as cocoa, white hair waving over his ears.

I stopped by the two women and asked, "Is Malia here?"

They did not answer; just shook their heads and went on with their weaving. I noticed then, for the first time, that there were no young people on the place. When Makaleha lived there the laughter of children echoed through every daylight hour. Maybe they had all grown up. But that wasn't possible; some had been infants in arms when I saw them last. Maybe they had been taken away. I turned from those uncommunicative people and walked around the point of land toward the swimming hole, half expecting to see the figure of David standing on the ledge with poised spear.

No one was there. Sunshine illuminated the place, shone through pale green waters on red and brown coral sprays massed on the ocean's floor, apparently soft as velvet, actually razor sharp, but beautiful to look at. Long rays of light pierced deep blue crevices in the rocky sides of the pool; little groups of black-and-white *kihikihis* moved in a serene ballet over mottled sand through miniature gardens of coral and swaying green seaweed. I stepped down cautiously—distances in that translucent chrysoprase water are deceptive—found I was waist deep, and floated toward the deeper end. It was like floating on silk, cool and yet warm, and when I turned an ear into the sea I could hear the chuckle and murmur of it under me. I forgot about Tony, the village, and relaxed into bliss, lying on my back and floating with eyes fixed on a cloudless azure sky.

Eventually I rolled over and began to swim out toward the edge of the undersea bowl and then back. As I turned and started toward shore I became vaguely aware of something following me. A momentary glimpse, lost in the movement of water and my own body. Involuntarily I quickened my stroke, then slowed again, remembering that there could be no sharks in this place; they wouldn't come through the narrow opening to the sea. I swam back to the spot where I had glimpsed a figure and saw something dimly, under the surface. I trod water for a moment, then jackknifed down with my hand outstretched.

And touched the dead, staring face of Malia.

What happened under water took only seconds, yet every detail was as clear as if I were there for hours, staring at the Hawaiian girl. Her black hair floated out behind her, moving in the current, her eyes stared into mine, and she poised with one foot on the coral at the ocean's floor, like a dancer frozen in an arabesque. I clung to the rocky ledge until need for oxygen forced me to rise to the surface. As I trod water and gulped air my mind kept repeating insanely, "But she can't stay there, she can't stay there—" I looked around for help, but there was no one—I might have been the only living human being on this planet—just the ocean rising and falling around me, not a voice, not a human sound. When I turned my eyes downward I could see her below the surface, still swaying with her black hair streaming out like some living submarine thing.

I dived again and my face brushed her thigh. I grasped her arm and it moved docilely as I pulled, but Malia's body swayed toward me reluctantly, one leg still extended straight down toward the bottom of the pool. It was then that I saw the rock which anchored her, tied to her ankle with something white—I forced myself down to clutch it and the stuff broke in my hands . . . I released my hold on her arm and shot up to the surface. And Malia's body began to move slowly after me . . .

It was then that I panicked.

I flailed arms and legs until I reached water shallow enough to stand in, then I began to run, oblivious of coral under my feet, falling, rising, and stumbling on, letting out terrified whimpers between gasps for breath. When I reached dry land I continued to stagger over lava rock, sobbing and gasping as I climbed the hill and ran toward the Averys', across the green lawn, toward a small group of people seated there. I heard someone exclaim as I neared the house, and I tried to tell them, crying, "Malia! Maha! She's down there—" before the earth reeled under my feet and I collapsed into darkness.

CHAPTER EIGHT

I GRADUALLY came awake in a world which seemed black, then gray, then brown—a sickly dirty brown like the taste in my mouth, like the thick brown tongue which I moved over parched lips. I lifted leaden eyelids and saw a gray room, a room filled with mist, where something moved before two lighter squares of gray, and something filled the air just outside those lighter squares with an indecent racket. My head ached with every raucous note, and I moved it on the pillow, trying to escape the hurting sound. With movement I came to full consciousness, and knew it was mynah birds I heard outside the window, squawking, making my head ache with their squawking.

Someone spoke. "Are you awake now?"

I opened my eyes wide and looked at Lily Wu.

"Oh, Lily," I said, "I'm so glad you're here." And I began to cry. "My head aches so," I said, as apology for the tears.

She came to the bed with a glass of liquid and held it toward me. "Can you lift your head for a moment? That's good. Now, drink this."

I swallowed a mixture which tasted awful, and lay back again. Presently my headache abated, and although I felt numb with heaviness more deep than exhaustion, I could talk.

"When—how did you happen to come here?" I asked.

"I telephoned from Kauai in response to your message. I was told that you could not come to the phone, you were ill. I flew over."

"What time is it?" I asked irrationally.

"It is two o'clock."

"You made good flying time," I said foggily.

Lily said, "I arrived yesterday."

"Yesterday? Then I've been—"

"You have been unconscious for about twenty-six hours."

Twenty-six hours out of my life, blank, which I could never recover. I raised my head quickly, then let it fall back again. "May I have another pillow?" I asked. "I don't feel like moving much just yet."

Lily brought a pillow from the chaise longue and put it behind me. She sat in a chair by the bed and regarded me with a grave expression. "It is not necessary for you to move," she told me.

Then she said, "Do you want to talk about what happened?"

I shuddered and asked in a low voice, "Did they find Malia's body?"

"That is what I want to talk to you about. There was no body in that pool, Janice. And no one in this house seems to know or even to be able to guess what happened to you."

I told her then, haltingly, of the message I had received from Tony, of my solitary swim in the pool, my discovery there, my subsequent panic and flight. After my collapse on the Averys' lawn I drew a blank.

Lily frowned. "There is no reason why you should have been unconscious for such a long time. When you fainted, it just happened, I was told, that a guest was present—a Dr. Atherton. He gave you a sedative by hypo-dermic and put you to bed. He says he prescribed a mild form of barbitu-rate, in case you were nervous when you awakened, and he can account for your long unconsciousness only by assuming that the shock you had was very great. Do you remember being given any other medicine?"

I closed my eyes. I could remember nothing. All I could think of at that moment was my relief at having Lily with me. I told her this, trying not to cry again.

Lily smiled as she said, "I saved your life once, remember? That makes me, according to the beliefs of my ancestors, forever responsible for your welfare."

Her tone was bantering, but beneath it was the Chinese girl speaking, who, while she might make light of some of the ancient codes of her people, respected and obeyed them because of a sense of honor as inflexible as that of Confucius himself.

She resumed our former subject. "Janice, I have taken the liberty of telling your friends that my cousin Ethel is your personal physician and will take care of you."

"I thought she lived on Kauai."

"These are the Honolulu Chuns. There are many," Lily said smilingly, "in the Chun tribe. You met Ethel on the *Lurline*."

"Is she a doctor?" The only impression I retained of Mrs. Chun was a round, laughing face with bright black eyes, and a plump, bustling figure.

"She is a gynecologist, her husband is a pediatrician; they share offices here."

"Fine," I said vaguely. "When is she coming?"

"She called here last evening to examine you. Her opinion is that you were given something much stronger than a mild sedative. Whether it was administered by Dr. Atherton or was an additional drug given you orally by someone else after he left the house, we do not know. But no further chances will be taken."

"Are you going to stay here, Lily?"

"I am staying here," she said. Amusement glinted in her dark eyes as she added, "Although my presence is causing discomfort to a certain Mrs. Benson. I believe she is slightly appalled at taking her meals with a heathen Chinese."

"She'd be hostile to anyone less than St. Peter himself," I said, laugh-ing in spite of my headache. "I hope you brought some chopsticks."

"Nothing but my Oriental cunning," Lily said. "That will disconcert the lady sufficiently."

She took a cigarette, offered me one, and lit it for me. "Now," she said in a brisker voice, "you're feeling better, I can see. Let's get down to facts.

Tell me again what happened yesterday."

I tasted my cigarette and stubbed it out with a grimace. I repeated my story—more coherently now, as details came vividly to mind.

"You say the girl was anchored underwater. It would require an expert swimmer to pull her below the surface and stay there long enough to tie her to a rock."

"That wouldn't be necessary. The rock was big, but it moved when I pulled her toward me. It could have been tied to her ankle before she was put into the water."

"She was murdered."

"Oh yes," I said wearily. "I am sure of that."

"But her body has not been discovered. Perhaps there is a reason why it is not desirable to the murderer that her body be found."

"The opening in that basin is narrow," I told her. "A man can swim through it—I've done so many times. But I doubt whether the tide would carry a body through."

"Possibly it wasn't the tide. Let's consider that later."

I frowned, trying to think clearly. "If she floats out to sea she may never be found. If her body is washed to shore along here—the coast is rocky beyond Wainiha—there will be no way to determine the cause of death, unless she was shot, and somehow I am sure she was not shot. She was choked, or hit on the head, and dropped into the water with her body weighted, so that even if she recovered consciousness immediately, she would drown before she could free herself."

"Then her death was meant to look like an accident."

"Either accident or—" I became silent as I tried to remember some Hawaiian superstition about death by drowning, but details eluded me.

"You'll think of it later," Lily said, reading my mind as she so often does. "Now. I think it might be advisable for you to lose your memory for a while, or at least be very confused about what has happened. We cannot help the dead girl by reporting this to the police. It may be best to let her death go on record—or her disappearance, if it turns out to be that—as accidental, unsolved, or whatever her murderer wishes it to appear. Forcing an investigation at this point is not necessary. And I have an intuition that the less you seem to know, the safer you will be."

"Lily, why do you say that?"

"I'll tell you later, when I have all the facts in order. What I want to know now, before we see any of these people in the house, is what has been happening since you arrived. Do you feel like going back and telling me all of it?"

I turned and raised on one elbow, and in doing so moved my feet for the first time. They hurt. They were wrapped in something. I threw back the sheet and saw that both feet were bandaged, and when I moved them again, movement was painful.

"What's the matter with my feet?"

"You have some rather bad coral cuts. Ethel and I cleaned them out as well as we could; I hope we got all the coral. You will not be able to walk for a while, Janice."

I sank back on the bed, so dismayed that I was speechless. Fleeing from the scene of Malia's death, I had forgotten caution, all sense had forsaken me in the urgency of my panic. Coral cuts are not only painful but dangerous, since coral breaks into almost microscopic particles which seem to continue their growth in human flesh, causing swelling and infection. They never heal until the last particle of coral is removed.

"You see," Lily said, "you will be immobilized for a while. That is why it is best for you to lose your memory. You would be a sitting target for someone who thought you knew too much."

The realization that I was helpless generated a sense of outrage in me which swelled into anger so strong that I began to shake. "Give me a cigarette," I said, and almost snatched it from Lily's hand and began to smoke the thing in spite of its disagreeable taste. The resentment I felt at being unable to walk was more bitter than the aftertaste of any drug.

Lily laid a slim hand on my wrist. "Janice," she said, "do not waste your vitality in such a manner. Can you not see how very angry I am? Let my anger serve for both of us now."

I looked at her and relaxed a little. Lily was indeed angry. It showed in the icy calm of her, the steely quality of her voice, in every controlled movement. The more deeply Lily felt an emotion, the more quiet she became.

She was right. I needed to recover from what had happened to me; I could not waste my strength in helpless fury. Lily's control under stress was always a reminder that I should learn to discipline my more volatile nature. She had taught me by example several times that anger, unless converted into action, was enervating to the point of weakness.

I waited for a moment until I could control my voice and then said, "Let me tell you what has happened here since I arrived." I began with meeting Walter Benson on board the *Lurline* and told her everything I could remember up to the present hour. The narration took a long time.

Lily sat utterly still, as if listening with each delicate pore of her body. When I finished she nodded and said, "So. That is how it is. This is more complicated than I thought."

"What do you mean?"

"Tell me," she countered, "do you believe that there are supernatural forces active in the Hawaiian village?"

"I do not!" I said quickly. Then I went on, in a reflective voice, "But,

Lily, if I were Hawaiian, I might believe it. The night I heard the drums I believed it enough to be utterly terrified for a while. You must experience these things yourself to understand what a spell they can work on one who—" I broke off, confused and disconcerted by my own confusion.

Lily rose and went to the window to look out toward the village. She pulled aside the sheer curtain, and I could see past her the rocky slope covered with thorny bushes, over which a pale sky arched, at the foot of which sapphire waters glinted in sunlight. The mynahs screamed, a palm crackled like raindrops on a metal surface, and faintly one could hear the sound of waves on the shore near the house.

Lily dropped the curtain and faced me. "I have not seen the place," she said as she returned to her chair. "I have not heard ghost drums in the night, either. But I think that even if I heard them I would not believe in such things."

She kicked her small white slippers to the floor and sat in her favorite position, with feet under her. "We Chinese are possibly the most complete realists in the world," she said with a smile. "Twenty-five hundred years of Confucianism have given us an ineradicable sense of reality. We do not accept the inexplicable, which means the supernatural. I believe that everything which is happening here is being made to happen, for a reason. And starting with that premise, I intend to find out why. I have an advantage over you at this point, Janice."

"Why? I don't understand."

She held up slim fingers and counted reasons. "First, as I said, I refuse to accept the supernatural as explanation for anything. Second, I have no memories of the past connected with this situation, so that I am not tempted to imbue either place or individuals with qualities which might no longer exist. Third, I do not know these people: the Averys or the Bensons, the Hawaiians in the village, or the woman who lives next door. Actually I am not interested in them, nor do I care what happens to any of them. I care what happens to you. And since I am not involved emotionally, my observations will be more exact."

I said, with the frankness permitted by our friendship, "You look like a beautiful doll, Lily. You sound like Nemesis. Heaven help the woman—or the man—who tries to outmaneuver you."

"Women I don't bother with," she said with equal frankness. "There have been a few men"—amusement raised the corners of her mouth—"but someday I shall meet the man who wants to be partner instead of opponent. I shall nab him," she finished inelegantly, "so quick!"

We relaxed into laughter, and it was at this point that someone knocked on the door. It was Luther, carrying an enormous box of flowers.

"How are you feeling, my dear?" he asked in a tone of deep concern.

Luther looked tired and worried, and his eyes when they met mine held abject apology for what had happened while I was under his roof.

"Luther," I said, "please don't be upset. I'm perfectly all right except for some cuts on my feet, and that's not your fault. I knew better than to walk on live coral. It was just that I was scared and forgot."

He stood at the foot of the bed holding the flower box. "What frightened you?" he asked. "We could not get any idea of what had happened except that it was something about Malia. And then you fainted."

Here was where I had to tell my first lie to an old friend. "I thought I saw someone swimming after me in the water. It looked like Malia. Actually I was never close enough to be certain who it was—it might have been one of the women from the village—or just shadows in the pool; you know how water distorts your vision. But I was terribly frightened and tried to run."

"It could have been one of the Kanakas—they swim there," Luther said thoughtfully. "But Malia is not around. She told us she was planning to sail for the mainland, and we paid her wages up to date. The *Lurline* has sailed, and she was probably on it. The girl said good-by to her friends a few days ago."

Malia had not intended to sail on the *Lurline*. She had changed her mind about leaving because of what I told her about a movie being made in the village. I did not speak of this. But I wondered where the Hawaiian girl, who wore a shabby cotton dress and walked in grass sandals, had got enough money for passage to the mainland. Perhaps Faye had given it to her; perhaps Faye told her of fame and fortune to be earned in a night club. Malia had reason to know how her talent was appreciated, and not only by local tourists. She had danced for audiences in Washington, Tony said. I made a note to tell Lily of that.

Luther laid the flower box on the foot of my bed. "Shall I open this for you?" I nodded and he did so. The card inside was from Tony. The box contained long stalks of yellow roses on a nest of damp ferns. Beside the yellow flowers was a roll of waxed paper in which was a ginger *lei*, the special kind which few tourists see, made with the creamy ginger petals woven flat like feathers. In Hawaii, a man gives the *awapuhi lei* only to his sweetheart. For one who didn't know the islands well, Tony was adopting Hawaiian ways remarkably fast. Or, a suspicious afterthought suggested, someone was coaching him.

"I'll tell Suka to put these roses in water," Luther said. "You'll want to wear the ginger, won't you?" His eyes smiled approval at this evidence of a romance.

He turned to Lily, who remained seated but had quietly slid her feet back into the white slippers. "We have given you the room next to Janice," he said. "I am sorry that it is so small, but we have several other guests at present. Your room was occupied by Mrs. Avery's nurse during her recent illness."

He said to me, "This girl was so worried over you that she slept on the chaise longue beside your bed last night. But we'll make her more comfortable now."

Lily gave him a smile that was calm and sweet. "Thank you. I am sure I shall be most comfortable. I stayed with Janice until she regained consciousness because Dr. Chun ordered a nurse for her. Since I've had some nursing experience, and since I am a close friend . . ." Her words trailed off and she smiled again.

Luther sighed. "We are very glad to have you here. Especially since we are understaffed at present. Poor old Suka has all that she can handle with the housework and cooking."

He unwrapped the ginger *lei* and laid it across my lap. "*Wikiwiki* with your recovery, Janice." His hand rested on my shoulder for a moment. "We have missed you since your accident."

After he had gone Lily picked up the card from the florist's box. "Tony Davis interests me. I called him last night to ask what happened at that pool when he went there to meet you. He said that he did not meet you and he sent no message."

"But Suka told me he phoned."

"Yes. That is how I knew about it before you were able to tell me. I asked Suka what happened yesterday. She said it was a man who called, and that was all she knew."

She bent a corner of the card and regarded it thoughtfully. "Someone wanted you to go to that place, Janice. Someone wanted you to find the body of Malia. Just as someone did not want you to be able to tell about it after you discovered the dead girl. The question is: are they both the same person? It does not make sense that they should be. And if someone other than the murderer knew of her death but did not want to make the discovery himself, yet wanted it to be made—you see where that can lead us?"

"Into confusion."

"Yes, at first. But confusion can be cleared gradually, step by step. We will take the first step tomorrow by trying to understand the first incomprehensible thing which has happened: Tony's interest in you and his failure to explain why. We will investigate Tony Davis."

"How? I can't even walk. What can I do?"

"A great deal. First, continue to lose your memory. And get Tony out of his hotel by inviting him to lunch. If he says he has another engagement, burst into tears, reproach him, say you're ill and lonely or you have something terribly important to tell him—use any trick to get him here. When he comes, keep him for at least two hours. While you entertain this clever young man I will visit his room and see what I can discover."

"You have a nerve!" I exclaimed. "How do you think you're going to get into his hotel room?"

Lily's smile was mischievous. "The hotel has Chinese houseboys, doesn't it? Arrangements will be made. Do not worry about my activities. You handle your friend Tony."

"All right," I agreed.

I sat up against the pillows, and the pain of moving my feet was a sharp stimulus. I winced, then gritted my teeth. Anger was at last being channeled into purpose. My calm was almost equal to Lily's as I said, "I'll be looking forward to that."

CHAPTER NINE

THE next day I felt practically normal again, except for my painful feet. I dressed with Lily's help, in a kimono which Julia loaned me, an exquisite thing of powder-blue crepe printed with chrysanthemums in colors from apricot to bronze, the flower petals tipped with gold. It was too large, and consequently made me feel smaller and more frail—a feeling I welcomed, since I needed to capitalize on my helplessness. We heightened this effect with makeup: light powder, blue eye shadow, and pale coral lipstick.

"Elizabeth Barrett had nothing on me," I told Lily, and she agreed, standing off to study the effect and nodding approval.

Luther came to tell me he had provided transportation in an aluminum chaise longue with rubber-tired wheels. He carried me down to the *lanai* himself, although I protested.

"I'm used to this," he insisted. "Until Julia could use her canes, I carried her up and down the stairs every day."

Walter Benson looked over the edge of the *Sunday Advertiser*. "And that chaise was Julia's means of locomotion for several weeks, wasn't it, Julia?"

Julia agreed. "I never imagined," she added in her tired voice, "that you would ever need it, Janice."

"She will be walking soon," Lily said. She had followed us, dressed for her role in white. "But in the meantime," she admonished in the authoritarian tone of a nurse, "please see that she gets enough rest. I must go out for a few hours today."

Maude Benson had not raised her eyes from the book she held, a volume titled *Daily Devotions*. She closed it now with a snap. "You can do some errands for me, Lily," she said, indicating her determination to regard my Chinese friend in the status of servant. "There are a few things I want you to get from the druggist."

Lily lit a cigarette and blew smoke delicately in Maude's direction. "I am sorry, Mrs. Benson, but I shall not have time for errands other than my own."

Maude jerked erect in her chair and glared at Lily, who blew another cloud of smoke and regarded her serenely.

"I'll go, Mama," Ellen volunteered in haste, trying to bridge the explosive moment. She smiled at Lily Wu. "Perhaps we can drive to town together. What time are you going?"

"You're not going to drive anywhere, Ellen!" her mother snapped.

Walter dropped the newspaper to his knees. "Why can't she take the station wagon? Ellen's a good driver. You're the one in the family who has all the accidents." His glance at his wife was openly hostile.

Maude scowled at him. "Because," she said with equal hostility, "I may need the station wagon myself."

Walter subsided, looking puzzled.

"I can take you now, on my way to the office," Luther offered from the doorway.

Maude turned her thick body to look at him. "Working again—on Sunday?" she said.

"It's the one day I can really concentrate, when none of my draftsmen are there," Luther explained. He repeated his offer to Lily. "Can I give you a lift to town?"

"Thank you, but I am not ready yet. I must get my patient settled for the morning."

"Koji will drive you two girls to Honolulu," Julia said after Luther had gone. She asked me, "Is there anything you want—books, magazines, writing paper?"

"Nothing," I answered. "But you asked the other day if I wished to invite someone here. Today I should like very much to ask a friend to lunch. Tony Davis. Perhaps you remember meeting him at Faye's party?"

"Of course. Shall I call him for you?"

"I'll do it later, thanks."

Maude looked interested. "He's the man you went to meet at that swimming hole, isn't he? What really happened to you there? We've all been wondering, since you made no sense whatever when you came running back from the place, screaming."

If there was ever a disagreeable way to phrase a sentence, Maude invariably chose it. I told her—while the others listened with interest—the same confused version I had told Luther. Surely he had already repeated it to them. I wondered whether Maude questioned me because she sensed the incompleteness of my story and hoped I'd make a slip of some kind.

Ellen murmured sympathetically when I finished, while the rest were silent. Walter made a tent of his fingers and stared through them at his feet. Julia looked deeply unhappy; her mouth drooped and her eyes were somber. Maude sniffed. Disbelief? Or was it contempt because I chose to go to a rendezvous in a bathing suit which weighed four ounces? I kept my expression blank as I pictured briefly what the lump of lard she wore for a body would look like in such a garment.

"I walked over there early this morning," she announced. "There's nothing in that pool but coral and seaweed. However—I did find this!" She opened her big bag and produced a small water-soaked book.

It was another Bible.

"May I see it?" I asked. I had not been given a chance to examine the first one closely. Reluctantly she handed it to me, and I opened the damp pages. A name had been written on the flyleaf with indelible pencil; the letters were blurred but still legible. I read aloud: "*Jennie Kalani, May 1943:*"

"It might have been a birthday gift," I hazarded, "or a Sunday school prize. I wonder where she is now."

Ellen said in a reminiscent voice, "We had a girl named Jennie Kalani in our Bible class several years ago. Her father was one of the ranch *paniolos*."

She smiled at her father and said teasingly, "Daddy used to live in Sonora, Janice; he gets a kick out of knowing that our first Hawaiian cowboys were taught by Mexican *vaqueros*. That's where the word comes from, isn't it?"

"Yes," Walter said absently. "*Españoles. Paniolos.* Joe Kalani was one of our best. I had to fire him recently, for drinking. He used to head for Wailuku and go on a bender every payday. When he had enough liquor in him he got superstitious, talked about the *kahuna* who lived in the mountains on our place—I let Joe live in a cave on our land—" He broke off abruptly and sent an apprehensive glance at his wife.

"That crazy old man!" Maude's words grew shrill with agitation. "You told me you had gotten rid of him!"

"Don't excite yourself, Maude," Walter said. "I told you that because I didn't want you to go out there and badger him. The old fellow was just senile and full of notions—what harm could he do to our land? We've got plenty of food; what was wrong with our people taking a little of it to him once in a while?" He shrugged resignedly and finished in a bitter tone, "Well, he's gone now, of his own accord. I rode that way recently and found his cave deserted."

"I will have no witch doctors and no drunkards on my land!" Maude's dark eyes blazed. "The ranch hands are decent Christians, they go to our church regularly. Otherwise"—her voice hardened—"they don't work there."

She was an awful bore with her single-track, narrow-gauge mind. I wondered again at the lack of resemblance between the two sisters, whether it was innate or had been brought about by the difference between their adult lives. They seemed to have not one attribute in common.

"Do you wish to make your telephone call now?" Lily reminded me. She needed to know whether I could get Tony out of his hotel before she went there. Julia offered again to make the call for me, but I said, rearranging the ginger *lei* with a self-conscious gesture, that I would rather do it myself. Lily wheeled me into the library and I called Tony's hotel. He sounded pleased to hear my voice.

"I want to thank you for the flowers," I said. "Will you come to lunch, so I can do it personally?"

"Janice, I'd love to, but I have another date." He seemed genuinely regretful. I looked at Lily with a wry expression before I turned back to the telephone and went into my act. With a pathetic quaver in my voice I urged: "Please come, Tony. I'm anchored here with both my feet cut to ribbons, I've had a dreadful experience, and I need to see you!"

"But, darling girl, how can I possibly——" he wavered.

"Besides," I went on in a softer voice, "your lovely *lei* reminded me that there's some unfinished business between us. I've been thinking a lot about it and——" I broke off as if embarrassed at my own forwardness.

That did the trick. He agreed to cancel his date and to arrive at the Averys' at noon. I wondered whether the date was with Faye and hoped it was. Then I wondered how I'd handle the "unfinished business" which I had no intention of discussing, how I could drag that nebulous situation out for the two hours Lily's errand required. Finally a solution occurred to me and I proceeded to make arrangements.

When Tony arrived he found me on the lawn under the big tree, smoking a cigarette and drinking vermouth and soda from a tall glass. He came toward me with a smile which changed to an expression of concern as he drew near enough to take in my costume and the artful look of frailty.

"Janice, are you sure you should be out of bed? You look awfully pale."

The warmth and solicitude in his voice were enough to tempt any woman to wallow in a little self-pity. I wanted to succumb to it, to be completely honest and tell him the whole story. For just a moment the impulse lasted. Then I remembered his duplicity.

And I remembered that Tony had known Malia.

Here we were, preparing to eat delicious food in a garden bright with sunlight and flowers—and where was Malia? Nobody mentioned her, the ardent girl who had been murdered before she had even begun to live. While we sat at ease with the Pacific crooning at our feet, was she floating on the same waters not far from us, dead eyes staring into the sun, brine crusting her face? Or was she impaled by the tide somewhere on sharp lava rocks? I remembered a drowned fisherman I had seen once, brought ashore after two days in the sea. He had been identified only by his clothes, since his features . . . I blanked that memory out fast.

I looked at Tony, and now, although my smile was wistful and my voice was tender, not one gesture was spontaneous.

"I feel better since you're here," I said. "Will you have a drink?" I indicated the tray of bottles and thermos bucket of ice on the table.

Tony mixed himself a rum collins and refilled my glass before he sat down. As he lit a cigarette and tasted his drink, he kept watching me. Finally he said, "You puzzle me. Most girls are pretty much of a pattern, either one type or another. You're not. You're like these Hawaiian skies, always presenting a new aspect. First you're the sophisticated shipboard companion. Then you're the girl who is half native, who goes swimming in secret ocean pools and talks about catching squid and eating Kanaka style. Now I find you've got intellect, you're an authority on Hawaiiana—you've even written a book. Why didn't you tell me?"

What a line he had! "Who told you that?" I asked, wondering what lie he'd give me.

After brief hesitation: "Faye Clarke told me."

Faye said Luther had told her. But Tony acquired a dossier on me before he arrived in Honolulu. I shrugged.

"I don't talk about it because I'm tired of the subject; a book that's finished is the deadest thing on earth to its author. Let's find something more interesting."

I shifted my position until I lay Récamier style, and slipped my bandaged feet from under the folds of the blue kimono. Tony stared at them.

"What's the matter with your feet?" he demanded.

When I told him, his surprise seemed genuine. He was quick then to say, "I didn't leave any message for you."

"So Lily tells me. Who do you think did?"

"Some joker, possibly. There were people all around us when you were telling me about that swimming pool." He leaned forward. "What happened when you got there?"

Again I told my story, accenting lights and shadows of the pool, distortion of the water, my own panic. I finished by asking a question before he could question me. "Tony, what did Malia want with you that night? Remember she drew you aside and asked you something. What was it?"

Tony grinned. "She asked for money. Once in Washington I had a drink too many and made the mistake of handing her a twenty-dollar bill when she danced at one of Faye's parties. After that the girl wanted money every time she saw me."

He swirled ice in his collins. "Remember Malia said she was going to do a special dance later that night?"

"Did she dance?"

"She certainly did. Faye wanted to put on a little private show for the senator, something to remember Hawaii by. He'll remember, all right—his eyes almost popped out of his head. And one of the Kanakas, Malia's boyfriend, gave the performance proper drama by carrying the girl out of the room kicking and screaming."

He set down his glass and said casually, "You're familiar with the native village where she lives, I'm told. What's this rumor about idol worship, and primitive practices being revived? Anything to it?"

An icy finger touched the back of my neck; my spine went tight. Was this what Tony wanted from me? I stalled for time by taking along drink, and regarded him over the rim of my glass. He was studying me with a half-smile on his face; one hand held a cigarette while the other turned a packet of book matches over and over against the surface of the table. I couldn't draw my silence out forever, I had to say something. I clutched my glass with both hands and leaned forward.

"Tony," I breathed, "it's just too dreadful. If I could only tell you—" I stopped and exclaimed brightly, "Here comes our lunch!" as Suka appeared, toddling across the lawn behind a tea wagon. We waited in smiling tension as she set the table, and I glanced surreptitiously at my watch. Just as Suka bowed and started away, my other guest arrived, exactly on time. I had called her immediately after I called Tony. Saved by the gong.

Stephanie Dugan, called Steve by her friends and many other things by her enemies, was a reporter for one of the local papers, the one who had been at Faye's *luau*. She was a ginger-haired woman with arms and legs which seemed loosely attached to her big frame, so that they dangled in all directions. Her walk was more like a lope, she wore a size nine shoe, and her horsy face had a smile that was wonderful to see.

"Hi, baby!" she called loudly as she galloped toward us. "Hope I'm not intruding, but I was driving by and thought I'd stop in to say hello. Also to commiserate with you for being such a dope as to walk on live coral. Hey, is it lunch time already? Looks good, whatever it is. And do I see a bottle of demon rum at your elbow?"

"Hello, Steve. It's fine to see you. You're intruding, but now that you're here, why not stay? And that is a bottle of rum, and help yourself. You know Tony Davis, don't you?"

She bobbed her head at him as she poured a generous jigger and reached for ice cubes. "Sure. Met you at Faye Clarke's the other night. Nice to see you again."

She swallowed straight rum and grimaced. "Need a bracer," she said, grinning. "I met Maude Benson coming out as I started down that damned driveway. Took ten bucks' worth of paint off my fender when she forced me against the wall. What a driver *she* is! No reflexes at all."

I watched Tony repress irritation at this interruption of our privacy, silently applauding his social presence as he greeted her affably and offered to squeeze lemons for a collins. At the same time I recognized further proof of his agility as a liar, deciding I'd prefer Steve's blunt honesty any time. But Steve was playing a part too, and doing it well.

She thanked him and kept up a line of chatter while he went to work, commenting sulfurously on our dear senator, a visiting movie star she had just interviewed, and various local gentry either notorious, infamous, or sanctimonious. The stories Steve knew and hadn't written would have filled several editions of the local Sunday papers with no space for advertising. She gave the impression of being always on the verge of laughter over some enormous private joke, and possibly she was, for she knew the secrets of most of our local V.I.P.s and the haughty respectability of some was vastly amusing to her.

Tony listened to Steve's monologue with apparent fascination while we ate, and as we sipped iced tea at the end of the meal he glanced at his watch with dismay. "It's two-thirty—have to go!" He rose and sent me a look conveying frustration and regret, shook Steve's hand, and departed through the hedge toward Faye's house.

I watched his retreating figure for a moment and then said to Steve, "While you were gabbing you reminded me of something I'd like to find out. What's the story on Julia Avery and Maude Benson? It's difficult for me to understand how two sisters could be so unlike. Do you know anything about their family history?"

Steve set down her glass and stuck hairpins back into the knob of gingery hair which had slipped down on her neck. "No ladylike scruples about discussing your hostess?" she asked amiably.

"Not now. There's something going on here, Steve, and I seem to be deep in it."

She nodded and lit a cigarette. "Yeah. The natives in the village. *Pilikia* there."

"Luther told me nobody knew about it!"

"Not many do. No one's going to talk. Not for a while, at any rate. But if a story breaks, you'll let me in on it?"

"Yes. "

There was no need to caution Steve about what could or could not be printed. She loved the islands as much as I did.

"Well," she began, "I don't really know very much. Ed Harrington, Julia and Maude's father, got his money in the usual way: inherited interests in sugar and pineapple and stock in various factors. He built this place, then retired and lived off income when the girls were grown up. He always liked the Hawaiians—I suppose you know most of this, don't you?"

"That's all I do know. I knew the Averys when I was a little girl, but we were never intimate friends; after my father's illness we hardly ever saw them, although Father and Luther kept up casual contact. I met Julia's sister only a few days ago."

"They generally stay on Maui and make a trip to the mainland every couple of years. The old gal, you may have observed, does not like to be any place where she can't be Queen Maude. Incidentally, she and Walter have terrific battles because he'd rather breed polo ponies than beef cattle. Every time he buys a new horse Maude raises hell, but she couldn't run the ranch without him—nobody would work for her." She chuckled. "Lord, how she hates the Hawaiians!"

"All Hawaiians? I thought she just hated the 'infidels.' "

"She hates 'em all. And, baby, for what a wonderful reason!"

Steve flipped her cigarette across the grass to the beach and watched it roll on the sand. Sea water came slipping in with a soothing murmur, and the Pacific stretching before us to infinity was blue as indigo under a cloudless sky. In front of Faye Clarke's house the dredger was at work, manned by two Hawaiians in swimming trunks. Steve saw it and said, "What are they doing? Dredging coral?"

"Yes. See that float anchored there? Faye's making a swimming beach. Let's get back to the subject. What is Maude's wonderful reason?"

Steve lit another cigarette, eyes narrowed as she watched the dredger. Then she shrugged and resumed her story.

"Maude was in love with a Hawaiian. Quite a guy, from what I've heard—a magnificent fellow, *paniolo* on the Harrington ranch, and one of the most popular boys on Maui. Maude was a sour-pussed gal about twenty-two; in spite of the family money, she'd been unable to snag a husband. Julia was younger and had just married Luther Avery, who was working for Lewers & Cooke. He opened his own office after their marriage and moved into this house. Maude didn't relish being an unwelcome third, so when Luther moved in she moved to the ranch to live with her father. That's where she met Kamuela. He taught her how to ride, and she fell for him and decided he was the only thing on earth she wanted."

Steve threw back her head and laughed heartily at some recollection. Finally she calmed down and said, "Excuse me. But the story at this point is so delicious I nearly bust every time I think of it. A wonderful illustration of the difference between two cultures. You see, when Maude started making eyes at Kamuela he responded in the way most natural to him. As he told it later—in all innocence, mind you—the girl wanted to be loved, so he obliged her. He never thought for a moment of marriage. That's where the wonderful difference comes in.

"After Maude 'gave her all' to Kamuela she took it for granted that they would marry. She told her father and there was a hell of a row. Maude threw hysterics for a week until the old man gave in. He summoned Kamuela and told him he would permit the marriage and that he intended to give the boy the luckiest break of his life, by making him foreman of the ranch. Kamuela was dumfounded. He said he didn't want to get married, he wasn't interested in being ranch foreman. Fortunate fellow, he had no ambition. He wanted to be exactly what he was: a happy-go-lucky *paniolo*. Old man Harrington raved and swore, but Kamuela just laughed. When Maude's father threatened to run him off the island, Kamuela packed his gear and went to Hawaii, where he got a job on the Parker ranch. Harrington couldn't make trouble for him without letting the whole story out.

"But it leaked out anyway, another of those island scandals that never saw print. Maude's father sent her away to school, and when she came home she brought a husband—Walter Benson. He was riding master at her school—crazy about horses. They moved onto the ranch and have been there ever since. But she never forgot the humiliation a Hawaiian had given her. Maude hated the natives; she became so disagreeable that all their help began to quit. Finally Walter took over, to keep them from going bankrupt, and Maude had to retire from ranch management. So she turned to good works, built a church, and now she persecutes the poor Hawaiians on the grounds that they're heathens."

I was silent when she finished, assimilating what Steve had said. Maude's act had fooled me, possibly as it fooled Maude herself. I had thought she really was worked up over the Hawaiians' reversion to primitive life. It wasn't the first time a corrosive hatred had been sublimated into religious fanaticism.

"But I still don't see, Steve, where she and Julia are at all alike."

Steve cocked her head on one side and looked at me quizzically. "They're alike. They've both got enormous pride. Julia's never had her self-esteem challenged, that's all."

She stood up. "Thanks for the lunch. When you decide to tell me the truth about how you cut your feet on coral, call me up. I'm busting with curiosity, but I can wait. Something tells me when I hear the whole story it'll be a good one."

CHAPTER TEN

LILY arrived with my new doctor soon after Steve left. Ethel Chun looked just as I remembered her, dressed in navy-blue linen frosted with white, moving with the brisk cheerfulness of any plump, efficient Chinese house-wife on her way to market. Instead of a shopping bag she carried a black medical case. She twinkled at me as she said hello, stuck a thermometer in my mouth, and felt my pulse. She read the result with an enigmatic expression and asked, "How do your feet feel? Any throbbing or swelling?"

"Yes, in the right one. I'm trying to ignore it."

"We'll have a look. Let's get her upstairs, Lily; I want to give her some penicillin."

I felt all kinds of a fool being pulled up the stairs in that awkward chair by two tiny Chinese women. But Julia couldn't help, Maude and Walter had disappeared, and Ellen hadn't returned. I was unable to walk; I tried once and couldn't bear weight on my right foot. Lily and her cousin hauled the chaise up the red-tiled stairs with considerable rocking from side to side, wheeled me into my room, and rolled me efficiently onto the bed.

Once I was prone, Dr. Chun opened her black bag, swabbed my rear with alcohol, and proceeded to give me a shot in the stern with a hypodermic needle which looked to my apprehensive eyes big enough to use on an elephant. She was so deft that it hardly hurt a bit. Then she examined my feet and announced that there was still some coral in the right one, since the heel was inflamed and swollen. The process of removing it took a few minutes which seemed more like hours and was too unpleasant to dwell upon. She packed her little black bag, twinkled at me again as she said she thought I'd be all right now, and bustled out en route to her office.

After she had gone Lily closed the door and pulled a chair over near my bed. "How was your luncheon party?"

"Delightful," I said crossly. "Tony and I talked in circles. Just when he was starting to ask questions, Steve Dugan showed up on schedule. He left at two-thirty for the house next door. I hope you had enough time for your little errand."

"There was enough time. And the errand was successful."

I started to sit up, discovered that since Dr. Chun's injection my rear was getting very sore, scowled and lay on my uninjected side. Lily stuffed pillows behind me and said, "Temper, temper. Relax and I'll tell you about it."

I sighed with resignation. "Okay, I'm relaxed; begin."

"What did Tony tell you about the kind of work he does?"

"He never talked about it much. Something to do with statistics, he said."

Lily's red mouth curled in a smile. "That is correct. He works with statistics—of a certain kind. Do you remember the paper on which his notes about you were typed?"

"Copy paper, wasn't it?"

"Yes. Tony Davis is a feature writer, formerly free-lance, now employed as roving editor by—" and she named a digest magazine with mighty influence and international circulation. Its numerous minor editors were paid fabulous salaries, since the book earned such astronomical profits that its owners had to spend them somehow before paying taxes. Little Marvel printed stories dramatizing faith in God and in God's children and especially in God's country. At the same time it distilled warmongering in subtle form, made devout obeisance to Big Business, and waged unremitting attack on unions and liberal political factions.

I was silent for a while, surprised and yet not surprised, trying to fit Tony into the pattern Lily had given me. I was also remembering an evening I spent in New York with a writer who sold regularly to that market. Max Bloom, a publicity man I knew, had brought him along for a double date, and later I crossed the new acquaintance off my list and marked the experience as Things a Girl Learns in Making Her Way Around New York. My bruises faded in a couple of days. I remembered vividly the writer's lecture on how to sell to his market: "If you can get the right angle—or a good gimmick—" Was I an "angle"—or a "gimmick"? I looked at Lily. "What does Tony want from me?"

"A story. On paganism in Hawaii. 'Do the Hawaiians really eat human flesh? Do they actually sacrifice beautiful virgins in their secret temple rites?' And so forth. He has a list of questions written down, apparently ideas for his lead paragraph."

"But he can get all the history he wants from the library, the Bishop Museum, the Archives, half a dozen different sources."

"Tony wants a story of today. He's writing about your village, the one next door." She gestured toward the window which overlooked Wainiha. "And his story is going to be 'As told by Janice Cameron, daughter of Emmett Cameron, scholar and recluse whose lifework was compiling Hawaiiana. Sacred secrets of the natives, never before revealed.'"

I gasped. Before I could say anything, Lily opened her bag, brought out a sheaf of papers covered with typescript, and handed them to me.

"These are copies of notes and correspondence." At my look of inquiry she explained briefly. "The boy who helped me is a stenographer; he took shorthand notes and transcribed them during his lunch hour."

"How did you persuade him to let you into Tony's room?"

"He is Chinese; his small daughter is a patient at my uncle's clinic."

"What did you tell him?"

"The truth," she said succinctly.

I began reading the typed pages. Lily sat impassive, watching me as she smoked and waited. There was a letter signed Joe (I couldn't remember his surname), the writer who dated me on that ill-starred evening. He expressed congratulations and envy because of Tony's job and his proposed trip to Hawaii on his first big assignment. Apparently Joe had gone to Tony with the idea for a story and abandoned it when he found it involved traveling six thousand miles on speculation.

He mentioned things I had told him about Hawaii—that was in the days before I learned to keep my mouth shut concerning a world outsiders couldn't understand—when I tried to correct his misconceptions of island life. At his challenge I had cited my father's research, his scholarship and years of personal experience, as my authority. This foolishness of mine had spawned the "gimmick" with which he approached Tony. All to be tied up with my forthcoming novel and the movie to be made from it.

Joe's letter finished with a warning: "The gal is nuts on the subject of the natives—handle with caution."

Tony had taken it from there. He had done some preliminary work already: there was sketchy data from Porteus, Fergusson, Burrows, Alexander, and Malo, which indicated that he intended to do some research in addition to pumping me for specific information about Wainiha. Scribbled notes said: "*F.C. says ghost drums heard—ask J. If no dice, approach M.B.*" "*If* heiau *not used for human sacrifice, inference can still be made . . .*"

As I read I felt nausea rising in my throat. I knew the slick way the story could be written; it was easy to hint, to write vaguely of unnameable obscenities and practices indulged in when the moon was in *Ku*, or when the Shark God must be propitiated. Easy to describe a life hundreds of years past and then to ask: "Do these natives still . . . ?"

As I thought of the Shark God a vague memory stirred and subsided. Something to do with Malia, but again it eluded me.

I read on. The sickness in me changed to acute apprehension as I realized that if I refused to talk to Tony he could still, through his contact with Faye, find another to give him the story he wanted. "M.B." That meant Maude, tormented by her hatred of Hawaiians, ranting about paganism and depravity.

When I finished reading I took Tony's *lei* from around my neck and flung it toward the wastebasket. I laid the papers on the bed, my fingers slipping them together automatically as my thoughts raced.

Lily asked, "What are you going to do?"

Characteristically, where a personal problem was concerned, she preferred to let me make my own decision first.

I bit my lip, concentrating fiercely. An idea was presenting itself, still nebulous but taking form. I began to think aloud. "If I refuse to give him any information, Tony will go ahead on his own and write the story. He'll get it from Faye, or from Maude. Maude was born on this land; her byline wouldn't have the publicity value of mine but it might look even more authentic."

Lily nodded, waiting.

"So the wise thing for me to do is play along with him and either stall him off as long as possible—"

We looked at each other and nodded simultaneously.

"—or give him information which is completely false—"

"—and let him know that it is inaccurate after the magazine has already gone to the printer—"

"—so that the entire issue will have to be withdrawn!"

We nodded at each other again, and my smile was grim. I was reflecting wryly: what is that old aphorism about the woman scorned? Her wrath doesn't exceed by one centigrade that of the woman tricked! Pride was part of it, of course, but deeper than lacerated vanity was my anger at the callousness with which a group of warmhearted, generous people were to be publicly degraded—just for a gimmick, a headline.

Finally I said, "I'm going to do something else which will prevent Tony from using my material or anyone else's. Wheel that chaise over here, Lily."

Lily never asked silly questions. She pushed it over to the bed and I rolled onto it.

"Luther's study is down the hall at the front of the house. I saw a telephone there, and I'm going to put in a call to New York. Let's go."

The study was really a drafting room, with a long, high table and the stool on which he worked, a fluorescent light angled over drafting sheets protected by brown paper. Luther's tools were neatly arranged at the right end of the table: pencils with hair-thin points of extra-hard lead, the sandpaper stick on which he sharpened them, art gum, T-square, tacks, a slide rule. On a stand by the pillow-covered *punee* was the telephone. I picked it up.

"Lily, will you go down to the library and stand guard over the extension? I don't want anyone to overhear this."

She turned toward the door. "Tell the operator to charge the call to Dr. Ethel Chun," she advised. "I'll explain to them later."

"Right."

It was nearly dinnertime when my call went through; late at night in New York. I got Jo Ames, my agent, at her apartment. There was noise of people and music at first; finally she moved her telephone on its thirty-foot cord into her bedroom for our conversation.

"This is Janice," I told her.

"So I gathered," she said dryly. "I don't have any other clients who'd call from Honolulu at this hour. What's on your mind? It can't be money, because that last check was enough to keep you in grass skirts for the rest of your days." Jo dropped the bantering tone; her voice became warm and normal. "What is it, Janice?"

"Remember that story you wanted me to write?"

"Which one?"

"About my island childhood and my Hawaiian friends in the little village."

"Sure I remember. Changed your mind about writing it?"

"Yes. I want to do it now. On one condition, Jo: that it is published before December."

Jo laughed. "After all my lectures about publicity, and all the times you said you weren't interested—what's the—"

I interrupted. "Jo, this is important. Can you place it for me?"

"Sweetie, I know a couple of editors whose inventories are just crying for that piece. About four thousand words, with pictures. I'll confirm it tomorrow. What time is it out there, for heaven's sake?"

"We're about to have dinner."

"And I'm about to go to bed, as soon as this gang leaves. Good night, Janice, thanks for the call. I'll call you back tomorrow. Hey, how about that Hawaiian village—getting things lined up?"

I gulped. "Yes. Everything's fine. Good night, Jo, and thanks."

When Lily came up she said, "I listened downstairs. That will keep you busy while your feet heal."

I nodded. "I've got to get some boxes out of storage now, to find the right pictures."

"Where are they stored?"

"In my garage. After Mother died, Saito moved from the servants' quarters into the house. When I rented the place I stored personal stuff, papers and books, in the room she used to use. I've been worried about insects getting at those things; they're packed in wooden boxes, all except Father's notebooks. I put those in a steel filing case."

"You can get them tomorrow."

"Right. Let's dress for dinner. Would you bring me that white blouse with the navy taffeta skirt? I feel like wearing something special, to compensate for these bandages and my wounded ego."

Lily went to the clothes closet and opened the door. "You're compensating already," she told me.

I was glad I had taken pains with dressing that evening when I saw that the Averys had guests. There was a new maid serving canapes, an Oriental girl wearing a dark uniform with white apron. Suka watched her with an anxious eye from the door of the dining room, but she needn't have worried; the girl was very efficient as she moved from one guest to another.

Dr. Atherton was talking to the judge, who had been at Faye's party; the judge's son, Fred, was listening politely to his elders and smiling across the *lanai* at Ellen, dressed in the blue frock which was so becoming to her.

Julia and Walter were speaking low-voiced with heads together; Maude was not to be seen. Faye Clarke and Tony stood by the cocktail table, laughing over something one of them had just said.

Our entrance had to be slightly dramatic, since Luther carried me and there was some business of getting settled in the chaise near the edge of the *lanai*. Lily seated herself near me and smiled refusal of Luther's offer of a drink; she relaxed at once into the stillness which I knew meant that every sense was alert, that she wasn't drinking because she did not intend to blur any impression she might get from this group of people. She wore a Chinese panel dress of sage green with jade earrings and bracelets set in Chinese gold. Her makeup was simple; she did not want to look conspicuous, and with her chameleon ability to absorb atmosphere, or, rather, to recede into it, she succeeded in giving the impression of being a rather plain and unassuming little person. I saw Tony glance at her with a puzzled expression; he was probably remembering the scene in our stateroom. But his glance passed over her quickly, lingered on me with very convincing affection, and then returned to Faye.

She was in white, with gardenias in her hair. Her golden skin was smoother than the petals of the flowers she wore, her mouth was invitation, the pose of her ripe body was promise of delight. To a man, that is. She set down her glass as Luther approached the table, and said, "Luther, I'd like to talk with you later this evening, about those plans. I think I've found the property I want. There may have to be some changes."

"Any time, Faye," Luther said wearily. I wondered how many changes he had already made for her.

The Avery station wagon skidded around the driveway in a spray of gravel and stopped with screeching brakes in front of the garage. We all glanced in that direction as Maude's dumpy figure emerged and began trudging toward us. She hadn't changed; she was still wearing the brown dress, and it looked wrinkled and soiled. She seemed surprised when she saw us, and said, "Dinnertime already?"

"Where have you been, Maude?" Julia asked. "Suka looked everywhere for you."

"Oh," she answered vaguely, "I went to a movie. I must have gone to sleep in the show—I had no idea it was so late."

Maude didn't look like a woman who had been relaxing in a movie. She looked more like a traveler just returned from a long and uncomfortable journey.

"I'll go and change," she said, and disappeared into the house.

There were voices suddenly coming from the beach, shrill young voices, sharp with excitement—and fright. Like puppets we all turned in that direction and saw a group of children running toward the house, half a dozen wiry little boys dressed in swimming trunks, running and calling, "Mister Avery! Mister Avery!"

Their hair was wet, and their trunks. Their eyes—all colors of eyes, from the liquid dark of the Portuguese youngster to the pale blue of the Caucasian child with yellow hair—were wide with fright. The tallest boy—part Hawaiian and part Chinese, from his features—reached us first, panting.

"What is it, boy?" Luther asked.

"Mister Avery!" the child gasped. "We found—down there in the water—a woman! She's drownded!"

"I know her," a second boy said. "She used to live here. It's Malia."

Later we got a more coherent story. They had gone to the place in a gang, to fish and swim. One of them had dropped his spear and dived for it near a ledge a few hundred feet past Wainiha. He had found Malia's body under the ledge, thrust there at low tide, imprisoned, when the water receded, by her long hair which tangled in the rock. I thought quickly as I listened to their story. It was improbable that the tide could have carried her out the narrow opening in the rocks through which water rushed into that swimming hole; improbable, but not entirely an impossibility. She had floated then, farther down the coast, to be thrust under the ledge and held there until her body was discovered.

Lily and I did not look at each other during the recital of this discovery.

"We stopped at the village, but the people went in their houses and wouldn't talk to us," one boy added resentfully.

"So we came on here. What do we do now, call police?"

Luther set down his glass with a hand that shook. He swallowed and then said slowly, "We will verify this first, boys. You lead the way."

He started off, accompanied by all the men in our party, plus Ellen and Lily. Julia and I were immobilized, and Faye apparently didn't wish to ruin her white slippers. She sat down and said thoughtfully, "*Lumahai.* Sacrifice by drowning. Isn't that what it's called, Janice?"

She was right, and of course she knew it. I had been trying to think of the word ever since I found Malia in the pool. I didn't want to think of its significance.

"Malia was trained as a temple dancer," Faye went on as if thinking aloud. "She decided there wasn't enough excitement in dedicating herself to religious *hulas*. Temple dancers have to be virgins. Isn't there a superstition that the Shark God takes those girls who violate their vows of chastity?"

There was a gasp from Julia. She sank back, clutching her chair, while her face went white. "No, Faye! You must not say things like that!"

Faye shrugged ever so slightly. "There has to be some explanation. Unless the girl was killed by that Hawaiian lover of hers. She was a good swimmer. It's not likely that she fell in and just let herself be drowned."

"Why don't we wait," I suggested, "until—" I bit off the words. I wanted very much to declare my certainty that Malia's death was from no supernatural cause. But if I carried through my intention of giving Tony a lurid account of native superstitions, I'd have to keep quiet for the present. He would undoubtedly check with Faye. The two women were waiting for me to finish, and I said, "—until we find out what really happened."

"Wait! That's what everybody keeps saying!" The outburst came from Maude, standing in the doorway, her face contorted with violent emotion.

"Wait until we find out what really happened!" she mimicked. "Julia says it, even after one of the Kanakas pushes her down the hill and tries to kill her! Luther says it, when he knows those filthy natives are contaminating the entire community, bringing shame on all of us because their disgusting practices are tolerated! I say let's get rid of them, get them off our land. Julia says no, we must wait, we must—"

She stopped and stood staring over the lawn, while the rest of us followed her gaze toward a procession which had appeared on the trail leading from the village. They walked in single file, like figures in an ancient frieze, silhouetted against amethyst sky and purple sea. Luther was in the lead. In his arms he carried a sodden thing which dripped water in dark splotches over his white linen suit. The others followed in a slow, silent cortege.

Up on the ridge which separated us from Wainiha other silent figures stood, dark against the paling horizon. Then one of them began to chant. Malia's death dirge.

The police officer who came to the Averys' was an immense Hawaiian named Kamakua, possessed of coffee-colored skin which made his perfect teeth seem startlingly white, and a soft voice with which he spoke meticulous English. He was island-born and a graduate *cum laude* of the local university, with two years of postgraduate work on the mainland, plus several years of Army Intelligence to his credit. This meant that he could probably speak several Chinese dialects as well as Japanese and Hawaiian. Without a doubt he also spoke wonderfully expressive pidgin. I looked at Captain Kamakua and decided that he would be great fun on a party and I should like to see him do a *hula*. It would be wicked.

He wasn't showing his private personality to any of us now. He was the alert officer, quietly in command of himself and of the situation, seemingly casual in his questions but aware of every nuance of voice, every betraying gesture. He sat on the *lanai* and asked questions of each of us in turn. The questioning was brief, since some of us—Lily and I, Judge Coffee and his son—had no acquaintanceship with Malia. Luther and Julia explained that she had been in their employ briefly, because of a shortage of domestic help in the house. Maude and Walter corroborated this; when Captain Kamakua looked at Ellen with a raise of eyebrows, she nodded further corroboration and he did not question her.

Faye had the most to tell: that she had taken Malia to the mainland as her personal maid, that the girl had been insolent and sulky, and had been discharged because she began to steal small things: lingerie, costume jewelry, stockings. Faye also added, in a calm voice, that the girl wanted to earn money, and she had paid her for dancing at the *luau* for the edification of the senator and her other *malihini* guests.

"The senator was a friend of ours in Washington, Captain. I promised him that when he came to Honolulu I'd produce a real *hula* dancer. It was at his request that I asked Malia to give a private performance for a limited number of my guests." She finished by describing the interruption by David and his carrying the furious Malia out of the house.

Tony and Walter repeated Faye's story of Malia's performance. As Walter admitted being part of the audience Ellen gasped, looked at her father and then quickly at her mother. Maude was the one from whom a strong reaction was to be expected. She stiffened as Walter acknowledged his presence when the scene between Malia and David took place; she looked at him in surprise and resentment, but behind her regard was also an attitude of withdrawal, of intense contemplation, as if she were considering his behavior not only as her husband but in some other light. Her somber eyes studied him, her lips were pressed tight together, and she said nothing.

From the time Malia had been carried from Faye's house, nobody in our group had seen her. David had apparently pursued her to the village, and from then on, nobody knew what had happened.

Captain Kamakua rose and tucked his notebook in his breast pocket. "Thank you. That will be all for now."

There was no need to caution any of us about leaving, as is customary in mainland police inquiries. We were on an island.

Dr. Atherton walked with the police officer toward the garage, where Malia's body had been laid in an empty bedroom of the servants' quarters. Conversation was desultory after they left, but when the doctor returned and said briefly that Captain Kamakua was on his way to the village to interview David, some of the tenseness left our group. We ate a silent and hurried meal, served by the new maid, who was deft but unsmiling, and by Suka, who looked as if tears had recently been dried on her soft, round face.

After dinner the judge announced that he thought he would drive over to Kaneohe to visit a client, and asked if Ellen and Fred would like to go. Ellen's face lighted and she looked at her mother for permission. Maude nodded absently, still immersed in the deep waters of her private conjecturing. Luther went to his study for Faye's plans and walked through the hedge with her to discuss them at her house. After they left, Tony came over to talk with me, but at that point I realized how tired and depressed I was, how much I wished to be alone. He carried me upstairs and deposited me on the bed, then sat down for a cigarette before leaving.

"How about lunch tomorrow?" he asked.

I preferred never to see Tony again. I couldn't let him know how I felt, not yet. "I'd love to," I said with phony enthusiasm, "if I finish working in time."

His eyebrows went up. "But I thought you didn't even want to think about work! Writing another book so soon?"

"No indeed." I put regret into my voice. "I have to do some revisions. I'm afraid my memories of the village were inaccurate. Since I've been home I've discovered—" I bit my lip, as if reminding myself not to be indiscreet, and was silent. Tony waited.

I said, reluctantly, "I have to go through my father's notebooks again to look up certain details. It's a nuisance; they're stored in the garage of my house in Nuuanu and I haven't looked at them for years." I shrugged. "Let's not talk about it now, Tony; I'll tell you sometime, if you're really interested."

"You know I am." He got up from his chair and came to sit on the bed next to me. "I'm interested in anything that concerns you, Janice. And aside from that, I'm a writer, of sorts. You're mistaken to think I'd be bored with shoptalk. But just at this moment—"

He put both arms around me and pulled me against him; his mouth brushed my throat. I didn't want Tony to kiss me again; I didn't want him anywhere near me. But I had a part to play.

I said, pushing him away, "You can't stay up here, you know. This isn't proper. The Averys are very straitlaced people, and I'm their guest."

Tony smiled as he rose. "Right. I'll call you tomorrow."

Lily came in after he left, to help me undress. She gave me some ointment for my feet, and as I applied it and rewrapped them, we talked.

"As we expected," Lily told me, "it will be difficult to discover how Malia died, unless a weapon was used. She had been in the water too long. The crabs—" She shivered delicately. "But everyone thinks that the Hawaiian, David, killed her in jealous rage and threw her into the sea."

"How about the Shark God?"

"A suggestion which was violently rejected. Of course it looks very bad for the Hawaiians. Religious fanatics have been known before this to insist that a death—or a sudden cure from illness—resulted from superhuman causes. And there is some thing about such an idea which fascinates even the most outwardly sensible people. Do you remember the thousands who made pilgrimages to the Bronx and left offerings on a vacant lot where a little boy saw a vision? This happens all over the world."

"I read about that and saw some pictures. There have been such things here too. Years ago, on one of the plantations, someone claimed to have discovered a stone of the old healing god, Lono. Hundreds went there, left flowers and money and other offerings. Not only Hawaiians, but people of all races and religions. The plantation owners tried to get rid of it and ordered one of their men to push the stone over and remove the offerings. He did as he was told, and the next day he was found dead. People whispered that he was killed by the god. The plantation owners had to replace the stone and leave it there, and the people kept on coming."

"The man who died—was he Hawaiian?"

"He was Japanese."

Lily's dark brows drew together slightly; she sat silent. Finally she said, "I do not like this. We must find out why this is happening. There is a reason, and we must discover it.

"What are you going to do now?'"

She took a compact from her purse and traced lipstick over her mouth with a tiny brush. She made a little moue of distaste as she said, "I am going to play bridge. Maude Benson has gone to her room, and I am asked to make a fourth. Good night."

She hated bridge, and I didn't blame her. Most people who know the subtleties of mah-jongg find bridge a dull game. Chinese are individualists of the first order, and mah-jongg does not require working in a partnership where all the player's skill may be useless if his partner happens to be unable or unwilling to cooperate.

I wished her good luck and settled with a novel which I tried to read. I found fiction dull compared to the frightening reality which I was living. I laid it aside and turned out the light.

There were no drums throbbing in the village. I had half expected to hear them.

I lay in darkness, for the moon had not risen, listening to night sounds interspersed with vague murmurs from the game downstairs, thinking of Malia and wondering where her body would rest. No one had ever mentioned that she had any family; Julia said she lived in Wainiha with relatives but did not define their relationship. I thought of Tony and how fond of him I might have been if he were a different person, and I wondered again what Faye meant to him. Such thoughts were disquieting, so I began to arrange work in my mind, a process which is almost always soporific.

I do not know how long I had been sleeping when I woke again. The house was still, darkness was absolute, and I lay tensely wondering what had brought me to consciousness. There was a faint sound from the balcony outside my room, as if the heavy bougainvillea vines there were being rubbed against the stone railing. There was no wind to sway those vines so markedly. I turned toward the opened French doors and stared, trying to penetrate absolute blackness. Distantly the Pacific sighed on the shore; a palm leaf broke, falling with a sudden rattle to the earth. The movement on my balcony stopped and there was utter stillness, the stillness of waiting.

I raised my head on the pillow, straining toward the doors. A form almost imperceptibly blacker than the darkness through which it moved came swiftly toward me; the bed jarred as someone bumped against it. My heart jumped in a tattoo of alarm, but I couldn't scream. I started rolling toward the other side of the bed.

A strong hand grasped my arm and held me; another hand pressed hard over my mouth. A low voice said, "Don't make noise. Don't turn on the light."

I began to tremble; I reached out my free arm and touched warm, bare flesh. It was a man, a man who wore no clothes. He released my mouth just enough so that I could whisper, "Who are you?"

"David. David Kimu. I want to talk to you."

CHAPTER ELEVEN

"DAVID!" I whispered. "David! Why did you come?"

"I came to talk. Sorry about what happened the other day," he said. "I didn't recognize you."

He lapsed into Hawaiian: "*Auwe, Kulolo, heaha heia? Lapuale, kela hale, lapuale no.*"

Alas, Kulolo, what are you doing here? This house is no good. I translated slowly, unused to the language. David sensed my difficulty and went on in English. "Kulolo, why do you stay with these people?"

"I have to stay for a while." I told him briefly of my hopes for a movie filmed at Wainiha and explained that my own house was rented and the Averys had invited me to visit them.

"Did you tell Malia about this movie company?"

"Yes. "

"So that is why she wouldn't go away. I understand now."

For a moment the strongest emotion I felt was the relief which flooded me. When your only living relatives can be counted on the fingers of one hand, old and dear friends have great value. This was the second time since my return that I had been called by my Hawaiian name, and the warmth it generated told me how much I had missed these childhood companions. Now the separation of years was forgotten in one moment. David hadn't changed. He felt the same *aloha* for me that he had felt when we were playmates.

"What do you mean—this house is no good?" I asked.

"You do not know what they are doing?" David's voice held surprise. He continued, "Of course not. This began before you came home."

"I know that something very nasty is going on in your village," I said, "and I don't like talking in the dark." I reached for the light, but his hand closed over my wrist. "Wait."

I heard him move, and when I turned on the light, David, wearing a red *malo* and nothing else, was sitting on the floor. Any watcher from ground level could have seen only my half-upright figure with a reading light burning by my bed. I picked up the discarded novel and held it, to complete the illusion.

"I do not have much time, so we must talk fast," David said. "Now that they have found Malia, I am going away."

"You didn't kill her."

"No. But it is intended that someone from the village be blamed for her death. The night she died, I did go into that woman's house and take Malia away—she was shaming us all. I hoped that she would sail on the *Lurline* as she planned. She told me she was going to get money because she knew a secret; somebody was paying her to leave the islands. Then she decided not to go, and she was killed."

My indiscreet confidence had caused the girl to make a decision which brought about her death. Malia would have been permitted to live if she had gone away and taken her dangerous knowledge with her. A secret about what? It concerned someone in this place, or Faye Clarke; Malia had been closely connected with both houses.

"Are you the one who telephoned for me to meet Tony Davis at the pool?" I asked.

"Yes. We wanted a *haole* to find her. Malia was put in the pool so her death would be connected with our village. We were supposed to find her body when we went to bathe in the morning. Added to other things which are happening in Wainiha, her death would have been the final incident to cause real *pilikia* for us. There is already plenty *pilikia* now."

"Yes, I know." I looked searchingly at him. "David, I heard the drums, I saw the blood on the *heiau*. What does it mean? And have there really been processions?"

David's eyes would not meet mine. "I have seen none. Malia says she did. And Henry Mahea is dead."

"Is that why Makaleha moved away? Who are those new people there?"

"The new people—" He looked intently at me for a moment from his cross-legged position, then said evasively, "None of the old-timers are there now."

I had been growing puzzled over David's manner. When I knew him he spoke carelessly, like many other islanders, a mixture of pidgin weird and picturesque to hear, and remarkably expressive. Now his entire bearing, as well as his speech, was altered. I asked him about it.

White teeth flashed in his bronzed skin. "I'm a college man now," he said. "Majoring in sociology. Got a scholarship."

"And you're going around in a *malo* putting on an act of being a simple fisherman."

"For the time being it is necessary. I find out more that way."

"What do you mean," I asked, reverting to the subject of the village, "the old-timers have moved away? Is it because of the *kahuna*? Is there really a *kahuna*? Who are these new people? Are they the ones who throw Bibles into the ocean and make sacrifices at the *heiau*? What is going on there?" My voice rose with each question.

"Sh-h!" David's face became grave. He shrugged and spread his hands out, opening the fingers fanwise in a typically Hawaiian gesture.

"I do not—" he started, and gestured toward the light. "Turn it out!"

Before I could reach the bedside lamp, the door to the bathroom opened and Lily Wu came into the room. In her flat embroidered Chinese slippers she moved without a sound. David had half risen, but I motioned him to stay put. Lily closed the door behind her and moved a chair against it. She went to the hall door and locked it. She sat in the chair recently occupied by Tony and said, "You do not use caution, Janice. I could hear you talking as far as my room."

David's face had settled into a wary mask, but he resumed his sitting position on the floor. He said to me, "Who is she?"

"She is my foster sister. Her name is Lily Wu— You can trust her."

He relaxed then. "I am glad you have a sister now. Welcome to Hawaii, Lily."

Lily smiled briefly at him. "You are David. You were Malia's sweet-heart?"

He shook his head. "Not her sweetheart. She was my calabash cousin, related as you are to Janice." Lily nodded comprehension; she knew of the Hawaiians' fondness for children and their casual way of taking strays and orphans under their wing without formality of legal procedure.

David said, "I am going away for a while. Let Kamakua think I killed Malia. I have told you that I did not kill her. But if police hunt for me they will not bother the people in the village. Turn your light out now, so I can go."

"One moment," Lily said. "Do you know which one of these people tried to kill Mrs. Avery?"

His expressive brows went up; he nodded approval. "So you have found that out already. Mrs. Avery came to the village shortly after the *kahuna* arrived. She wanted to see him but he would not appear. As she started down the trail to go home, she stumbled and fell. I was not there, but I was told that she jumped as if something had hit her in the back, and then lost her balance. Malia was working in this house at the time, and I asked her what happened. She said Mrs. Avery claimed someone had hit her with a rock. I asked our people and they all denied doing that thing."

"Then who did it?"

"The next day I went up on the old path—the one you and your father used to take, Kulolo. I found marks where someone had been standing—long enough to smoke many cigarettes. I stood there and threw stones. It was easy to hit the path below."

He sighed. "You see, it is better that you do not go to the village. Take care of yourself." He gathered his feet under him to rise.

"Will we see you again?"

"I will get in touch with you. Don't worry; the police will not find me. Good-by, Lily. Good-by, Kulolo. Turn out the light."

I did so. His figure made a moving blot in the darkness of the doorway. Then he was gone.

When I related our conversation to Lily she said in a thoughtful voice, "That helps somewhat. Now we know there really is a *kahuna* in the village, and the Hawaiian people are protecting him. Why?"

I let out a shaky sigh. I couldn't understand it and said so. At that moment I wanted to cry, and it infuriated me because I knew tears wouldn't solve anything.

Lily didn't help. Instead she reprimanded me sharply for being so careless. "You should know better than that," she said, not sparing my feelings. "I was not asleep, and perhaps that is why I heard you through the bathroom door. But you must remember that there may be others here who do not sleep. Janice, this is no pleasant house party. You must not expect these people to behave as if it were. Please be very careful."

I lost my inclination to weep when I heard her sharp words. She was right, and if she had been my flesh-and-blood sister I couldn't have wanted more to slap her lovely face for being so right.

"Have a cigarette?" she offered, smiling.

I took it and said, "What do we do now? I want to go and see Makaleha, I must get my things from Nuuanu, but if I can't walk—"

"You'll be able to walk very soon. Tomorrow I must go out for a while. Your job is to be quiet and observe without seeming to observe. Look helpless and blond and dumb." She dimpled at me. "It shouldn't be too difficult."

I couldn't respond to her teasing. It took effort to subdue resentment at being so restricted. I said slowly, disciplining my thoughts, "I have to wait for that call from Jo. And I must get that story written. Tony asked me for a luncheon date, but I'll refuse when he calls. Sore feet or not, I'm going to Nuuanu for those boxes."

"Please wait until I can go with you. I'll be free later in the afternoon. Suppose you keep the date with Tony and then meet me at your house at four o'clock." She rose, yawning. "You'll have a busy day. Take your New York call, write your story, keep the date with Tony, and meet me at four o'clock. You'd better get some sleep now."

"Good night, eavesdropper."

"Good night, loudmouth."

With these affectionate parting words we separated.

* * * *

The next day I began walking with a sort of lopsided hobble; my left foot was almost healed and the other would bear my weight briefly. I sat on the *lanai* that morning, waiting for Jo to call, chatting with Ellen while her parents read the papers. To my surprise, Julia joined us; she seldom appeared so early in the day. She made her way painfully across the flagstones to a chair and began to speak immediately of Malia's death.

"I was worried about her funeral," she said, her eyes fixed on the floor. Julia looked ghastly; her hands shook and her skin was dry and bloodless. "The police told us," she added, "that a relative had appeared and would make all arrangements."

"Did they determine the cause of her death?" I asked.

"Oh yes. She was drowned. Very likely it was an accident. She may have had a dizzy spell . . ." Julia's voice trailed off and her mouth twitched. She didn't believe in a dizzy spell any more than I did.

"The girl was probably drunk," Maude said flatly.

"She might have been," Walter agreed. "The night she danced for us she seemed unnaturally stimulated. And her costume—" He glanced toward his wife, who regarded him with hard, calculating eyes.

"Tony told me," I said, "that she was wearing the pink nightgown I gave her."

They all looked at me.

"When she helped me unpack, the day I arrived, she admired the gown and I gave it to her. Malia told me she was going away and wanted to wear it on board ship. She said," I added innocently, "that somebody had given her the money for passage."

Let them stew over that. It might make David's guilt seem more likely, but at the same time someone in this family might also begin to wonder who paid Malia's passage—and why.

"Then that's why he killed her!" Maude said. "Jealousy!" She stared hard at Walter and then looked down at her plate. Walter wiped his bald head with an already damp handkerchief and shrugged. Ellen's face was strained; these ugly undercurrents between her parents made her suffer.

At that moment we heard the telephone ringing. Walter jumped from his chair and rushed to answer it, like a man expecting important news. He came back to say, "New York is calling you, Janice."

I rose and limped to the library, aware that they were wondering why I should receive such a call. They would all listen.

Jo said, "Hello, you lucky girl. Sorry to tear you away from your ukulele."

"Go ahead and talk—it's your nickel. What's the verdict?"

"Four thousand words, and send pictures. November publication. Can you get the story to me by clipper in ten days?"

"Can do. Thanks a lot, Jo."

"Think of me slaving away in this hot office while you're eating pineapples and coconuts. But get the script in the mail."

"You'll have it."

I went back to the *lanai* and told the others that my agent had just asked me to do some revisions on my book and I intended to start work immediately. Ellen looked disappointed; she had probably hoped we could spend some time together.

"What revisions must you make?" Julia asked.

"Just one chapter, about Polynesian temple rites," I said evasively, adding, "I shall have to get Father's notebooks out of storage—they're in my garage—to check for accuracy."

Nobody made any comment. I excused myself and went to my room to set up typewriter and paper on the desk by the window. I didn't want to sit at a typewriter. I wanted the release of physical activity. Malia was dead— "drowned." Her funeral was arranged. David was a fugitive from the police. And nobody cared.

The people of this house were sitting comfortably downstairs; it did not concern them. Luther had gone to his office—Faye's plans must be finished. Faye herself was no doubt finding diversion somewhere, probably with Tony.

Tony. If I didn't get to work, his story would be published. Nobody could tell the truth about Wainiha except me. If Tony's version ever reached those millions of readers, no amount of denial or retraction would undo the damage. I took a deep breath. Then I sat down and began to write. At noon I lit a cigarette and read the first draft, finding it overemotional but holding together fairly well. It would do. I'd get the pictures from storage today and type final draft tomorrow. As I raised my eyes I glimpsed a human figure at the edge of the Avery property. I pulled the curtain aside in order to see better.

It was Maude, wearing flat heels and a big hat, stalking along the path which led to the Hawaiian village. There was determination in the way she moved, putting her feet down solidly and never hesitating on her course. Her figure disappeared as the path descended the other side of the hill, and then I saw Walter, in pursuit. He went swiftly but with caution, and as he reached the top of the hill he ducked behind a high shrub, raised binoculars to his eyes, and crouched there, watching. I wondered if somebody else in the house was watching him as I did.

Tony called shortly after that, to ask if I could meet him at Waikiki for lunch. Since I had time to kill before I met Lily, I agreed, welcoming the prospect of getting away from the house. I chose my frock carefully—a scoop-necked sheer voile, cocoa-colored with a jade and raspberry floral print, set off with a white straw bag and the only thing I could wear on my feet, flat white sandals attached by a T thong. My hair went up obediently, and when I added raspberry lipstick and the jade button earrings Lily's father had given me, the effect was gratifying. Tony's eyes when we met told me so.

We ate on the *lanai* of the Moana Hotel. Drinking bacardis and gazing out across Banyan Court at human activities on the beach, I felt that I wanted to sit there forever, forgetting all problems. While Tony ordered food I counted colors in the ocean: milky green, lapis, jade, purple, mauve, emerald—a thousand shades constantly changing with the moving waters. A boy ran out with a surfboard and cast it and himself flat on a receding swell, paddling with arms and feet as he traveled toward the reef. I watched until he merged with other dark spots which were the heads of surfers waiting for a perfect roller on which to race toward shore.

At last one came, and scores of surfers rushed toward shore, flat on their stomachs at first, paddling hard to catch the crest of the wave, then rising gradually to stand with arms outstretched as the boards reached proper position to skim with the water's impetus. One feminine figure rode her board like a goddess emerging from the sea: head high, swelling breast raised proudly to the spray, arms back as if she were about to fly at any moment.

"Look at her, Tony! Isn't she marvelous!"

"Which one?"

"In white—next to that boy in the orange trunks."

Tony looked and said, "That's Faye. They tell me she's one of the best."

And I had taken for granted that she wouldn't be any good at sports, except the indoor kind. I had scoffed inwardly at the idea of Faye making her own swimming beach, thinking it merely an ostentatious gesture. I watched her swerve her board toward the Outrigger Club with a skillful shift of balance, and I agreed—she was one of the best.

Watching the swimmers in that cool water made me want to join them, and I said, "Would you like to swim?"

Tony looked surprised. "How about your feet?"

"Sea water will be good for them—it's healing."

"Okay. Where can we get suits?"

"How about getting our own? A drive to the Averys' will give our digestions a chance."

"Okay with me."

We went to Tony's hotel first, for his trunks, and then directed the taxi driver to the Avery house. The place was quiet in midday heat except for Suka's kitchen radio; no one was in sight. I climbed the stairs slowly and my light sandals made no sound; perhaps that is why my arrival wasn't heard. The door of my room was half open, but I thought nothing of that— the new maid might be in there cleaning. As I approached, however, I heard sounds inside; not the brisk activity of a housemaid at work, but stealthy movement, and a rustle of paper. I slowed my step and then stopped as I caught sight of the intruder.

It was Julia. Moving easily, without her canes. She turned from my desk and bent over the suitcase which contained my notebooks, leafing rapidly through them. The script which I had done that morning, and had left weighted by the typewriter, was spread over the desk. I retreated silently and backed down the stairs halfway, then started up again, singing "Alikoki" cheerfully as if to myself. I took time reaching the door, and when I entered the room my manuscript was back in place and Julia was ready for me.

She stood leaning on both canes, gripping them so tightly that her knuckles made white ridges. She smiled as I entered.

"Janice, my dear. I hope you will not mind my coming into your room. I wanted to make certain that you are comfortable. The new girl is untrained, Suka is busy, and Maude forgets things."

It was a long explanation, and unnecessary. Since the first night of my arrival, when Julia discovered Maude's laxness in hospitality, my room had been supplied with flowers daily and there were plenty of ashtrays. I smiled at Julia and said, "Thank you. I'm very well taken care of, but I appreciate your thoughtfulness, especially when it's so difficult for you to get around."

She gave me a long, somber look. "I'm improving all the time. Now, if there's nothing you can think of that you need . . . " She turned, leaning heavily on the canes, moving with awkwardness.

"I just came for my bathing suit," I told her. "Tony and I are going swimming. Do you have a membership in the Outrigger Club?"

"Oh yes. Tell them you are my guest." She went out.

I picked up my suit and cap and departed. When I reached the lower floor I went to the library and telephoned my own house—the tenants were using my telephone under the old number—and told Mrs. Allison that I'd be over that afternoon to pick up some personal belongings. She said she would try to straighten things out a little for me. ". . . you know how the Navy is; we travel with hundreds of boxes, and I took the liberty of putting some of them with yours. I hope you don't mind."

"Of course not. There's plenty of room. I'll be there about four this afternoon."

Tony had come to the door to listen. He took my arm with a proprietary gesture as I joined him. "Not going to call off our swimming party, I hope."

"No. There's plenty of time."

At the Outrigger Club we separated to go to our dressing rooms. When I emerged Tony was waiting by the beach entrance and indicated our umbrella, a red-and-green one halfway to the water. We picked our way past prostrate bodies in all degrees of color, including the bronzed skin of Hawaiians and a few Waikiki regulars, the deep brown and lighter biscuit tan of other swimmers, as well as the shrimp red of *malihinis* who had toasted themselves too well and would soon be peeling and regretting.

It was one of those days when Waikiki is at its best: a perfect surf rolling in from the distant reef, cottony clouds tossing in a serene blue sky, even an occasional breeze to stir the hot air. Carefree people around us; children playing under the watchful eyes of their mothers or assorted nursemaids, young couples lying on their stomachs with heads close together, a pale *malihini* prone on a surfboard, getting a *lomi-lomi* with coconut oil from the beach boy whose services he had hired for the day.

Everywhere there was color: in the yellow sands, the green of trees, bright bathing suits and umbrellas, variegated waters tipped with white froth, and sounds of laughter, the swish of waves, tinkle of ukuleles and steely sigh of guitars from a group making music in the shade of an overturned outrigger canoe.

I tried to push worry from my mind as we reached our umbrella and knelt on the sand. But it was as if I wore dark glasses which dimmed the brightness of the day. I kept thinking of disquieting things: Julia's shocking deception, her search of my room, David hiding like a criminal, Maude's solitary visit to Wainiha while her husband spied on her from behind a hillside shrub, John Atherton, who professed to admire my father and perhaps had given me a drug, Luther's grim expression when the Hawaiians were mentioned. I was sure now that the Averys hadn't told me all they knew. Everyone was concealing something—including this glib liar at my side. Tony was spreading towels for us to sit on. He looked at me and said, "There you are—*kuu ipo*."

I forced myself to meet his mood. "Where did you learn to say 'sweetheart'?"

He grinned as he stretched long legs in front of him. "If you must know the truth, I learned it from a Portuguese taxi dancer on River Street during the war. There was a shortage of girls here at that time, as you probably remember. Leilani weighed half a ton and had pimples, but she could shake a wicked *rhumba* and her disposition was wonderful."

"Did you give her an *awapuhi lei* too?"

He picked up one of my hands and traced the edges of my fingers. "I did not. I gave her fifty bucks. Janice, don't tell me your eyes ought to be green instead of brown!"

I leaned toward him so that our shoulders almost touched.

"Do you think I have a chance against the kind of competition I've got?"

His eyebrows went up. "You mean Faye? Baby, you flatter me—Faye pitches only in the major leagues. Not that you couldn't," he added hastily. "But you're not the type, thank God. The truth is that our relationship is strictly business. Faye has offered me—"

"Talking about me?" Faye said. We looked up and there she was, water standing like diamonds on her golden skin, arms raised as she shook dampness from her hair. Cold drops fell on us, but she didn't apologize.

I said, "We watched you surfing a while ago. You're marvelous."

"Thanks. Come on over and have a drink." She nodded in the direction of three blue umbrellas grouped together farther down the beach. She waited, taking our consent for granted, and we rose and followed her. Several of Faye's friends were there, including the radio actor with his blond wife and a New York broker with a beautiful redhead, his bride of two weeks, his junior by two decades. They were drinking a local novelty: coconuts to which rum had been added, the liquid then sipped through straws stuck into the coconut holes. I took coke instead.

Faye sat down and tossed her cap on the sand. She poured suntan oil on one palm and massaged her legs, and as she rubbed she began talking about Malia, telling the story of her death as if it were some amusing bit of local color, pointing up David's jealousy and the scene he made, finishing with the in formation that he was wanted for questioning.

"He was such a beautiful man!" The radio actor's wife sighed. "Do you think they'll find him?"

Faye finished one leg and started on the other. "Of course they will. These Kanakas are really quite dumb, you know. He'll do something stupid or sentimental like visiting his sick old mother, and he'll be picked up:"

She rolled over on her stomach and held the bottle of oil toward Tony. "Put some of this on my back, will you?"

As he began to anoint her smooth back Faye pillowed her head on her arms and sighed. "Ummm! Very nice."

I turned my eyes away. I pushed my hair under the cap I carried and rose to my feet, accidentally kicking sand on Faye as I did so. I didn't apologize. "I'm going to swim," I announced. "I have to leave soon."

"What's your hurry?" someone said. "It's ninety miles around the island—no place to go."

"I'm going to Nuuanu to get some things out of storage."

Faye half turned, smiling lazily. "What have you got in storage, Janice? Calabashes, feather helmets, some old shell *leis*?"

"All of those," I answered smoothly. "Also some college records my father kept. And his notebooks and family stuff like that."

Faye knew what I meant by college records. She turned her face onto her arms again, but not before I had caught the glint in her eyes.

I waded into the water without asking Tony whether he wished to join me. When I began to swim I forgot about him in delight at being in my element again. Soon I heard Tony calling and slowed to wait, then started off again when he reached my side. He had a fair stroke, but I had learned from David, and outdistanced him without effort. I turned back eventually, then we went out toward the reef together and tried some body surfing.

Enjoyment of the water didn't last long. I kept looking at the big beach clock and wanting its hands to move faster. Twice I started to leave, and allowed Tony to talk me out of it. At three o'clock I waded determinedly ashore.

"But there's plenty of time," Tony protested, following. "You're not supposed to be there until four."

"I know," I said over my shoulder. "But I want to go now." I turned at the entrance of the Outrigger Club. "There's no need for you to leave, Tony. Why don't you stay and enjoy yourself—there's Faye signaling now. Tell them all good-by for me, will you?"

For a moment Tony's face was sulky, then he smiled ruefully and agreed. I hurried in to shower. The dressing-room attendant brought a fresh Band-Aid for the one deep cut on my right heel; the others were practically healed. Limping slightly, I hailed a taxi on Kalakaua Avenue and gave the driver the address in Nuuanu.

The shower trees in front of my house were in bloom; they spread over the lawn with drooping pink clusters swaying in the cool wind that swept the valley. There had been some "liquid sunshine"; a rainbow tilted across the mountains, while deeper in Nuuanu another shower approached like white chiffon floating down from the Pali. It would reach the house in about twenty minutes, I judged, and hoped that Lily would arrive early so that we could carry boxes to a taxi before the rain began.

Mrs. Allison, pink and pretty in a blue cotton dirndl and white blouse, seemed surprised to see me. "I'm very glad to meet you, Miss Cameron. It's nice that you decided to come after all."

Peculiar, I thought. I had told her to expect me at four.

She ushered me into the living room, said wouldn't I have a drink of something, and I accepted iced tea, wanting to prolong briefly the strange sensation of sitting as a guest in my own house. I hadn't seen it for so long that I could look at the place with new appraisal. The furniture was oddly mixed: a tired sofa, peel chairs, a teakwood opium couch with pillows covered by raw silk in brilliant colors, an ebony Bechstein on which my mother used to play Chopin, a faded old Sarouk, vases of Chinese porcelain and cloisonné, shelves overflowing with books which might be worm-riddled by now, a big desk of carved camphorwood with brass locks, a painted silk scroll on the wall.

Father's masks and *tapa*s and Tahitian drums had been put away somewhere. In the dining room the Sheraton mahogany was polished, and on the sideboard I glimpsed my mother's Revere tea service on its shining tray. Mrs. Allison's maid kept the place immaculate, and I decided with relief that other rooms would be the same and my possessions equally respected there. One reason I had postponed this visit was fear of finding a different kind of tenant in occupancy and being unable to do anything about it.

While these thoughts occupied me, I asked a few questions from the top of my mind, made light comments as Mrs. Allison chirped away about problems common to navy wives: travel, housing, the boredom of protocol. As I finished my cigarette my tenant said, "I can't tell you how much I love your house, Miss Cameron. Such a relief after some of the horrid accommodations we've had. I don't know how I'm going to live without that heavenly camphorwood desk!"

"I'm glad you're enjoying the house," I said, and meant it. I rose. "I'm expecting a friend to meet me here at four. But I think I'll go out now and look over the things in the storage room."

Her pink mouth opened. She said, "But I just gave your friend the key to the room; I thought you had decided not to come and had sent someone else."

"Oh. Good. Then we can get things moved before that rain reaches us. Please don't come out—we can manage without bothering you any more."

I opened the door to the garage and stepped inside, sniffing the smell of damp and mildew. My boxes were all together in the center of the room, an island in the midst of other cartons and cases stenciled ALLISON. I heard a foot scrape on the floor and called, "Lily!"

No one answered.

The door swung shut behind me and I felt, too late, the sense of an alien presence. I started to turn, but the other moved faster. Something hit me on the side of the neck and agony flowed through every nerve center; my knees sagged and I dropped to the floor.

CHAPTER TWELVE

I WAS never completely unconscious. I was paralyzed. I felt myself dragged over the floor and propped against a wooden box, and could not move a finger to resist. A hand thrust my head back, forced my jaws open, and stuffed something dry and unclean into my mouth. It was half of a pocket handkerchief; the other half went around my head to hold the gag in place. When my head went back I saw the man—a short, wiry Oriental in khaki cotton trousers and white shirt. A Japanese, possibly, since he gave me a jujitsu blow on the neck. He didn't say a word as he tied my wrists with a rope from one of the Allison boxes. He worked quickly and in silence, and as soon as I was bound he picked up one of my boxes and went out with it. I heard a car enter the driveway and stop near the garage door, and then he returned, just as I was struggling to my feet. He came over and kicked me efficiently, as one kicks a log out of one's path. I collapsed on the floor, moaning with the pain of his shoe against my ankle. He picked up two more cartons and took them to the car, not bothering to look in my direction again. He was carrying out the last and heaviest load, a steel filing case, when I heard the sharp tattoo of Lily's heels on the driveway.

She spoke to the man. "Where is Miss Cameron? Inside?" Apparently he nodded, for she said, "Thanks."

Lily took him for someone who was working for me.

I choked and kicked on the floor and could make no sound because of bare feet in sandals. I was scooting around to reach a box I could tip over to warn Lily, when the door opened and she came in. She stood there an instant, until her eyes found the dim corner where I sat. She exclaimed with alarm and started toward me, and the door closed with a snap. Lily ran back to it and tried the knob, but it was locked. As she pulled on it we heard a motor start and then there was the sound of the car backing out of the driveway.

Lily turned back to untie the handkerchief around my head and remove the gag. I opened my mouth and rubbed my arm across it; I wanted to scrub my teeth, I wanted to gargle, I wanted to scream with rage and humiliation. The set look on her face told me that her emotion was almost equal to mine, and I bit back the things I wanted to say and concentrated on getting myself picked up and brushed as clean as possible.

"Did he get everything?" she asked. I nodded. I went to the door and tried it myself, knowing it would not open. He had snapped the lock.

"I have a key in my purse," I said. "But the lock opens from the other side. We could get Mrs. Allison out here eventually, by screaming."

"Do you want her to know about this?"

"There is no reason why I should worry her."

Lily glanced around the room. "Is there any other— How about that window?"

The rain had begun, and the dusty pane streamed with water. I limped across the floor and opened the window. Rain blew into my face and it felt good on my hot cheeks, it felt clean and fresh. I turned back to Lily.

"I'm filthy already," I said. "I'll climb out.'

"What's outside the window?"

"Nothing but some oleander trees."

"Neighbors?"

"Not for several hundred feet."

She was peeling off her dress and shoes. "I'll go. I'm smaller than you. Let's push this box closer. And give me the key."

It took her less than a minute to slip through the window and unlock the door. As soon as she was dressed again we walked down the driveway to the street, where a Packard sedan, borrowed from the Chuns, was waiting at the curbing. As we rode slowly through the rain toward Honolulu, I told her what had happened. There wasn't much to tell, and certainly my part in it had been ignominious.

"Did you know that man?" Lily asked.

"No."

"Would you recognize him if you saw him again?"

"Hardly. There are thousands of Orientals here who wear cotton pants and white shirts. You spoke to him. Would you know him on the street?"

"I doubt it. I didn't even notice his car, except that it was a small, dark sedan. I thought he was your taxi driver."

"He might have been a taxi driver. Or some Water Street bum. I don't think his identity is important. Except that if I ever get a chance to kick him like he kicked me—" I choked on the words. Then I said, more calmly, "He was just earning his pay. It wasn't his idea to steal my things."

"How many people knew you were going to get those boxes today?" Lily asked.

"Everybody at the Avery house, except Luther. He had left when I got that call from New York. But if he came home for lunch or phoned and happened to inquire about me, anyone there might have told him."

"And Tony Davis?"

"He heard me telephone Mrs. Allison to say I'd be there at four. And Faye Clarke knew; I mentioned it at the beach."

"I should have expected something of the sort," Lily said, "after your bag was mislaid. I remembered later that I saw Koji taking it to the Avery car the day we landed. When you said your luggage had been searched at the same time the Hawaiian girl took your nightgown, I dismissed my suspicions."

She went on more slowly: "I have made the same mistake I warned you against. I underestimated this murderer."

"Don't be ridiculous!" I said, speaking sharply to keep my voice from trembling. "You're not omniscient. How could either of us have expected a thing like this?"

Lily was silent, concentrating on the rush of traffic caused by office workers homeward bound at the end of the day. "You must have something important, Janice," she said at last. "Something which somebody wants very much. Do you remember what was in those boxes?"

"Nothing but personal things: old letters, pictures, and Father's memoranda. After his death I couldn't bear seeing those reminders of him. I haven't looked at his papers for years.

"You're right," I added, "in saying I must have something somebody wants." I told Lily about finding Julia in my room.

"So the lady is not so handicapped as she would like us to believe," Lily said. "That is very interesting. Has it occurred to you that there is more than one person doing this searching? Someone kept your bag downstairs, waiting for an opportunity to examine it. Someone ransacked the luggage in your room a short time later. Now Mrs. Avery does the same thing. Three searches have been made, and one was possibly Malia looking for the gown. That means at least two different people want something which they think you have."

The Averys were showing me a fine example of Hawaiian hospitality, I thought bitterly. We drove on. The windshield wipers clacked, cars passed us with tires hissing on wet pavement, headed into the valley.

"Lily"—I voiced the feeling which had been growing in me with every turn of the car's wheels—"I don't want to go back to that house. I can't."

"You don't have to go back. I left a message that we would be out this evening. We are going to meet someone who may be able to give us information."

"Where?"

"Fuji Gardens. We'll have dinner there; I've reserved a room. First I must stop and make some telephone calls."

We stopped at the house of one of Lily's island friends, a girl of whom I had heard but whom I had never met. She was a photographer who had recently published a book on Oriental gardens, illustrated by superb pictures. Mary Tong met us at the octagonal moon door and acknowledged

Lily's introduction with quiet courtesy, then nodded gravely as Lily began speaking in staccato Mandarin.

To me she said, "Come in. You can wash, and then we'll have some tea while Lily uses the telephone. You'll find towels in the bathroom, through that door."

Her house was small, furnished with the exquisite austerity seldom achieved by any except Oriental people. One entire side of it, overlooking a garden, was a window wall, the center doorway extending onto a balcony with a red railing. Light filtered through silk-screened teak grilles running horizontally along the top of the wall and lay in patterns on the dark shining floor.

I was sitting in a low teak chair looking at the framed Chinese calligraphy on the wall when Mary Tong returned from the kitchen with a steaming teapot and three fragile cups. Lily took hers into the tiny adjoining bedroom and promptly began dialing the instrument. I sat with our hostess and tried to make small talk but could not—I was beginning to feel too deeply depressed even to sustain normal social intercourse. The slim girl sitting opposite me seemed to comprehend—she stopped talking and we sat silent. Lily made two calls. Although I couldn't understand anything she said, it was evident that she was asking questions, then giving orders. I waited with the untasted tea in my hand, sunk in apathy, useless.

It is a strange and unnerving thing to discover that you have an enemy whose identity you do not know, yet whose activities are directed toward you with ruthlessness and cunning. If I could have understood why, I told myself, I should have been able to take it better, to fight back. I had known there was evil generated in the village, but that it would involve me personally, making me victim as well as the Hawaiians, I had never considered. Now I faced it, and the result was that I felt utterly confused and miserable.

When Lily finished her calls I looked at her for comment, but she said merely: "Now. Something is being done." She put her cup on a low table and added, "I apologize, Janice. This should never have been permitted to happen."

"How could you have helped it?" I asked wearily. "Shall we go now?"

Fuji Gardens is a Japanese teahouse set in a garden with a stream winding through it; I hadn't been there for years, and at any other time would have enjoyed seeing it again. Now I wandered over circular bridges, past ponds in which golden carp waved filmy tails among blue lilies and green water plants, and hardly looked at them.

At the door of the teahouse Lily took off her white pumps while I removed my sandals, we slid our feet into Japanese slippers and put cotton kimonos over our dresses. We seated ourselves on cushions on a grass-matting floor while a kimonoed maid placed before us a lacquered table just high enough to go over our knees, then knelt to prepare our dinner. As we waited for food, and for the third guest, we read the evening paper.

The front pages contained no mention of Malia's death. It was an unimportant inside item; Avery influence had insured that no details of location were given, and the report did not even name David. He was just "an unidentified Hawaiian" who was being hunted. I tossed the paper aside with contempt.

The door to our private room finally opened to admit our guest, a brisk, dark-eyed girl wearing a white straw hat and carrying a bag to match. They looked incongruous against the kimono and grass slippers she had slipped on at the entrance to the teahouse. When she took off her hat and smiled at me I recognized her, although I didn't know her name.

She was Julia's new maid.

"Hello," she said. "Sorry to be late, but I had difficulty getting away. I'm not supposed to take time off this week. If it weren't for my sick old grandfather . . . " And she giggled in a manner which was contagious. Even through my depressed mood I found myself smiling.

She was Taeko Nakamura, and she was a friend of Lily's. She was also a very good housemaid, and I told her so.

"I ought to be," she said. "I teach domestic science."

"I hope Mrs. Avery likes you," Lily said.

"She does. Equally important, Suka likes me. She has been lonely there—and overworked."

After our silent little cook had departed, with bows and smiles at our murmured "Arigato's," Taeko talked.

"I have heard some interesting things in the short time I have been there," she began as she balanced chopsticks and picked up a morsel of food.

"There are many hidden currents in that household. To begin with, Mrs. Avery is having incessant battles with at least three people: her husband, Dr. Atherton, and her sister, Maude."

"Start with Luther Avery," Lily said.

"There is something wrong between them, because they do not share the same bed. He sleeps in his study, although nobody knows it. She goes there every morning as soon as he leaves and makes his bed, leaving hers for me to do. I watched her yesterday. Did you know that she can walk quite well without those canes?"

I nodded. I knew that, as of today.

"Have you been able to hear anything the Averys say?"

"Not specifically. From the sound of their voices, I think he is urging her to do something which she rejects. She sounds angry, at times hysterical, while he seems worn out with argument."

"How about Maude Benson?"

"That one is very angry. She also urges action which her sister won't consider—I've heard the words 'Kanakas' and 'disgrace' and 'refuse to tolerate' over and over."

"Does Maude Benson also fight with her husband?" I asked.

The Japanese girl nodded. "Yes indeed. She keeps telling him she won't stand for it any longer, she is the owner of the property and he must do as she commands."

"What does he say to that?"

"His conversation is mostly oaths, laced with some kind of desperate anxiety. He wants to go somewhere, while she refuses permission."

"They were booked to sail for the mainland," I said. "Maybe that's it."

"Possibly. He called some airport this morning and asked about flying schedules. I heard that while I was dusting in the hall. His daughter is worried. I think she listened on the extension in Mr. Avery's study; she ran upstairs as soon as he began to dial."

"How about Dr. Atherton?" I asked.

"Mrs. Avery talked to him for a long time this afternoon. He arrived just after you left with your bathing suit."

"What did they talk about?"

"The doctor keeps telling Mrs. Avery she has simply got to do it— whatever it is, I don't know. She cries and says she has tried and he doesn't know how hard it is, and he insists that he does know but she must do it anyhow, her future depends on it."

Lily turned to me. "Eat something, Janice. Your food is getting cold." I balanced the bamboo chopsticks and began picking out mushrooms.

"Have you heard anyone talking about cartons or boxes to be picked up or delivered somewhere?" Lily asked.

Taeko's hairline brows contracted. "No. Is it important?"

Lily explained briefly what had happened and urged the Japanese girl to be on the alert for any telephone calls or mention of the stolen boxes.

"I'll try," Taeko said. "But I haven't dared hang around the telephone since Suka caught me listening to Mr. Benson talking with the airport. She blistered me thoroughly and said there was another maid who spied on people and now she is dead. That was the Hawaiian girl, eh?"

"Yes," I said, laying down the chopsticks. I couldn't eat any more. I thought of the grinning old *mama-san* and gulped before I asked, "Is Suka mixed up in this too?"

"Oh no. She's a dumb old darling. Just loyal to the family, and worried about them. Apparently the only one she hated was the dead girl. Suka keeps saying, 'Too bad, that kin',' and that's all. I'll work on her some more as soon as I can. That Koji is no company to her; he stays in the garage or in the garden, and she's happy to be able to talk Japanese with another woman. But it will take time for her to trust me."

I had a fleeting glimpse of the lonely lives of countless Oriental servants in *haole* houses: unable to speak English well, and with no one at all near enough to speak their own language except on weekly days off. Living their time out in the service of people alien to them. Our own Saito had been one of those, and for many years I had taken her services and her devotion for granted. The Averys' attitude toward Suka was identical.

"Are you thinking of Suka?" Taeko asked, with sudden perception. I nodded.

"Don't waste your sympathy. She lives in quarters more comfortable than anything she has ever known. Her father was a contract laborer on a coffee plantation; he sent her mother out to work as a scrubwoman to help him buy up his contract so he could go into business. The business was a gambling house near plantation land, where he could meet the workers on payday and invite them in to lose their earnings. Suka and her five brothers and sisters slept on the floor, while their mother stayed up all night serving hot *sake* and cleaning up after the drunks. Suka's brothers went to school, but she was only a girl and couldn't go. Her wages from the Averys have helped send two nieces through college. Times are changing, and Suka is playing her part; she knows it and is satisfied. She remembers the life her mother had."

Taeko wasn't smiling now. Her voice was sharp, her dark eyes met mine with a challenge. "Don't look at me like that," I said. "I am not responsible for such a social system."

She bobbed her head. "I'm sorry. It's a sore subject with me, and I have a temper."

"Control it while you're working at the Avery house," Lily warned. "Otherwise you'll be of no help to us."

"I shall be a model domestic. And I'd better get back to the job, now that my grandfather is feeling better." She rose and picked up hat and purse. "I'm getting a taste of high life tonight. The glamorous Mrs. Clarke has offered me five dollars to serve at a party she's giving." At the door she turned. "Thanks for the dinner."

"Thank you for the information."

We waited for a while after Taeko had gone. Lily said, painting her mouth with a lipstick brush, "How do you feel now? Are you ready to go back?"

"I don't want to," I said. "I don't want to spend another night in that house."

"You do not have to go. The hotels are probably filled, but you can stay with the Chuns, or with Mary Tong. I must return to the Averys'. "

"You? Why?"

"The telephone calls I made were to arrange surveillance of every individual who might possibly have engineered today's theft. I believe your boxes will not be delivered until after dark. If my supposition is correct, the moment that any of these people goes to keep a rendezvous with the driver of a small, dark sedan, someone will call me—at the Avery house."

I was already up, taking off the kimono. "What are we waiting for? Let's get out of here!"

Driving past the Waikiki Tavern, we saw many bathers disporting themselves in the water. This was the early evening hour, that time of relaxation when office workers forgot the day's pressures and went swimming in the mellow light of sunset. Lucky people, I thought; after their swim they'd stroll back to their bungalows for a shower, a cooling drink, an evening spent chatting with friends, dancing, or making love. None of them were headed for a household where inimical currents eddied through every room, leaving uneasiness and distrust. At least, I thought, I'm not going back there the unsuspecting soul that I was. I've been alerted, and thanks to Lily, something's being done about it.

I said, "Lily, I know you have friends and relatives here, but surely they can't put aside their private lives on a moment's notice to help us. How did you recruit enough people for this surveillance?"

"I got the idea when I saw that gang of youngsters who found Malia's body. Ethel and Harry's oldest boy, Richard, belongs to a *hui*, a secret society, which has a dozen or so members and requires a blood initiation and fearful oaths of allegiance. I called Richard and told him what had happened, then asked if he could recruit a few friends to help us out. I do not have to tell you what his reaction was. There will be a member of Richard's gang trailing every one of these people."

I regarded that information dubiously. "How old are these boys?"

"In their early teens."

"But how will they manage to avoid curfew, and family restrictions?"

"Ethel and Harry know about this; I obtained their consent first. Even if they hadn't consented, Richard would have managed. Do not worry; his crew will be handpicked."

The certainty in her voice relaxed my doubts. I knew from experience that when Lily said so, it was so.

Swift Hawaiian dusk was settling over Avery land as Lily nosed the Packard onto the driveway and shifted into second gear for the steep descent. Koji was watering the front lawn as we stopped, and Lily asked whether there was room for her car in the garage. He nodded and said he would put it away when he finished watering. We went on into the house.

Taeko was serving coffee to the family on the *lanai*. We stopped there, and Lily answered, in response to an inquiry from Julia, that we had enjoyed our day very much. My brown dress, fortunately, didn't show marks from the dusty floor.

"Where did you go?" Ellen asked.

"To a friend's house, in Kailua," I said, and told the story Lily and I had agreed on. "We started out to my place in Nuuanu, but it was such a fine day, and we had a car loaned to us, so we drove to the other side of the island. I'll pick up my things later," I finished indifferently.

"Julia says you have to revise your book," Luther said. "I hope you don't have too much work to do."

"I've decided to cut instead of doing a revision. After all, I'm supposed to simplify the story, not complicate it." They gave me the politely blank responses which I expected. I said, "I must get upstairs to work; I want to put that script in the mail tomorrow."

Lily settled into a chair by Ellen and joined the others in wishing me good luck with the job. I limped across the tiled floor and up the stairs, determined to finish my writing stint that evening; it would help to pass time. I looked at the typewriter, at sheets of blank paper, and groaned. Then I took a tepid shower, pinned my hair on top of my head, and got down to work.

After a long session I finished, in that state of numbness which follows prolonged concentration. Too keyed up to sleep, too tired to read, all I wanted to do was get rid of the incubus. I sat at the desk thinking, I'll tell Lily to ask the boy at Tony's hotel if he can type it for me. But how about pictures? Maybe if I call Steve, she can help me. I turned in the chair, preparing to rise.

"Pssst!" The sound came from the balcony.

David's back, I thought, and wondered what he wanted. I walked out to the balcony and bent over the railing as if for a sniff of air. Bougainvillea vines rustled near me; I saw dark oblique eyes set in a round young face, and the boy said," You're Janice. Where's Lily's room?"

I moved nearer the mass of vines and murmured, "Wait. I'll turn out my light."

When I returned to the balcony a yellow square at the other end indicated that Julia was still awake. I made a cautioning gesture and moved along the wall of the house until I could see into her room. She was sitting up in bed, writing on a tablet. Letters, probably. I went back to my end of the balcony and said, "Come." He followed me soundlessly.

Lily and Richard and I had our conference in the bathroom, ready to shove the boy into the shower at any sign of interruption. He was a chubby fellow wearing a yellow T shirt and starched chinos. His coarse black hair, probably slicked back daily, stood in erratic tufts on his round head. His black eyes glittered with excitement as he said, "The stuff was delivered two hours ago. I had to wait until the people downstairs went to bed so I could get up here."

"Delivered? Where?" I asked.

He jerked his head sideways. "Next door. Mrs. Clarke's house. She's giving a party; there's a mob of people." He looked at Lily with scorn. "You're a fine one, telling us to watch for a small, dark sedan. It came in a truck, with some cases of liquor. If I hadn't kept my eyes open, nobody would have spotted it."

Lily grasped his arm. "Where did she put the boxes?

"Upstairs. I didn't dare go in the house. But I heard one of the drivers swearing because he had to carry some of his load up the back stairs."

Lily murmured something in Chinese. He blinked at her, gulped with pleasure, then grinned. "Whatta we do now?" he asked. For this embryo Superman nothing was too difficult; she just had to give the word.

"Go back to the house. Try to contact Taeko Nakamura—you know her? Fine. Tell her to locate those boxes and then be ready to take us in through the service entrance. We'll be there soon."

"Right." He slipped through the door and vanished into the blackness of the balcony.

Lily and I began dressing. We went barefoot down the stairs, carrying our shoes. There was someone in the library; we saw light streaming onto the hall floor and heard a radio announcer speaking softly. We tiptoed through the foyer and out the front door, and I thanked heaven my foot was sufficiently healed for that stealthy gait. We couldn't take the car, so we skirted the house on the *ewa* side by the kitchen and worked our way through the hedge behind the garage to Faye's land.

There was music coming from her house, and sound of voices, not in the "letta go your blouse" spirit of a *luau*, but with restraint. The music wasn't Hawaiian, either; Faye had hired a string quartet which was playing Mozart. A figure in white which signaled from the kitchen door proved to be Taeko. She said tersely, "In her dressing room. I'll show you the way, then you're on your own. Up these back stairs."

Faye's dressing room was mirrored on one side; the wall opposite was clothes closets with sliding doors. The room was papered in shell pink and silver, with peacock-blue carpeting on the floor. Also on the floor were my boxes, their lids pried off and splintered, their contents scattered in every direction. My face grew hot and my heart began to thud angrily as I recognized treasures I had almost forgotten; an ivory-and-lace fan of my mother's, my Punahou yearbook, snapshot albums, Makaleha's feather *lei*, family photographs. A faded chiffon scarf I had kept because I wore it on the night I met my Big Romance, a yellowed pair of white kid gloves, and papers, papers, papers, tossed in corners, wadded as if in anger, torn in bits, everywhere on the peacock-blue carpet.

I began to tremble. I clutched Lily's arm so hard that she winced. "This is definite proof! Now I'll fix her! That rotten, contemptible, sneaking bitch! She'll be sorry she ever heard the name of Cameron! I'll denounce her before all her guests; I'll bring them up to see this evidence right here!"

I stooped and picked up crumpled paper and smoothed it out with shaking fingers; it was my parents' wedding photograph. Scalding tears began to trickle down my cheeks, but I hardly felt them; I turned blindly and started toward the door.

Lily caught my arm. "Janice. Janice! Wait a minute. Please stop and think what you are—"

I jerked away. She reached for me again and I shoved her aside. "Let go of me!" I said between gritted teeth. Lily ran to the door and stood against it. "Janice, listen to reason for just one moment."

I'd have to drag her from that door. I said grudgingly, "Say it."

"What do you think you'll accomplish by exposing Faye Clarke at this point? Don't you realize that you'll jeopardize everything we're trying to do?"

"I don't know what you mean. How can she deny what she's done here?"

"She will deny it. Flatly. Or she'll say that these boxes were delivered here by mistake and she opened them to find out what was inside. Everybody knows you were supposed to get them from your house today. She'll get out of it somehow. Even if she doesn't, even if you prove her a thief— what will you gain? You'll put her on guard, and from now on she'll outmaneuver us at every turn. Janice, we're trying to find a murderer, not a petty thief."

"Petty!" My voice raised in outrage.

"I know these possessions are of personal value to you," Lily soothed. "But actually, compared with a human life, their value is nothing."

My trembling legs would support me no longer. I was on the point of collapse when Lily led me back to the dressing room and pushed me onto a bench.

"Listen, Janice," she said urgently, "I am convinced that Faye knows the truth about Malia's death. I think she is involved in what is happening at the Hawaiian village. But so far there isn't a shred of evidence to prove it. If you confront her now and put her on guard, our chances of finding the truth are gone. All she has to do is get aboard the next clipper and leave the islands—you can't do a thing to stop her. But if we wait for—"

I made an impatient gesture, and Lily said, "Oh, I know waiting is difficult. Patience requires much more will power than taking immediate action. But that is the way— What are you looking at?"

For my eyes had found something I missed before. Over in a corner at an angle, scarred and dented, but still obdurately and blessedly locked, was the steel filing case in which I had stored Father's precious notebooks. It was the sight of that battered thing, still inviolate, which saved my reason. I caught Lily's wrist.

"Look!" I said triumphantly. "She hasn't been able to—"

"Shhh!" Lily's acute ears had caught a sound. Then I caught it. Hurried footsteps coming toward the bedroom door. I rose and started in that direction automatically, seeking escape, for it was our only means of exit. Too late. Faye was speaking just outside the door, and the knob was already turning.

CHAPTER THIRTEEN

"I'LL take it in here, Taeko," she was saying. "Hang up when you hear me talking."

She came into the bedroom and slammed the door shut. She snatched the telephone from a table beside a satin-upholstered slipper chair. Faye was wearing ice-blue chiffon which swirled as she moved; the cold fire of diamonds shone at her throat and in bracelets which swung from her wrists. Her hair was swept into a coronet which circled her head, and the coiffure gave her dignity. She was dressed for the role of hostess to Mozart lovers and looked the part—until she swept magazines and a cigarette box off the little table and kicked them viciously across the room.

"Hello," she said, and waited for the click of the extension. Then: "You everlastingly stupid fool! What do you mean by calling me at this hour?"

I had been staring without thought of concealment. Lily took my wrist and pulled me toward the clothes closet, one door of which was open. We stepped into it, pushing aside chiffon, satin, and lace, and backed against the corner. Once the clothes had fallen into place again, we could hear clearly.

"No, I haven't found anything," Faye said. "If I had, I would have let you know. I've looked through all her junk except a steel filing case, and I can't get that goddamned thing open . . . . Because it's steel and it's locked, that's why . . . . No, I can't. I've broken two fingernails on it already . . . . I can't, I tell you. Did you forget that I have guests tonight? I should be down there now, instead of up here listening to your— Why the hell should I invite you? We're together too much already. . . No. No. Do you want to know every time I go to the toilet?"

Silence. Then a conciliatory tone. "Now listen, darling, you're being unreasonable, you know . . . . Of course. You know I do. But there's too much at stake for both of us. We can't risk-—What? She is, is she? Well, you can handle that. Just don't get panicky, that's all. And for Christ's sake stop worrying. I'll get the damned filing case open tomorrow as soon as I get up . . . . No, don't. You know I sleep late. I'll call you instead. Now, I really must—"

A second feminine voice said, "Oh, excuse me, Mrs. Clarke. I was looking for the dressing room. So sorry to interrupt."

Faye's voice, gracious and sweet: "You aren't interrupting a thing. Good-by, Eddie—thanks for calling."

We heard the receiver click, then heard Faye say to the other woman, "That was my liquor dealer wanting to know whether his delivery arrived safely. One of his trucks was in an accident. The dressing room is across the hall—I'll go with you."

"Oh, thank you. This is a charming party—so delightful after the usual sort of evening one spends here. Everyone is saying—" The door shut and we heard no more.

As we went cautiously down the back stairs Lily whispered, "I've thought of a plan. We can get your filing case out of the house before Faye touches it again, if we do it tonight. I'm sorry about the other things, but it is best not to remove them."

"All right," I said unhappily. Now that my hysterical anger was gone, I realized that Lily was thinking of the larger issue involved and regretted the loss of my personal possessions almost as much as I did. I was remembering a time when Lily had searched for, and finally recovered, something more precious than anything of mine which lay on the floor of Faye's dressing room. It was like her not to remind me that she had shown infinite patience and calm in the face of a graver problem.

Richard materialized from behind a mango tree near the kitchen door as we emerged from the house. "Was that the stuff?" he hissed.

"It was," Lily said. "You have done a splendid job."

The lad looked crestfallen; his evening of detective work was proving too brief. His face lighted when Lily told him there was still plenty to do, and as she outlined her plan to him, he began to giggle like the very young boy that he was.

"My partner's waiting up on the road," he said. "Let's get going!"

I started with them. Lily stopped and said, "Janice, don't you think you had better go back to the house? It would be wiser—"

"No. I'm going with you," I said. "I've had too much sitting and worrying; I'm going to have some action."

Lily knew that I meant it. She smiled at me as we went up Faye's driveway together.

On the road just beyond the drive a car waited; as we drew nearer I saw that it was a small ambulance, on which was painted KAPIOLANI ANIMAL HOSPITAL. DR. KAPSUNG LEE, VETERINARY SURGEON. A boy about Richard's age was at the wheel; as we approached he said eagerly, "Mission accomplished, sir?"

"Okay, Kappy," Richard answered. "One half the mission. There is still danger ahead."

He scrambled into the car and opened the rear doors so that Lily and I could climb inside. There was a strong smell of animal and antiseptic; something massive and warm was huffing and snorting from the floor.

"What is that?" I squeaked as the huge form rose and a hot breath fanned my face.

"Just my dog. Down, Dynamite!" Dr. Lee's son said. Dynamite went down. Lily and I sat on the floor of the car, and I wished for a cigarette to counteract the various smells. Dynamite had been eating fish.

We turned in another driveway and entered the Chuns' house by the service door. The house was in darkness; it was nearly midnight. We went through a large kitchen to a hall, and Richard called, "Mom! Hey, Mom!"

Ethel Chun appeared immediately, dressed in a black kimono, and laid a hand on her son's arm. "Everything all right?" Lily explained what we wanted, and the plump little woman reflected for a moment and then said, "I'll give you one of my old files." She looked at me. "What color was yours?"

"Dark green."

"Fine. Mine is the same. In here."

We went into an office, where she emptied a file of miscellaneous medical pamphlets and old correspondence, which she laid on a leather sofa. Richard and Kapsung, in the meantime, brought down from Richard's room an assortment of articles picked at random. We filled the filing case with three calabashes, a skull, some large shells, a string of boars' teeth, the iron barb from an old fishing spear, a pair of wild goat's horns, and a box of rock specimens which gave necessary weight. We locked the drawer and the boys took it down to the ambulance.

Dynamite had accompanied us into the house. He proved to be a Great Dane, pure black. He must have weighed as much as Lily Wu. His toenails, I observed with amazement, were painted scarlet. Kapsung Lee said scornfully, "My dopey sister does that. He's a fierce dog, really. If anybody tries to stop us when we get back to the danger zone—"

Nobody tried. We went right down the driveway to the kitchen door. If anyone had challenged us, the boys were to say they were answering an emergency call and had come to the wrong address. The only challenge came from Taeko, who stuck her head out inquiringly when we arrived.

Richard beckoned and she came to the car. He handed her the little bottle Lily had brought, which contained *syrupus chloral*, vulgarly known as a Mickey Finn. It was to go in Faye's next drink. Taeko took it and nodded, then scooted back to the house. Dynamite laid his head on my lap and drooled comfortably while we waited.

Presently we heard people coming out of the house in small, flustered groups. Motors started and cars drove away. One woman said, "What a shame! She seemed such a charming person." After a while the house was quiet. We went in to find Faye sprawled on the living-room floor; Taeko said she had gone to sleep abruptly, in the middle of a conversation. It would be some time before Faye gave another soiree for that particular group of Mozart lovers. As I stood and looked at her, my foot itched.

Lily laughed softly: "Go ahead, if you want to. You owe somebody a kick."

I turned away. "She wouldn't feel it."

The boys made the exchange of filing cases quickly, placing the phony one in the exact spot where the other had been. I watched as they took mine out to the ambulance, and sighed with relief as the car pulled away. Then I gave Faye one last look before we left the house. She slept peacefully. She looked utterly beautiful.

* * * *

Walter did not appear at breakfast the following morning, nor did Maude. As I was dressing I saw her heading toward Wainiha again, determination in every line of her thick, stubborn body. Julia was not in sight either, and Ellen said Luther had gone to his office. The girl looked worried; there were dark shadows under her eyes. She evaded looking at Lily and me, and sat fiddling with the table silver. Once she started to speak and decided against it. She excused herself with her meal half eaten and went back to her room.

As soon as we were alone I said, "I wonder how Faye feels this morning. Do you suppose she has a headache?" The last was said hopefully.

"Probably."

"I'd like to be there when she gets that file open." I stood up. "Lily, let's go to your cousins' house and unlock mine."

Lily reminded me, "How about your story? Is it ready to mail?"

"Damn!" I sat down again. "It's ready. But I must have pictures. I was wondering whether Steve Dugan might have some in her office."

"Newspaper pictures? For a story so personal as yours?"

I sighed. "They wouldn't have any of the village. But David might—or Makaleha. Let's go and see her now."

Maude returned to the house just as we were starting toward the garage. She was exhilarated by some inner excitement—and a sort of ugly triumph which shone in her dark, hollowed eyes.

"Where's my husband?" she demanded.

We hadn't seen him.

Maude strode to the foot of the stairs and called, "Walter! Come down here!"

Walter did not appear. Ellen came instead and said, "He isn't here, Mama."

"I want to see him. Where is he?"

"I—I don't know."

Ellen did know. She was naturally a truthful girl and the lie was an effort. Maude was too distracted to observe her daughter's distress; she heard the words but saw nothing. There was a kind of blindness in Maude that morning; in one sense she had always had impaired vision, but at that moment the disease was fully developed.

"I suppose Luther is gone too?" she said. Ellen nodded, turning away.

Maude stood indecisively for a moment, then tromped to the garage, and presently we heard the roar of the overaccelerated motor. The car emerged in jerks and backed off the driveway against a blue glazed jar which held a gardenia tree. Maude exclaimed and shifted gears, ignoring the wreckage. The station wagon roared around the house and up the driveway and was gone.

Ellen had gone into the hall and was standing at the door of the library uncertainly, looking at the telephone. Julia's face appeared on the stairs then, a white face taut with apprehension. "Ellen!" she called, and Ellen turned toward her.

"Let's go," Lily said quietly. We left, unnoticed.

Puunui hadn't changed. The valley has narrow streets with no sidewalks; the houses are old, nestled deep in luxuriant shrubbery which makes up for lack of paint on weather-worn wooden siding. We parked the car and walked down the street looking for the number David had given me. A stream gurgled near by, and far ahead the sun shone on a sharp peak deep in the valley, highlighting exquisite variegations of green. Beyond the peak, mysterious crevasses of the Koolau Range lay in a violet shadow blotted with dark green and deeper blue. We passed the home of a Japanese family; several pairs of grass sandals stood in a neat row on the steps, and through a window I caught a glimpse of a shining brass god; smoke from joss sticks feathered out through the window and dissolved into the sweetheart vine climbing there.

From the next house came a shrill ki-yipping, and a fat little *poi* hound tumbled out and rolled on the ground. A child's voice cried: "You—puppy! Bad dog! Don't make *kukai* here! Go outside!"

There was the sound of a hand smacking bare flesh, and a woman said, "Wassamatta you, Sammy! Don' hit puppy, he's baby dog. When you baby boy you *kukai* in pants. Shame you fo' hit puppy!"

The screen door opened and a naked youngster tumbled out after the puppy. Reconciliation took place under a mango tree to the accompaniment of tail-wagging and pink puppy tongue, small-boy hugs and pats on a joyously wriggling little animal.

Farther along the street was the place we sought. A white cottage, badly in need of paint, eyebrow deep in ginger and hibiscus. Two girls in slacks and faded cotton shirts sat on the back steps in dappled sunlight; one played a ukulele. They were singing "Maui No Ka Oi," their black hair hanging carelessly around their faces. A husky Hawaiian boy stood on the lower step, tapping one bare foot, occasionally joining in with a phrase or two.

Then I saw Makaleha. She was sitting near the bank of the stream under a breadfruit tree with bare feet spread apart and a lap full of white ginger, stringing the fragrant blossoms into a *lei*. A zinc washtub filled with flowers was at her side, and opposite sat her sister, similarly occupied. As soon as I saw the other woman I recognized her; she was the *lei* vendor who spoke to me the day I arrived. They would work until midnight, because tomorrow was steamer day, and tomorrow these *leis* would be sold.

Makaleha looked up incuriously as we approached. She stared at me for a moment, then dropped the flowers and heaved her monumental bulk from the ground.

"*Kulolo! Aloha nui loa!* So good to see you!"

She waddled forward and enfolded me in her embrace. I hugged her tight, tears stinging my eyes.

Eventually we sat down beside the two women and I introduced Lily. Makaleha nodded. "I know. David tol' about you. Good t'ing you come, take care dis *wahine*. She too much *lolo* sometime. She need *kokua* now."

"Is David all right?" I asked anxiously.

Makaleha gave me a broad smile. "Don' worry fo' heem. He *pololei*, no *pilikia*."

Her brown face grew serious. She said, "You do like David say, no go Wainiha now?"

"I haven't gone, Makaleha, although I've wanted to." I moved closer and put a hand on her fat arm. "Please tell me—the awful things happening there, ghost drums, blood on the *heiau*—what do they mean?"

Her big dark eyes grew angry. She yanked a leaf from the breadfruit tree and began to shred it as she talked.

"Don' believe dat stuff. 'S all lies, dat. Malia was bad, *pilau*, dat *wahine*." She tossed green shreds from her. "She do bad t'ings fo' money. Now she make-dead."

She launched into a rapid recital in a mixture of pidgin and Hawaiian. Malia had learned in the *hula* temple to play the sharkskin drums. The night that I arrived, she waited until others in the village were asleep, slipped out of her shack and poured chicken blood on the *heiau*, then took her drum back into the valley where it would echo from the surrounding hills, and began to beat the weird rhythm which had summoned me to the village.

Malia thought that she was not seen, but there was a watcher. Someone from the village had been watching Malia for a long time.

It must have been either David or one of the strange women I met.

I said, "Who are those women, Makaleha? Where do they come from?"

She started to answer. Her sister muttered something about *wahanui* (big mouth), at which Makaleha sighed and remained silent. Then she looked at me with apology. "Kulolo, I like tell you. No can. Soon you know."

I was surprised and baffled. I had taken for granted that Makaleha would be completely candid. Something stronger than her *aloha* for me, stronger than her attachment to the village where she had lived so happily, had forced her to leave her home and to be silent about her reasons. We sat there; the two women began working deftly with ginger flowers, and for a while no one spoke. Young voices on the steps of the cottage near us continued their song; the ukulele strummed and tinkled.

Finally I said, "Can you tell me this much: is it all right, what they are doing at Wainiha?"

Both women nodded emphatically. Makaleha smiled, and mischief lighted her dark eyes. She said, "Dey plenty smaht. Don' worry."

I slumped on the grass, sniffing a ginger flower. Then I remembered the pictures and asked whether Makaleha had any, explaining why I needed them. Her sister had some, and sent one of the girls into the house to bring them. We looked at pictures for a while, and I chose four which Lily said Mary Tong would enlarge for me on glossy paper. We thanked the two women for their help and rose to depart.

Makaleha said, "I t'ink I go back Wainiha someday." There was wistfulness in her voice. Then she added, in a good imitation of her former cheeriness, "We have big *luau*, eh?"

"We will!" I said, and meant it. We would have the biggest, the most splendid *luau* in the history of the village.

As we left them, wearing ginger *leis* damp from the leaves in which they had been wrapped, I was obsessed with determination to get back to the Avery house and have a showdown. All of this deception and fear had to end. For some reason which I was utterly unable to comprehend, my arrival had been the signal to set off a chain of events which brought discord and catastrophe. Even murder.

I would talk to Julia, force her to be honest. I would question Luther,

Walter, Dr. Atherton. I would find out what Maude had discovered that morning which sent her from the house in such excitement. It was unthinkable to tolerate this hideous situation any longer. I would insist on knowing the truth—I would . . . My thoughts raced on in angry confusion, while cold common sense said that unless I possessed some lever stronger than my own anger and determination, a thousand questions would get me nowhere.

Lily knew what I was thinking. She said, "You cannot force a climax, Janice."

"I can try," I retorted stubbornly.

"Be patient. Let us find out first what Faye Clarke wanted from you. We can do that immediately."

"All right," I conceded. "The key to that file is in my dressing case. Let's go back to the house now and get it. I'll pick up my manuscript and leave it to be typed; we can give these pictures to Mary Tong on our way. Then I'll feel free to concentrate."

As we drove along the Ala Wai, Lily began, "When you told me what Ellen said about Tony Davis being here a month ago, I checked with the airlines. He made a round trip by clipper, with a week's stopover in Honolulu, just about that time."

"Where did he stay then? At Faye's?"

"No. At a hotel. When did you write to the Averys about your return to Hawaii?"

"Six weeks ago."

"Then it looks as if Faye is engineering something through him. It must have been planned during his first visit here."

"How about Joe? We read his letter to Tony."

"That letter predated Tony's first trip here. Let's try to guess what happened: Tony met Joe, heard about you, and wrote to Faye—who was island-born and who had returned to Honolulu—for corroboration. What she had to say was important enough for him to fly here to discuss it more fully. A course of action was planned, either by the two together or under her direction. I suspect it was the latter. Tony then returned to New York and began making inquiries; when he discovered you were in California, he followed. Knowing agents and writers as he did, it was easy to ascertain your whereabouts. He checked with the Matson Line for your sailing date, then arranged to sail with you. We know the rest so far."

"Then do you think Faye is planning some sort of revenge on me? For a humiliation suffered years ago?"

Lily said slowly, "It is possible. But—"

"That's it. *But.* First, if she did feel strongly vindictive, she's not the sort to be satisfied with such a small revenge. All she can do, actually, is prevent me from seeing Wainiha used as background for filming my story.

She knows as well as I do that on the other islands there are spots even lovelier, where we can make a picture with full cooperation of the people.

"Second, although Faye may very well have put Malia up to those disgusting tricks with the drums and the chicken blood, she has nothing to do with the people who are now in the village, or Makaleha would have told us so. When a Hawaiian is as secretive as she is about the *kahuna* and about those strange women, it means that they are very important and directly connected with the Hawaiians themselves."

"You are right," Lily said. "It is possible that someone, perhaps Faye, started something in that place which has gotten out of control. I believe that is the case now."

"And the Averys are involved."

"Undoubtedly. They are involved, and the Bensons also."

"How about Dr. Atherton?"

"Ah. He remains the dark horse. But we must include him. He is very close to that family, especially to Julia Avery. Now we know there is some hidden conflict between them."

I thought, regretfully, of how much I had liked the doctor at our first meeting. Then I thought with deeper regret of how happy I had been at the prospect of being the guest of these old friends of my father's. Now, as we stopped the car in front of the Avery garage, I dreaded entering their house.

Julia and Ellen were on the *lanai*. Dr. Atherton was there too, an unopened magazine in his hands, his face set in a stern anger I had never seen him display before. As Lily and I approached he commanded, "Come here, you two girls!"

"What is it?" I asked, glancing at Ellen and Julia. The girl looked frightened—and worried. Julia's expression was more than fright; it was terror. Her eyes darted from side to side, her thin hands clasped and unclasped one another; she looked as if she wished to flee from the spot but hadn't the strength to move.

The doctor had been looking first at Lily and then at me, searchingly. "What is it?" I repeated, facing him. He tossed the magazine to the floor and leaned forward.

"Has either of you," he demanded, "removed anything from my medical bag?"

"Your medical bag?" I repeated. "I've never even seen it." I turned to Lily, who added, "Nor have I."

"Where did you leave it?" I asked the doctor.

His eyes evaded mine now. "I haven't been bringing it in with me recently. It was in my car, at the side of the house."

"What is missing?" Lily asked.

He said evasively, "A certain drug which I always carry. And a hypo-dermic needle." He was silent, and we waited. Finally he said, in a voice which was almost pleading, "Are you sure, absolutely sure, that neither of you has touched that bag?" We did not bother to answer.

Dr. Atherton wanted one of us to say that she had been the thief. That admission would have been immeasurable relief to him. Then the dark fear which was in his eyes would not have to be recognized. As he looked first at one of us, then at the other, he sighed heavily, and he seemed to grow older in a few seconds. His fear must be faced.

I turned and walked to the edge of the *lanai*, so that Dr. Atherton could not read the expression on my own face. Looking for some distraction, I welcomed the sight of a swimmer in the distant ocean. Faye was enjoying her expensive new beach. I wondered whether she had a hangover from the Mickey Finn. Probably not—Faye seemed indestructible. I wondered what she thought of the odd things she found in my filing case. I might never know. She climbed up on the float, poised briefly, and made a clean dive into the water. At that moment I envied her—she was so strong and hard that nothing could touch her. I was the one who worried, for reasons more personal than an abstract sense of justice. My love for my island birthplace was part of my personality; anything which sullied these islands injured me also.

Taeko appeared and said, blank-faced, "Luncheon is served, Mrs. Avery."

Julia started to rise and looked toward John Atherton for help. He sat still, although his hands clenched on his knees. Julia sent an imploring look in his direction, and he stared hard at her, not moving. She bit her lip, then raised herself slowly from the chair with the aid of her two canes. My own lip wanted to curl as I watched her; Julia no longer had my sympathy. We started in a straggling group toward the table.

At that moment there was a loud crash from the front driveway, then a wavering, terrible scream. Glass shattered and metal crumpled against stone. Lily and I were first to get around the house in time to see Maude's car still shuddering amid wreckage of the driveway retaining wall. Dust hung in the air. All that was visible of Maude was her head and shoulders and one outflung arm. The rest of her body lay under twisted metal and rubble. Lily reached her first and knelt by Maude's head, which was moving back and forth. A tongue of flame licked from the motor as she did so.

"Get away from there!"

Dr. Atherton reached the wreck and dragged Lily back toward the house just before the gasoline tank exploded.

Some time later, after the fire department had gone, after the police had taken our statement about the accident, and after Maude's charred body had been removed to a mortuary, Lily told me what she had seen in that instant before the explosion.

We were in my room, talking in low murmurs. Lily was pale, but her voice was under control as she spoke.

"When I knelt on the ground by her, Janice, I saw a series of red marks on her arm—the tracks of a centipede. The insect was running away across the ground. It was a blue one, about eight inches long. And there was another just crawling out of the neck of her dress."

I sat and looked at Lily and wanted to retch, wanted to shriek with horror. I couldn't even speak.

CHAPTER FOURTEEN

WALTER didn't appear until late that afternoon. He came into the house like a man moving in a state of exhaustion and shock. His face was dark with stubble, there was blood on his white shirt and on the whipcord breeches he wore, dust on his boots. Dirty and disheveled as he was, Walter looked for the first time as if his clothes fit his body. He had never seemed at ease before, because he was really himself only in the boots and breeches of a horseman.

"Ellen finally reached me," he said dully as he sank into a chair. "I was at the ranch." He wiped absently at stains on his shirt. "Excuse this appearance. My best mare foaled this morning. Barely pulled her through, poor girl. Didn't have time to change."

I wondered if he would speak of his wife. What could he say? Julia had already talked to him; Luther and Ellen met his plane. Walter had just come from the mortuary.

He reached into his hip pocket for a blackened pipe, turned it over and over as if the feel of the smooth bowl was comforting. I had never seen him smoke a pipe. After a while he said, "Maude was on Maui Sunday. Remember she said she'd been to the movies? Flew over and went to see Joe Kalani, asked him about the old fellow who lived in the cave. Hired a taxi to take her up to the ranch, and used our jeep to drive out to the hills where the old man lived. I guess she didn't believe me when I said he was gone."

He shook his head. "She was plenty mad when Joe told her those Bibles had been stolen from our own church. Poor Maude, I thought for a while that she was the one who took them. I still can't believe—" His voice broke and he put a hand over his eyes.

Ellen came in then and went to her father's chair. She sat on the floor and put her head against his knee. His fingers touched her hair, then went to meet her hand and clung to it.

"Daddy," Ellen said. "I'm not going to the mainland. I don't want to go to college. I'm going to stay with you."

Walter swallowed hard. He didn't answer, just clung tightly to her. I rose and walked out on the lawn, leaving them alone together.

As I reached the shore and stepped off onto white sand, Tony Davis came around the edge of the hibiscus hedge.

"Hello."

"Hello, Tony." I kept on walking and he joined me.

"Terrible," he said. The remark was perfunctory.

"Yes."

"Did you find out what caused the accident?"

I looked at him. "What do you mean?"

"Mrs. Benson came to Faye's house earlier today looking for her husband. She was terribly worked up over something about the natives there." He gestured toward Wainiha, which lay over the hill ahead of us.

"What did she say?"

"Nothing much. When Faye said we hadn't seen him, she went tearing out again. But if Mrs. Benson found out something those natives didn't want her to tell—"

"Well?" I said. "Go on."

He shrugged. "Could have been anything. I don't believe in these witch-doctor spells, but some people do, and when they believe in them, they die. Or they have accidents. Like Maude Benson—and her sister before her." He looked sideways at me, then away again.

Tony hadn't thought this up all by himself. Either he was extremely imaginative and superstitious—which I doubted—or someone had been planting ideas in him. I wanted to say a few things to him but remembered what I knew of Tony and my own unalterable conviction that talking to this man would get me nowhere. If he chose for playmates women like Faye Clarke, and if he gravitated toward the kind of job he had, he then possessed certain personal attributes which would make justice and truth less important to him than the goals which precluded them.

Lily would handle this character beautifully, I thought, scuffling along over the sand. Lily wouldn't let her emotions take control; she would play on vanity and cupidity for her own purposes, using the weakness of her opponent as tools. Well, I knew how it ought to be done. I could try. Tony wanted something from me. Let him disclose his hand now by making the first move.

We reached the end of the beach, where ages ago flowing lava had congealed into serrated rocks which marched, black and needle-sharp, into the ocean. Coco palms tilted over the sand there, and a grassy hummock at their roots made a natural backrest. Still waiting for Tony to say something,

I sank down on the sand and leaned back, looking at the water. The horizon was orange and crimson with the setting sun; heavy purple clouds, irradiated with gold from the light behind them, were moving slowly across the sky to blot out that glorious color. Behind us rose the trail to Wainiha, and from the village came a faint sound of voices and the thin sighing of a guitar as someone sang "Na Alii."

Tony sat beside me and offered a cigarette. "What's that song?" he asked, turning one ear toward the music.

"It's about the *alii*, the chiefs," I told him. "They were the royalty of Hawaii, the same as royalty or aristocracy of any country."

We talked about Hawaiian history for a while. Gradually my frazzled nerves were soothed in the murmur of a crooning surf, the whisper of palm fronds. Tony put his arm around me, and although I did not welcome the gesture, I forced myself to relax against him. When he finally brought up the subject which was foremost in his mind, I wasn't startled. I had been waiting for it.

"We've never had much chance to talk," he said, almost musingly. "I started to tell you about myself a couple of times and we were interrupted. I have a confession to make, Janice."

"What is it?" I asked. I hoped he couldn't hear the sudden thudding of my heart or sense the excitement which tingled in me. I wanted to urge him to go on, to tell me quickly. I said nothing, just waited.

"I didn't meet you by accident on board the *Lurline*, you know," Tony said at last. "I was pursuing you."

"But why pursue me?" I managed a purring little laugh of vanity. "I'm nobody important:'

His arm tightened. "You are. To me, now. At first you were an assignment. I can't tell you what a surprise it was when I found out what a swell girl you are. Most women writers are a bunch of aggressive old hags."

I forbore mentioning that he had received a very adequate description of me from Joe what's-his-name. "Go on, Tony," I breathed.

He went on. He told me about his job, in his voice the certainty that I would share his pride in it, possibly might even envy him a little. This was his first big assignment, to get the story of the village—with our double byline.

"Of course," he added in a voice that was ever so slightly patronizing, "the tie-up with your book is marvelous publicity—probably will double your sales. We'll schedule the two as close together as possible."

"What do you want me to do?" I asked, sure of his answer. He would ask me to write the story, and at this moment I couldn't, I was too heartsick. I'd have to get out of it somehow.

Tony surprised me. "You don't have to do a thing, sweetheart. Just okay my copy, and sign a letter to that effect which I'll send along with it. I've got the story here, in case you'd like to hear it."

So he had already written it himself. Then my hunch had been correct that if I didn't accede to his request he'd get somebody else to byline it with him. Only not Maude, not now.

"Go ahead and read it," I said, taking his arm from around my waist. He reached into his hip pocket as I leaned back against the grass. He began to read.

It was what I had expected, only more so. He wrote well, he was clever, he had an enviable knack for the neatly turned phrase, the economical sentence. And his powers of observation were good. He could have been a first-class reportorial writer, although he sounded very phony when he got all trembly over the power of the one true religion on primitive people. His editors could slick that up for him; it was their specialty. But the rest of it was there, the prurience, the sharp little mind rooting around in filth, the nasty little creature excreting more nastiness. The suggestion of erotic practices which couldn't be printed, pagan sadism which couldn't be described— all of that was there, including even the beautiful trembling virgin spread-eagled on the altar of black stones.

He read quickly and well, slurring over the religious tie-up at the end. "Have to put that in, you know. The Come-to-Jesus angle is a must."

He folded his script and put it in his pocket again, buttoning the back flap carefully. "What do you think of it?" he asked, his own opinion jubilant in his voice.

"Tony," I told him, "it's terrific! You ought to write fiction."

"I never cared much for it," he said.

I'll bet you didn't, I thought.

"Well, Janice?"

"But aren't you afraid to use such obvious descriptions of Julia and Maude? After all, nothing has been proven."

He laughed and fished in his shirt pocket for cigarettes. "It doesn't have to be. When Julia sells the land, and kicks the Kanakas off, that's proof enough."

A tocsin rang in my ears.

"What do you mean?" I realized too late how sharp my voice was. Tony became very still. Then he turned slowly toward me with a guileless smile. "Nothing. I was guessing that she probably will, since it will always remind her of her sister."

"Oh," I said, and lay back. But our moment of intimacy was gone. Tony was on guard now, no doubt remembering that Joe had warned him I was "nuts" on the subject of my Hawaiian friends.

I sighed, and began tracing a pattern in the sand with my finger, hoping

I'd find means to bring back his trust in me.

"I keep forgetting how things change," I said, and sighed again. "The village will have to go, of course. But I hate to think about it. It meant so much to me as a child. It's probably because I don't really want to be grown up." I glanced at him out of the corners of my eyes. "Do you think I'm grown up enough, Tony?"

This was the kind of talk he understood. He leaned closer, he murmured, "You're plenty grown up for me, sweetheart."

"I wish you could stay here in Honolulu," I said yearningly. "I'm going to miss you terribly."

Tony threw back his head and laughed. "That's the wonderful part of it; that's what I started to tell you at Waikiki the other day. I am going to stay here. I have a job."

"But I thought you just started with the magazine."

"I have. I'm going to keep both jobs. I'll be their Pacific editor and live right here at the same time. In one of the swankiest places this town has ever seen. It won't materialize for a while yet, but it's a cinch. And public relations—honey, I can do that stuff with one hand tied behind me!"

"Public relations for what?"

He grinned and put a finger under my chin. "I can't tell you yet. You'll find out pretty soon, though, when the story breaks. But don't worry about losing Tony; we're going to know each other better and better." He grasped my shoulders and started to pull me toward him. I moved away.

"Let's not start that; it's still daylight. And I have to go back to the house," I said in a sober voice. "You helped me forget for a while about the tragedy."

I hadn't forgotten for one moment. To Tony it apparently sounded natural enough.

He took his cue from that. We rose and brushed sand from our clothes, then started slowly toward the house.

"You'd better not go with me," I said, and he looked relieved.

"How about the story?" he asked.

An idea had been taking shape in my mind. "Go back and do your final copy, and write the letter for me. I'll stop by your hotel this evening and sign it."

That was exactly what he wanted, and away he went . . .

There was a little group of people seated in the Avery living room. Walter had changed to another shapeless seersucker suit which fitted him badly and diminished his personality. Ellen sat next to him on a brocade sofa, holding his hand. She looked older, from shock and grief. Part of that grief must have been guilt, too, that she could not really mourn for the mother who had been so difficult to love. Luther handed me a glass without speaking; he seemed to have aged twenty years, he stooped like an old man. John Atherton sat very erect in his chair, his look of good humor gone and his eyes hard with anger or suspicion. Lily was not present; she was too tactful to intrude on such an evening. I did not want to stay, either; I took the drink Luther gave me and set it back by the shaker.

"I won't stay, Luther. Lily and I had better go this evening." I turned toward Julia. "Could you send Taeko to help me pack?"

Julia said in a strange voice, "Sit down, Janice, for a moment. I have something to tell you."

I sat down, my eyes fixed on her. If Luther looked twenty years older, Julia seemed twice that. Her face was ghastly, white as bleached bones; her hollow-socketed eyes held a glare which was near the border of dementia. A muscle at the corner of her mouth twitched uncontrollably, relentlessly. Her hands gripped the two canes as if even seated in a chair she felt need of their support.

I said, "What is it, Julia?"

She wet her lips, and her face twitched. "I—I have decided to sell this property."

"No!" My cry was involuntary. "You can't mean it. There isn't another piece of land to compare with it on the island!"

She wet her dry mouth again before she went on. "That is why it is so desirable. A buyer made me an excellent offer some time ago, and I have decided to accept."

I went on, urgently: "But, Julia, this is your home, it has belonged to your family for generations!" Then I asked, in a thin voice, "How about Wainiha?"

Her eyes avoided mine. "That too."

"But you can't! Your father's will says so; it says that as long as the people live there peacefully they must be permitted to stay."

"Peacefully?" Julia's voice rose. "There has been nothing but trouble. And since my own sister—" She put thin fingers to her twitching face and could say no more.

I saw with despair that she was right. There were enough witnesses now to testify that the Hawaiians in the village were troublemakers. Nothing I could say in their defense would weigh against the word of the Averys, of Faye Clarke, even the senator. I knew his type. He would lick his lips over the performance of Malia's sensual dance, but the next day he would denounce Hawaiian depravity.

Luther came over and laid a gentle hand on my shoulder. "I know what a disappointment this is to you, my dear. Believe me, if there were any way to avoid hurting you like this . . ." He gave a weary shrug. "But there is not." I knew that he meant it.

"How about the Hawaiian people?" I asked.

"They will be given notice to remove themselves from the land." Julia's voice was hard now; it was under control. "I am also very sorry, Janice, but my decision is made. I will sign the papers tomorrow."

I rose and looked at her with contempt, and she looked back at me with the eyes of a woman in hell. "We will leave immediately," I said. "Thank you for your kindness and hospitality."

Taeko was already in my room, talking to Lily. They stood before the window which overlooked the village.

"That was a beautiful sunset," Lily said. Her suitcase stood by two of my bags which were already packed. All I had to do was put lingerie and toilet articles in my dressing case.

Taeko came over to sit on my bed while I emptied bureau drawers. "I managed to salvage your possessions," she announced.

I whirled, incredulous over this good fortune. I had given them up for lost, with no little resentment. "How did you do it?"

"Well, I knew Mrs. Clarke would be feeling pretty woozy this morning. So I nipped over there at eight, when her regular maid showed up, and gave her ten dollars to take the day off. When she saw what a mess the house was in she was glad to oblige. I called Kama Tomada, a friend of mine, asked her to substitute for a day, and told her to keep an eye on the things in Mrs. Clarke's dressing room."

"But how about Faye? Didn't she hear all this?"

"She was still asleep on the living-room floor. I phoned from upstairs. The lady woke up soon after that and got herself into a cold shower, yelling that she wanted black coffee 'and be damned quick about it!' Kama told me this, later."

Taeko giggled. "After she broke the lock on your filing case and saw what was in it, the air was blue for an hour. Then she ordered Kama to take the stuff out and burn it in the incinerator. Kama dumped it in that stand of bamboos near the garage. Let's hope it doesn't rain before you can get it out."

She stood up and said, "You owe me ten dollars. Do you want me to stay on here, now that you're leaving?"

"Please do," Lily said. "It will not be much longer, I think."

Taeko looked rebellious. "I don't like it. This is an unhappy house. And after that dreadful accident today—"

Lily went to her and put a hand on her arm. "That was not an accident, Taeko. "

The Japanese girl's eyes widened. For a moment I thought she was going to succumb to her fright. Then she said steadily, "I will stay. You will keep in touch with me?"

"Of course. You are perfectly safe. And you will hear from us very soon."

Taeko helped us carry the bags downstairs, and the silent Koji loaded them in the car. Suka was crying in the kitchen; I pressed some money into her worn hand and murmured brief thanks for the things she had done for me. Telling Luther and Julia good-by was even worse, but we got through with it quickly; Ellen gave us a faint wistful smile as we left.

Headlights of the car picked out a big gap in the driveway wall; the lawn far beneath it was burned and black, although the remains of Maude's car had been taken away. We reached the main road and started toward Diamond Head, but had gone only a few feet when a figure at the side of the road hailed us. It was David Kimu, dressed now in conventional clothes, which made him look older and much more serious.

"Come to Wainiha," he said. "You are wanted there."

He climbed into the rear of the car as Lily began turning. I twisted in the seat to say, "But aren't you supposed to be hiding from the police?"

David smiled. "Not really. Kamakua knows I have no reason to hide. That is why my name was not mentioned in the newspapers. You see, after Malia ran away from me that night, I fortunately went direct to Mrs. Clarke's swimming pool and joined the music boys. You didn't notice, Kulolo, but I was there when you were telling Mr. Davis about the pool at Wainiha. After the party was over we went to Waikiki to play poker. It was someone else who discovered Malia's body in the pool, about six in the morning. At that hour I was just cashing in my chips."

He leaned forward to touch Lily's shoulder. "Stop here. This is the path."

Darkness pressed around us like black velvet. The path was rough and steep; we could see nothing. David went first, extending a hand for me; I in turn held Lily's. We walked slowly. Once I stumbled and pitched forward; David's shoulder braced like a rock to prevent me from falling.

"Thanks," I whispered. He pressed my hand and we started again.

There were no lights in the shacks of the village. No normal sound of dogs barking or sleepy residents asking, "Who is it?"

They knew who we were. They waited for us. In the place where the *kahuna* stayed.

Faint light spread from behind the dense shrubbery at the end of the little valley. David moved branches apart and said, "Go inside."

It was a cave, cool almost to chilliness, with a strong crossdraft blowing from an unseen source. Light from several torches flared in the air current. It was a large place, but now it was filled with people, Hawaiian people. The men wore dark suits over which were draped cloaks of feathers dyed yellow, as were those worn by the ancient *alii*, the chiefs. The women were dressed in black *holokus*, with orange *ilima* in their hair and wreaths of *maile* vine around their necks. They stood straight and proud, grief chiseled on their faces, magnificent in their sorrow and their dignity. Someone was murmuring in Hawaiian; I could translate enough to recognize the Twenty-third Psalm.

There was a *punee* at one side of the cave, covered with *tapa* cloth, the ground beneath it spread with palm leaves. On the *punee*, robed in pure white to his feet, a figure lay, veined hands folded over his still breast, fingers interlaced. Silky white hair was brushed behind his ears; his mouth was open slightly; his sunken eyes were shut. It was the frail old man I had glimpsed a few days ago, dozing in the shade of a tree. Now the *punee* which was once his bed had become his bier. At his head and at his feet stood tall red-and-yellow-feathered staffs—*kahilis*—symbols of Hawaiian nobility.

The speaker finished, and another began a chant, low, vibrant with mourning, while women's voices wailed in unison the unforgettable Hawaiian death.

I couldn't move. I stood hypnotized, knowing that what we witnessed was the funeral service forever held secret from the white man. Why we had been brought there I could not know—I could only look with awe. After a certain time this white-robed figure would disappear, not to be seen again. The chosen few who carried his body to its secret burial place would never reveal its location. These people in the cave might pass us on the street unnoticed in their humble roles as bus drivers, housewives, policemen, bookkeepers, or clerks, but they never forgot that the blood of chiefs was in their veins. They had come to say good-by to one who apparently was their peer; after this night no one would mention the name of the frail old man with white hair.

And no one would forget.

A hand touched my arm, and I started. I saw a woman with gray hair and a tired, beautiful face. She turned and beckoned me silently to the cave opening; I obeyed, while Lily and David followed. She led us to the door of the nearest house, which was in darkness. Her signal stopped us there. The woman returned and pressed a paper-wrapped package into my hands, then grasped my shoulders and faced me toward the direction from which we had arrived. I began walking, and the others followed; as we started up the trail David stepped ahead and took my hand while I gave the other to Lily.

Not a word had been spoken.

When we reached the highway David got into the back seat again and said, "Drive to the first street lamp." Lily did so, and stopped.

I unrolled brown paper then, and we looked at the two small articles it had concealed. A small glass ampule marked DIGITALIN from which one end was broken. A hypodermic needle. Lily held out a hand and I gave them to her.

She said, "Maude was the one who took these."

"Yes," David said. "Digitalin is a heart stimulant. Today she used the drug to make the old man talk. He was feeble, near to dying, and she wanted to make him tell her who he was and where he came from. When she came to the village today we were unable to stop her from going into the cave. We did not suspect that she carried a drug. She was a very determined woman."

"Then he was the old fellow Walter spoke of!" I said. "Did he live in the mountains on the Benson ranch?"

"Yes. He was old," David told us. "Very old. And he was feeble from malnutrition, since Maude Benson forbade the ranch hands to take him any more food. Her injection killed him."

"And for that, Maude Benson died," Lily said softly.

"David," I asked, "was he really a *kahuna*?"

David hesitated for a long time. Then he said, slowly and with reluctance, "Let me put it like this, Kulolo. He was of an ancient line, and one of his names was Kane. Because of certain physical characteristics, all Hawaiians recognize those of his descent. His grandfather, his father, had knowledge, perhaps even powers, which the ordinary man does not."

He got out of the car and stood by the door. I opened my mouth to ask the question David had not answered, and could not. He laid a brown hand on my arm, and his smile was warm.

"Kulolo," he said gently, "I can tell you this much: he was a good man. There was no evil in him. That is why there is grief at his death."

He spoke across me to Lily. "Come back tomorrow, and we will do what must be done."

"Yes," Lily said.

As we rode on down the highway together I asked, "What did he mean, Lily—'what must be done'?"

Lily said, "Tomorrow we must try to prevent the sale of the land."

"How?"

"We will expose the guilty."

"Do you know who it is?"

"I think so."

"Then why," I demanded in sudden anger, "why don't you tell me?"

"You might find it difficult to accept. I want you, if possible, to find out for yourself. Perhaps your father's papers will give us the truth."

"Then let's get at them!"

"We must go to Waikiki first," Lily said, "to pick up that story from Tony Davis. We will have a drink at his hotel and then call his room. You must get yourself under control before you talk to him. He might be waiting, and he is sharp."

Tony was there; he saw us the moment we walked in. He looked spectacularly handsome in white linen, and he walked with a swagger. But he wasn't so sharp that night. Tony was celebrating, celebrating the sale of Julia's land. The hideousness of Maude's death hadn't touched him. Nor the death of the old man, for he didn't know about it. Those were incidents on the road to what he wanted.

"Come and have a drink with me!" he said, and urged us to a table near the sea wall. When our order came, he raised his glass and announced, "Tonight we can drink a toast, one that I know Janice will approve. To Tony Davis—*malihini* into *kamaaina*!" He pronounced the words carefully, correctly.

Newcomer into islander. That's rough translation; there's infinity of meaning in both words. Tony wouldn't be a *kamaaina* in a lifetime. Nobody who calls Hawaiians "Kanakas" with that subtle but unmistakable contempt ever really belongs to the islands.

Something dark moved in my memory, something I had previously refused to recognize. I tried to blank it out, unwilling to change preconceived ideas about my old life, old friends. It returned, that unwelcome realization, as if a stench from somewhere over the edge, beyond what's human and decent, had reached my nostrils. I picked my glass up, set it down, and moved my chair back, ready to rise. I had to get out of there, had to open my father's files; this game with Tony was intolerable.

Lily leaned closer to him and asked in the softest of voices, "Have you succumbed to the spell of the tropics? Are you giving up that wonderful editorial job Janice told me about?"

As she spoke, she kicked me under the table. The pain in my ankle, and her words to him, brought me to the job at hand. It was important, it had to be done now.

"Tony," I said, "that reminds me. How about letting me sign that letter now?" I giggled. "If I finish this drink I might not be able to!"

He nodded solemnly. "Of course. Must, mustn't we?" And went to get the letter.

Lily poured her drink on the ground. "Better do the same, Janice."

I wanted, I needed that drink. I poured it under the table.

"Let's get this over and get out of here!" I said. She nodded.

Tony returned with his manuscript in a manila envelope. He looked at our empty glasses and gave us an equally empty smile. The hovering waiter darted. Tony sat down.

"I was going to show this to someone else first," he said. "But I'll have the carbon. Here's the letter." He clapped his hands loudly; he must have seen that in the movies. "Boy! Bring me a pen!"

I signed the letter which corroborated Tony's story and pushed it over to him. He slipped it into the envelope and sealed it with a flourish. I eyed it covetously. Somehow we had to get that envelope from him before he mailed it. I flashed a glance at Lily; she had to help now, for I was almost at the end of my control.

"This is wonderful luck for me," I said. I made my eyes big. "Imagine how many books I'll sell after this"—I picked up the envelope—"is on the newsstands!"

"We're on our way to the post office," Lily said. "Can we send this off on the clipper for you?"

Tony hesitated, and my heart began to pound so loud I thought surely he would hear it. I touched his knee with mine. "I'm glad you've got that story finished, so we can begin to have some fun. Tony, I have some friends at Kailua who want us to come for the weekend. They're having some Hollywood people . . ." I picked names at random.

He was delighted. "Right you are, sweetheart. Mail the thing for me and let's forget about work."

I slid the envelope into my lap to get it out of his sight. As I did so, Lily caught his attention. "But I thought you said you have a new job. How can you forget about work?"

Tony laughed. "That job doesn't start for a while. Even when it does, it'll be the easiest money I've ever earned." He shook his head. "Brother, what a wonderful break!"

A Chinese man in bellhop's uniform approached. "Mister Davis? You are wanted on the telephone."

Tony rose hastily. "Excuse me. Be right back."

I started to get up. "Let's get out of here now, before he comes back! Lily, please!"

"Wait, Janice. Only a few more minutes."

She hit her glass and overturned it, spilling liquor across the table. She made an exclamation, and the Chinese bellhop turned, saw what had happened, and hastened to repair the damage. Lily began speaking to him sharply, in rapid Chinese. An elderly couple at a nearby table watched her with disapproval. The bellhop bowed and murmured apology, then hurried away.

I said, "What did you do that for? You know he didn't—"

"Shhh!" Lily looked up and smiled. Tony was approaching, slightly unsteady on his elegant long legs.

He frowned slightly as he sat down and said, "I forgot. I have an appointment. Can I give you a lift anywhere?"

"We have a car," Lily told him. "I just ordered it brought to the door."

"Okay." He had risen as we did; he frowned at the manila envelope in my hand.

In a minute he was going to ask for the return of that manuscript, so that he could put it in the mail himself. Lily knew it too. She said quickly, "There's the car now; I recognize the horn. Come on, Janice." We left in a hurry.

The Chinese who brought the car was the man she had scolded a few minutes before. They greeted each other amicably. She took the envelope from me and handed it to him.

"You know what to do?"

"You bet. It will be finished immediately. As soon as he leaves."

He was the one who had copied Tony's notes for Lily. Her pretended scolding had actually been rapid instructions. En route to the Chun house she explained. As soon as Tony left the hotel the other man would enter his room, rewrite the letter I had signed, with Tony's typewriter, on Tony's paper, and sign my name to it. The envelope would go out on the next clipper.

Tony's superiors could only conclude, when the denouement we planned for them arrived, that my signature had been forged.

What this would do to Tony's editorial career didn't bother me in the least. Deep inside me a slow and fierce anger was beginning to burn. With that flash of insight at the table had come my hunch about Tony's job. I leaned forward in automatic effort to force the car ahead, faster, and I opened my purse, feeling for the key to the steel drawer where the final truth very likely would be.

CHAPTER FIFTEEN

THE CHUNS were having dinner, and we had to join them. I wasn't hungry; I was tense with eagerness to get on with the evening's work. I could have groaned aloud at the prospect of meeting all those people, sitting down to a leisurely meal, making polite conversation. It had to be done.

There were five at the table besides Lily and me: Ethel and Harry Chun, their youngest son, Tommy, their baby daughter, Alice, and a grandmother. All except the old lady and the baby wore American dress; eight-months-old Alice wore a diaper and a bib, the grandmother was comfortable in Chinese trousers and jacket; both bulged with good food and contentment. Many an Occidental mother-in-law would give her eyeteeth to be as respected and as cherished as a Chinese *tutu*. Some of them are veritable she-dragons, breathing fire; this one was fat and indolent, surveying her brood with pride.

I looked for Richard, but he was absent. At a scout meeting, his mother said.

The dinner was Chinese style, superbly cooked, and after I had taken a few mouthfuls I began to eat ravenously, realizing that this was actually the first food I had relished in a week. Not one meal at the Avery house had been enjoyable; there was always tension at that table. Faye's *luau* was not a relaxing occasion; lunch with Tony I had taken guardedly; and the Japanese dinner had been no dinner at all for me, I had eaten about six mushrooms. I reached for roast duck with almonds, water chestnut hash, and smoked pork—it was wonderful.

Harry Chun beamed at me over his rice bowl. "You enjoy our food, I see. Try some of this fish." He loaded my bowl with steamed *opakapaka*. As he ate he said, "Our Chinese cooks consider it barbarous that a hungry man should be forced to hack and saw at what is on his plate before he can eat it; that's why our food is always cut before it is served."

I nodded with my mouth full, and nobody minded. The Chuns chattered comfortably as the meal progressed, switching from Chinese to English and then to pidgin, as they felt like it. The grandmother spoke Chinese; she cooed at the fat baby in her high chair and urged tidbits on her, and she paid no attention to me at all. I knew that she had already observed every feature I possessed and assessed my personality; her opinion of me would be exposed later to the family. I hoped it was affirmative.

After dinner we took our tea out through the living room to the immense *lanai* which overlooked Waikiki, the Ala Wai, and, farther distant, the city of Honolulu. Lights sparkled below us, and the night was fragrant with ginger which grew somewhere nearby. Ethel Chun was wearing a blue silk dress; over one ear she had pinned a white flower which I did not recognize. I asked her about it.

Her husband answered me. "That is Ethel's favorite, a Chinese blossom called *bok yok lang faa*—white-jade-flesh-flower. It grows in our garden." He sighed. "Ah, that reminds me of our honeymoon! We went to Bali on that delirious occasion."

His wife wriggled with confusion and said something to him in Chinese, at which he grinned broadly. "You'd never think she was a learned woman, a doctor now, would you?"

She hurled some staccato phrases at him, then they both burst into laughter. I saw that this was a household where happiness prevailed, where there were constant jokes and affectionate teasing. No wonder their eldest son was such an intrepid character. Lily was seated opposite me on a *punee* with her feet curled under her; she was at ease, yet aware of my state of mind. Much as I enjoyed these people, I wanted to get away from them.

After a while some guests arrived, and our hosts went to greet them. A maid began to set up card tables, and I saw with relief that a mah-jongg game would soon start. I finished my tea and put out my cigarette as Harry Chun came to the *lanai* and said, "Do you wish to play?" It was only a token invitation; I said no, I had some work to do. He knew what the work was; for a moment the twinkle left his eyes and he gave me a serious, sympathetic look before he returned to his guests in the living room.

"Can we go now, Lily?"

She slid her feet to the floor. "Certainly. Upstairs."

The filing case was in my room, a large bedroom furnished with dark mahogany and rose-flowered cretonne, a blue Chinese rug on the hardwood floor. Lily's room was next to it; we shared the adjoining bath as we had done at the Averys'. It was hot up there, and we took off our dresses and sat on the floor before the steel box to begin what promised to be a long and tedious search.

My father had been systematic. There were yellowed manila folders with typewritten labels, filed alphabetically for half the depth of the drawer. Behind those lay stacks of thin paperbound notebooks with ruled pages; he had preferred making his notes with a very fine pen in books which could be laid flat. Each was labeled: different islands, different communities on each island, names of individuals and genealogy charts for important Hawaiians, then books on plants, herbs, fishes, animals, rocks, shells—it was bewildering.

We started with the notebooks, since they were most formidable and would require greatest concentration. It was slow reading, and much of it brought back memories of field trips, of certain days we'd spent together and people we had met. More of it was new and previously unknown— none of it seemed significant. The book on *kahunas* I read with great care, not missing a word, and learned little I hadn't already known, except that a certain Honolulu dowager of great social position and wealth was known among her people to be a *kahuna* of importance. I found notes on a different kind of person on Maui who was a *kuni kahuna*, a dealer in slow death, and read how he had killed three people, under pretense of using a spell, by means of *limu make*—the poison moss which grows on lava rocks at the edge of the sea and which the government tries hard to eradicate. The *kahuna* was eradicated too; he went to jail for murder, and his supposed magic never got him out. I finished reading with a sigh and picked up the next book. Sitting on the floor near me, Lily was doing the same.

We read for hours. When we had gone through the notebooks it was almost midnight. Lily rose and stretched her diminutive figure to its fullest height, then yawned. "We need some coffee," she said, and went to her room for a kimono to wear down to the kitchen.

When the door opened I could hear voices and the clack of ivory tiles;

someone called "Kong!" and another player squealed with dismay. I lay on the soft rug and tried to relax until Lily returned with coffee.

We ate coconut cake and drank the scalding black liquid, smoked a couple of cigarettes, and went back to work. An insect began to buzz around the window screen; it was very hot and still outside the house. I took a dozen manila folders marked "A" from the file and handed half of them to my companion, moved to rest my back against a chair, and opened the first folder. It contained correspondence with my father's publishers, and I scanned the letters hurriedly. As I closed it I became aware that Lily was sitting very straight, reading with intense interest. I opened the second folder in my hand and tried to begin reading, but could not. I glanced at Lily again; her attitude told me she had found something. I sat and waited, watching as she read.

Finally she finished a page and turned quickly to another. I said, "Have you found something?" Lily looked up with a start.

"Yes," she said. "Take this first one and I'll go on with the others."

I took the sheet she handed me and began to read. When I reached the bottom of the typescript a slow pounding had begun in my temples. I held out a hand for the second, and she gave it to me and started reading the third. In that way we finished the entire contents of the folder.

The last sheaf of papers was the carbon of a letter, and I reproduce it here:

I long ago recognized you, my former friend, as an individual possessed of mediocre personal qualities and a suppressed itch for power. These two attributes did not concern me greatly since they could not affect our relationship, and I have never considered myself qualified to sit in judgment on my fellow men.

But I should have remembered that if an itch for power is dormant in a human being at one hour, it may become active ruthlessness in the next, providing the means of gratification is sighted. I have been thinking recently of what might happen if that hour comes for you, and it causes me deep concern. For you can jeopardize the welfare and security of other human beings, and I do not want them to be sacrificed to your weakness.

That is why I have recently been reviewing the substance and total of many remarks you have made to me in recent years, questions you have asked, which prove beyond possibility of doubt a desire, a half-formed plan, of which you may or may not be consciously aware. I consider that you are a person who might be willing to drift through life, bringing little of value to others but actually harming no one, unless an incentive presents itself and serves as catalyst to bring your wish to the surface and give you courage to act. In such an eventuality you may change from the ineffectual non-

entity you are now into a person capable of doing harm to a number of others. It is to insure prevention of such disaster (and it would be disaster for you as well as your victims) that I am writing this letter. I shall now review the evidence.

When I first met you, the day I brought my little daughter to your house and asked a servant for first aid, I thought you a genuinely warm person. Subsequent meetings helped to develop a friendly relationship between us, and when you decided to give water to the Hawaiian family I was convinced of your generosity and kindness. (It did not occur to me until later that if you had been really a kind human being you would have thought of the water yourself, long before I suggested it.)

After a while, when you began questioning me about the heiau, *and its former function in religious rites, I at first congratulated myself on having stimulated your interest in Polynesian culture. Later I became aware (tardily again, but sharply, very sharply aware at last!) that your interest was not in the culture of the people themselves, but in the more primitive aspects of some of their beliefs, and you sought this information for some hidden, ignoble purpose of your own. I began then to sift and analyze your questions, your remarks, segregating and isolating those which seemed to me to pertain to this dark desire of which I was becoming more and more certain.*

You were quite clever, in those long, friendly conversations. You flattered me, too, seeking me out in my study while Janice was at school, relieving my loneliness, feeding my not inconsiderable ego by your admiration for my erudition, your professed desire to learn. And the facts you really wanted to obtain were strewn so casually among the many questions you asked; if I had not already been on guard, I should never have been suspicious. But gradually the pattern began to emerge. And after you stopped making frequent visits, after you dropped even the pretense of friendly concern over my welfare or that of my child, I knew that the scholarly invalid had served his purpose, you did not need him any more.

It was then that I began to examine our past dialogues (for I had made scrupulous notes, setting down all our conversations as soon as you left my house) with the purpose of winnowing out your hidden wish and your possible future intent. It would take too much energy and paper to repeat the entire context here; I wish, however, to inform you that there is a file under your name which contains these notes in full. I will give you, instead, two statements: one a résumé and the other a prediction.

You made a significant slip one day when you remarked how easy it would be to turn this paradise into a hell by exposing the nitwit natives to a little bit of superstition. The Hawaiians are not nitwits. They are very wise people, having acquired through several centuries a vast accumulation of unwritten knowledge. This knowledge pertains to the winds and tides, to sunlight and storm, to flowers and fruits of the earth. And they possess a secret which one of your kind will always envy and can never know—the blessed secret of enjoying life.

You want to force the Hawaiians from your land. First, because in their instinctual way of living they remind you of the sourness of your own nature, and you hate them for it. Second, because you are aware that although the property is yours legally, you have no moral right to it. The land on the Waikiki side of your house, where the village now stands, was a kuleana *grant, from King Kamehameha to Liholiho Kanahele, a direct ancestor of the Hawaiian woman whom you know as Makaleha. How the first Harrington got the land from Kanahele is not clear, but the original ownership and transfer of title in 1867 are matters of record. The price paid to Kanahele at that time was eighteen dollars. No wonder you never visit Makaleha at the village; sight of her must always remind you that she belongs there, you are the trespasser. It was she, incidentally, who told me the history of the land, and her casual words sent me on my first investigations into your title.*

The last Harrington willed the property with the stipulation that so long as the Hawaiians lived peacefully in Wainiha they were never to be evicted. A sop to his conscience, no doubt. This stipulation must always be in your mind like a bitter ferment. And when the time comes soon that there is no more ocean frontage available in Honolulu, when opportunists who want to turn this beautiful land into another noisy and vulgar Coney Island approach you with offers for the property, then is when you will try to find means of getting rid of the Hawaiian people. I do not intend to give you here a blueprint for such means. But you are clever enough, possibly, to find them.

I told you that I was going to give you two statements, a résumé and a prediction. I now add a third—my warning.

I expect to die in the near future and have made preparations for my going. After my death you may not consider yourself free to act as you choose, for I have taken steps to prevent your carrying out those hidden plans. A copy of this letter remains for my daughter, together with all the notes I mentioned, and an outline of the possible course of action you may take to bring public disapproval to bear on the Hawaiian village. These notes are accompanied by my careful statement, which will be given to the proper authorities should the need arise. I assure you my word is respected there and what I say will be given absolute credence. Janice will know what to do if it becomes necessary, and my daughter will do it.

I hereby instruct her, and notify you, that if ever there is any disturbance of any kind at Wainiha, either purporting to be supernatural or aris-

ing from native religious practices, or if there is ever any mysterious hap-
pening related in the slightest degree to the outline which is attached to my
notes, Janice Cameron is to take this folder to my friends at the Bishop
Museum (she knows who I mean), and they will see that investigation is
made and your evildoing will be circumvented.

I sign myself on this date, April 4, 1945, in full possession of all my
faculties, Emmett John Cameron, your unrelenting enemy in life and after
death.

The letter was addressed to Luther Avery.

"It was Luther who searched my bags," I said at last. "Looking for this." I clutched the folder in my lap. "That's why he invited me to his house—"

"His wife's house," Lily corrected. "That is the important point. Luther Avery has nothing, not even a good architectural practice. When Julia married him, he was working for a firm where house plans were supplied free to owners who bought building materials from his employers. You told me yourself that the houses he designed were without distinction. The job suited his capacities. Luther acquired position and money only through his wife."

"But Julia also was searching," I said, then added, "Steve Dugan told me Julia and Maude were basically alike; they both have enormous pride, only Julia's has never been challenged. What is she trying to do—save face?"

"I believe so. She may suspect that Faye is Luther's mistress; from the telephone conversation we heard, I believe that she is. So long as the relationship remained hidden, Julia might have continued to tolerate it; she must have been suspicious for some time. But she wants to avert a scandal. Denouncing them would expose her own humiliation. She has been very stubborn in refusing to sell the land. Even after her husband tried to kill her, she remained obdurate."

I thought of Julia, recovered enough from her injury to walk normally, yet pretending to be a cripple, clinging to the support of crutches. Julia, afraid to stand up.

"The murder of the Hawaiian girl was a shock," Lily continued, "but she still remained silent. It took her sister's death to make her realize that Luther will stop at nothing."

"So," I said, "she will destroy the Hawaiian village rather than let the world know her husband is unfaithful."

Lily said dryly, "Julia Avery is not a noble character. Actually she and Luther make a very good pair. He is using her, and Faye is using him. Ironically enough, Julia does not know that it is Faye who wants to buy the land."

"But she said she had an offer."

"Yes. From Tony Davis. He is the dummy buyer. It was arranged during his previous visit here. He is posing to Julia Avery as a rich young man who has fallen in love with the islands and wants to build a home. Not an unusual story."

Nor was the use of a dummy to purchase real estate a new practice in Honolulu. I recalled the local excitement when it was announced that a national chain store, noted for selling good merchandise at low prices, had acquired enough land to build a retail establishment. The deal was handled through a dummy, so the story went, who conducted negotiations from the sanctuary of a private room in a local hospital. Screams of outrage from those who previously retained monopoly on department store merchandising shook the islands harder than the worst earthquake in Hawaii's history.

"So Tony is the dummy," I said, rather liking the appellation. "How did you discover that?"

"Taeko told me earlier this evening, before you came up to the room to pack. Her friend Kama overheard the telephone conversation when Tony called to tell Faye that Julia had consented to sell the land."

"Do you think she would still sell if she knew the buyer was Faye?"

"I do not know. However—"

There was a faint knock on the door, and I jerked nervously at the sound. "Come in," Lily called, at which young Richard Chun entered, accompanied by Kapsung Lee. Both were wide-eyed with news they brought.

"Turn around a moment," Lily said, "until we get some clothes on." She reached for her kimono and tossed me a silk robe from my dressing case. "All right now. What reports do you have?"

The surveillance by our young secret operatives had not stopped with last night's activities. Unbidden by Lily, Richard explained, he and his men had continued their investigations until this evening when they had to attend a Boy Scout meeting. Earlier in the day they had seen something. He and Kapsung had been working as a team—for safety, Richard explained gravely—and had witnessed a meeting between Maude Benson and her murderer just before she drove the station wagon through the Avery retaining wall to her death.

Richard began the story. "We were sorta hanging around between Mrs. Clarke's house and the Avery place, and we saw Mrs. Benson come tearing along the road. Another car was following her—he honked and she stopped, see? Then Mr. Avery got out and went over to talk to her. He acted funny. He leaned against the car, and while she couldn't see his hands he took a paper bag from his pocket, a little bag, like you get cracked seed in—"

"Don't forget, Richard, she was plenty *huhu* wit' him," his partner reminded.

"Yeah, she was burned up, all right. She kept yammerin' and he tried to hush her. While this went on he put his hand on the back of the seat, friendly-like, and opened the bag. He talked and watched it a minute, then he grabbed it away quick, said something to her, and away she went. He got in his own car and drove off fast toward town."

"Fast, boy! I'll say!"

"After he left we found the bag on the road and picked it up." Richard gulped. "We dropped it plenty fast. There was a big centipede in it."

"Right after that," his partner finished, "we heard the crash and heard her yell. When we got there the car was starting to burn and that white-haired man was pulling you"—he jerked his head toward Lily—"away from the wreck. That's when we scrammed."

They looked at us with questioning eyes. I in turn looked at Lily. Should we tell these children that they had witnessed a murder? Lily Wu didn't hesitate. She told them the truth, in simple words. As she spoke I realized, watching their faces, that it was the wise thing to do. They had known it anyhow, and her manner of speaking robbed the situation of complete horror and emphasized the importance of their contribution.

"Now, Richard," she said in conclusion. "Give me the paper bag."

They looked at each other in consternation. They had left it on the road. "Gosh!" Richard said. "Fingerprints!" He grasped his friend's arm. "Come on, Kappy. We gotta go back!"

"Just a minute," Lily said. "We're going with you. If we find it, we may have evidence to convict a murderer."

But our trip to retrieve the paper bag was useless. We found it ground to shreds by the tires of passing cars.

CHAPTER SIXTEEN

THE next day we sat together for the last time on the *lanai* of the Avery house. Not everyone was there. Fred Coffee had taken Ellen to visit his family at Punaluu. Tony was with Steve Dugan, who had called at his hotel with a request for an interview and confirmation of a big story.

The story, prematurely revealed by our bibulous senator, was announce-ment of a new development in Honolulu, an enterprise in which the senator was an investor: construction of a lavish "beach club." Such places had been very profitable in California, where miles of most desirable ocean frontage were acquired by private operators and made available to those people with enough money to pay for swimming privileges, called "mem-berships."

Honolulu's new club, as designed by Luther Avery, was to be the ultimate in luxury; guests would be able to make reservations only through certain channels. All of the beach from Faye's property to the end of the Hawaiian village was to be "restricted." The work of removing coral to develop a perfect swimming beach had already begun. In his job of "public relations," Tony would make his permanent residence at the "club," with frequent mainland trips to contact "eligible" members.

I thought of this with bitterness as I watched the people on the *lanai* and waited for something to happen. Julia sat near me, her eyes darting from my face to that of Lily Wu, impassive in the chair beside mine. Dr. Atherton, formerly Julia's devoted attendant, avoided looking at her; he seemed still to be in an emotional state, either angered or worried. Walter Benson was with us in body but apparently not in spirit; he smoked his blackened pipe and made rapid calculations on an envelope which he took from his pocket.

Captain Kamakua sat in the chair next to Lily, quiet, unhurried, sure of himself. His intelligent eyes observed all of us, noted each revealing gesture, but he said nothing, he waited. Kamakua was not there officially; he had come at our request, and had told us we must handle proceedings ourselves.

Luther arrived late from his office, where I had telephoned him. He recognized his guests with a gravely courteous smile and said, "I came as soon as I received your message, Janice. What is the reason for this meeting?"

I started to answer, but words stuck in my throat. Lily said, "There have been some developments in Captain Kamakua's investigation which are of interest. He thought we all should know."

Luther looked at the big policeman. "Investigation? Of what?"

"Of certain events in the Hawaiian settlement, which led to the death of the girl, Malia." Captain Kamakua was bland; his tone conveyed nothing.

Luther seemed surprised. He rubbed a hand over his face and said, "To tell the truth, we had almost forgotten that poor girl, in the shock of what happened here yesterday. Let us hear the developments, by all means."

He turned to his wife. "My dear, you're forgetting your usual hospitality." Julia stared fixedly at him and did not speak. Luther went to the door and called, "Taeko! Bring us something to drink. And a bucket of ice, please."

"I hope," he said as he measured rum into glasses and began squeezing lemons for collinses, "that this won't take too long. We have an appointment with our attorney at three."

At three they were to sign the papers which transferred the property to Tony Davis.

Lily said, "We will be finished before three. We are waiting for Faye Clarke."

Luther looked at her for the first time, and seemed surprised.

Lily was in black, her severely cut Chinese dress accentuating the pure green of earrings and circles of jade on her arms. Her black satin slippers had high heels, and she seemed, in spite of her diminutive figure, haughty as an empress, and as indomitable.

Luther pressed a lemon so hard that it went to pulp under his hand. He discarded the mess and started on a fresh half as Walter announced, "Here comes Mrs. Clarke now."

Faye had apparently been ready for a swim when she was summoned. She appeared in a white bathing suit, carrying her cap in one hand. "Hello," she said. "What's going on here?"

Lily rose. "We can start now. Sit down, Mrs. Clarke."

Faye gave her a long look, then sat on the arm of a chair and asked Luther for a cigarette. He gave her a light and went back to squeezing lemons. It gave him something to do with his hands.

"Janice," Lily said. "You begin the story."

My heart had begun to thud, and my hands were cold and wet. I was afraid to begin, because once we started we had to finish, and our performance was purely bluff. We had no proof.

"I think you all know," I said huskily, "why I have been so interested in Wainiha. It was a place very dear to me in my childhood, and to my father. When I came here recently, at Luther's invitation, I was horrified to discover that the village had changed, there were mysterious and frightening things happening there. The first night I was here, I went to Wainiha and found that the old *heiau* had been rebuilt and there was blood upon the stones. Later I questioned Luther and Julia and they told me a *kahuna* had appeared in the village and pagan rites were being practiced. The Averys said they didn't understand what was happening. But there are other people who know. We have asked them to come here and explain."

I finished with a sigh and looked toward the police officer. Kamakua went to the library and said, "Will you come out, please?"

David Kimu came out to the *lanai*, accompanied by two women dressed in *holokus*, wearing *leis* of *ilima*. They were the Hawaiians I had met in Wainiha. The eldest, a tall woman with gray hair, began to talk. She spoke in perfect English.

"We went to the village at the request of David Kimu, who lived there as a boy. Most of the Hawaiian people who had homes in the village had left, and the few who stayed were terrified. They said that a *kahuna* had appeared and was performing secret rites at the *heiau*, which he had rebuilt. We moved into one of the deserted houses and gradually made the acquaintance of the stranger.

"He was not a *kahuna*. He was a feeble old man who had no place to live, and he had been told that if he would come to the village he would be given food and shelter, in exchange for which he was asked only to rebuild the *heiau*, which had been in ruins as long as any of us could remember. He rebuilt the altar and he moved into a cave at the end of the village, where a bed and food were provided for him by Malia, who lived in the house across from ours.

"We watched Malia. She worked for this family as a servant, and we did not come here, but we watched everything she did at the village. Malia had some Bibles in a paper carton under her bed, and she threw them one at a time into the water at certain places where they would be found by members of the Avery family or their guests. We retrieved several, but not all. One night Malia did not come home until late; this was while the Avery family was away, visiting on Maui. We approached the house on that night and watched while she operated a film projector from the balcony so that moving figures were visible on the hill of the village, as if in a procession. The film was a picture of a Kamehameha Day parade in which people are costumed as old-time Hawaiians, in feather cloaks and helmets.

"Henry Mahea, the gardener, was also watching, and he thought that he saw a ghost procession. Henry was seventy years old and his eyesight was poor. He was very frightened, and he died of his fright. But we knew what the procession really was, and we knew who was responsible for Henry's death.

"Soon after that, Miss Cameron arrived. That night Malia poured chicken blood on the *heiau* and beat temple drums in the hills. Miss Cameron came to investigate, and when she saw the blood and the deserted village, she ran away. Malia watched her, and later we heard Malia laughing.

"The next night Malia went to dance at Mrs. Clarke's house. She came back from there crying. Much later, after we had gone to sleep, we were awakened by voices. Malia was arguing with someone by the pool, she was very angry. We listened and heard her saying that she was not going away on the boat, she was going to stay, and she wanted more money, or she would tell everything she knew. Then we heard no more, and we went back to sleep. The next morning we found Malia's body in the pool. We knew that if we reported her death, suspicion would be attached to the village, and we wished to avoid publicity, we did not want the Hawaiians to be blamed."

She stopped and looked at David.

He took up the story. "I arranged that Janice should find Malia's body, for I knew she would protect the people in the village if she could. But after Janice ran back to this house with the news, and when no one came to investigate, I realized that something had happened to Janice and the murderer was determined that the village should be involved in Malia's death. I removed the dead girl from the pool and put her body in the ocean, in hope that it would drift far from here. You all know what happened."

Dr. Atherton coughed irritably. "Why didn't you tell the police? That's what you should have done."

"Because," David said patiently, "we did not want strangers to come to the village for a few days. The old man was dying. We wanted him to die in peace."

Dr. Atherton looked at Captain Kamakua. The officer looked back at him without a flicker of expression.

"This is all very fascinating," Faye said, "but I don't see what it has to do with me, or why I was called over here."

"Relax, Faye," I said to her. "You will see."

She looked at me quickly, and wariness gathered in her blue eyes. She moved into a chair and sat there, very still.

Julia spoke then. "Go on. What happened after that?"

David looked at her without expression as he continued. "After Malia's body was discovered by the children, your sister began to visit the village. She looked into each house, trying to find the old man. Then finally she heard him muttering in the cave, and went in. He was too feeble to talk coherently. She watched him for a while and went away. Then she flew over to Maui and verified her suspicion that he had come from there, at the invitation of a member of her family.

"She came back; she forced her way into the cave again. We did not suspect that she brought a drug which would stimulate him so that he could talk. He spoke long enough for her to discover who had sent him to Wainiha, and under what circumstances. She went immediately to confront that person with the truth. She also died."

Walter looked up. "I told her not to interfere." He turned to David. "I suppose we'll never know what caused that accident."

Lily said, "You will know."

Someone's feet scraped over the flagstoned floor. Luther, walking to a wastebasket to dump lemon rinds.

"Give me a drink, Luther," Faye commanded. He started to obey, but stopped to listen as I took up the story.

"When I arrived here, my luggage was searched. I thought at first that it was Malia. Later I discovered that several people were interested in my possessions. You, Julia, who pretended to be a cripple—"

Julia gasped and clutched the two sticks at her side.

"I told you!" John Atherton said angrily. "I begged you to stop malingering and walk normally again. If you keep this up you'll really be an invalid!"

Luther looked at his wife. "So it has been an act all this time?"

She sat and stared at him, her face twitching. She didn't answer.

"Later," I went on more loudly, "after I announced that I was getting my father's papers out of storage, I realized what the searcher wanted, when the papers were stolen before I could read them. I recovered them from Faye's dressing room before anyone had a chance to open the files. I was certain then that the answer might be there."

Faye shrugged a smooth shoulder. "I have no idea what you are talking about."

"Taeko knows," Lily told her. "She is a friend of ours."

Faye looked at Lily with wide eyes, but behind that gaze one could almost see the thoughts racing, the quick searching of memory to recall what she had said or done in front of the Japanese girl. Her face was blank.

"Last night," I went on, forcing my voice to steadiness, "I read through my father's papers. I found the letter he sent to you, Luther."

Luther became very still. He looked back at me gravely. "What letter? I do not understand."

"I am sure that you do. The letter explains how you have done these things. Your relationship with Faye explains why. We know about the use which you and Faye intend to make of the land."

"Faye?" Julia cried. "Luther and Faye?"

"Yes, Julia. It is Faye who is buying the land. Tony Davis is only a front for the two of them."

Julia grew very white. "Luther, you promised—you—"

"Be quiet, Julia!" At the threat in his voice she cowered.

Luther looked at her angrily. "This is ridiculous nonsense. There is not one single thing which these hysterical girls can prove. As for the others, they're a group of illiterate Kanakas who can't even spell their own names!"

"No, Mr. Avery," Captain Kamakua said. "You are mistaken. David is an honor student at the university. And these ladies— Allow me to present Mrs. Grace Hamilton, of Kona."

The tall, slender woman bowed her head slightly. Her name was known the islands over, for she came of a famous family, and her husband, four generations removed from missionary ancestors who arrived in Hawaii before 1825, was a prominent attorney, one of Kona's most honored citizens.

"And Mrs. Lydia Brent," Kamakua added. The second woman acknowledged the introduction with a faint smile.

I had met Lydia Brent before, since she was on the board of directors of a residence for girls where I once worked as secretary. I hadn't recognized her in native dress, speaking pidgin. She could call herself by a Hawaiian name more important than that of Brent, if she chose. She was the widow of Gerald Brent, member of the Territorial Legislature, direct descendant of a former British Ambassador to the court of King Kalakaua.

"Mrs. Brent," I asked, "why did you go to live at the village?"

She turned toward me and said in exquisitely articulated English, "David Kimu is as dear to me as my own, since he and my son were friends through high school, and my husband's will provided for David's college education. When he came to me for advice about the trouble which threatened our people, I felt that I must do something to help. I discussed the situation with Grace Hamilton, who insisted on moving to Wainiha with me. Her husband has been our adviser, in daily contact with us since we went to live there."

I looked at the two women and wondered how they had enjoyed giving up modern, luxurious homes to live in a Hawaiian village. A glint in Lydia Brent's dark eyes answered my question.

Luther was looking at them too. For the first time he was beginning to lose composure.

"Luther! I asked you for a drink!" Faye said. He didn't seem to hear.

Lily spoke then. "There were two witnesses to your interview with Maude Benson yesterday. They will testify when you go to trial. They recovered the paper bag in which you carried the centipedes. Fortunately it retained excellent fingerprints."

Luther's face suddenly turned gray. He wet his mouth, looking from one face to another. Faye rose and went to his side. She grasped his arm with one hand while with the other she poured lemon juice into one of the drinks which stood on the table. She took a drink and then faced us with a scornful smile.

"You all know this is a lot of nonsense. You're talking like fools, trying to pull a bluff which isn't going to work. Luther didn't do any of the things you accuse him of." She laughed. "Even if he had, there's no proof. Otherwise he would have been arrested long before this and you would have saved your dramatics for the courtroom."

She finished her drink and set the glass down so hard that it broke..

"Now I'm going swimming in my nice new beach. And I'd like to see any of you try to stop me."

She patted Luther on the check and said, "Come over for cocktails after you finish with the lawyer. The senator is coming. We will celebrate *Tony's*"—she underlined his name maliciously—"latest real-estate deal!"

She started across the lawn toward the ocean, and no one tried to stop her. We watched in silence as she waded into the water and began to swim with long, easy strokes.

Luther stood as if stunned with relief, while color began to return to his face. He began absently picking up ice cubes and bits of glass from the table, and he said in a low voice, "She's right. She's always right."

Julia moaned. He looked at her with contempt and made a gesture as if to brush her from his sight. Then he started and glanced at his hand, which was bleeding.

"Faye broke her glass," he said, "her—" He picked up the pieces and examined the pattern. He whirled and glared wildly at me as he shouted in a dreadful voice, "That was your drink! I mixed it for you, you interfering little bitch!"

He looked at the water, where Faye was swimming toward the raft. He cried, "Faye! Faye, darling! Come back!" Then he began to run like a madman.

Kamakua and David both started to follow. They halted as Julia said, "Don't stop them. There's nothing to worry about. He had morphine in his pocket; he took it from John's bag. He said it was for me, that if I didn't do as he said he'd give it to me, only I would never know when—"She dropped her head into her hands, weeping. Then she looked up and said, "I took the bottle from his pocket this morning and put saccharin tablets in it. She won't be hurt. Nothing can hurt her."

John Atherton let out a ragged sigh, and his shoulders sagged. No one bothered with him. Every eye was turned toward the ocean.

Luther had reached the water. He waded in with all his clothes on, stumbling, falling, and getting up, then beginning to swim with weak floundering efforts. We could hear him calling her name as he struggled toward her.

Faye was at the float before she finally stopped and looked back over her shoulder. She turned then and swam toward him, and we saw Luther's arms go around her, saw her try to fight off that frantic grasp as he panicked and she was unable to free herself.

Suddenly they went under together, like two stones.

By the time David and Kamakua reached the spot both figures had disappeared. They were found six hours later, still locked in that fatal embrace. Faye and Luther drowned in one of the holes from which the Hawaiians had dug coral growth when she hired them to make her perfect swimming beach.

* * * *

We had the *luau* on the day Makaleha came back to the village. She traveled in style, riding on the back of a truck, her comfortable bulk sunk into a pile of *lauhala* mats, bare legs hanging over the edge. I thought of Queen Kaahumanu, who rode in a cart painted turquoise and filled with rugs, legs dangling casually from the rear of her conveyance. They were related, if not by blood, then by temperament.

Everybody helped Makaleha move into her house, which had been scrubbed for the occasion. Getting settled didn't take long: cooking utensils were hung on bare rafters over the stove, blankets spread on the new *punee,* fresh mats laid on the floor, a few cotton garments on hooks behind a *tapa* curtain, and it was done.

Other families were already reestablished. Word had gone out by coconut wireless that Wainiha was a happy place again. Children and adults crowded around Makaleha, kissing her, flinging *leis* over her head. The wreaths caught in her hair and the pins came out so that it fell to her waist. Makaleha laughed and fastened a pink hibiscus over one ear.

"Now I catch me numbah-one kin' fella," she announced, rolling her eyes.

"Me, I'll be your fella!" a gray-haired neighbor said, and she made a naughty suggestion to him in Hawaiian at which everybody roared.

"No more wase time now! Gotta *hanahana* if we make good *luau,*" she said, and the group scattered. Archie Kamaka went to the *imu* to inspect the fire over the stones; others got the long net ready for our *hukilau.*

I walked with Makaleha as she made the rounds of the little settlement. Her eyes missed nothing: the *heiau* now covered with flowers, garden plots which needed weeding, vines overrunning a cottage window, a sagging roof which must be repaired. She said little as we ambled over the warm earth, but gestures told her emotion: a hand lingering to touch a flowering tree, eyes resting on moving waters which once again were so near. Finally she faced the horizon with arms outstretched, palms up—the gesture with which a human being loves the earth on which he lives.

When we had finished our tour I asked, "*Au-au?*"

She nodded vigorously and went to her house to put on a bright pink *mumu,* that voluminous Hawaiian garment which is so comfortable. We swam in the pool and Makaleha washed her hair, shaking it in dark handfuls to dry in the sun. I left her there and went to smoke a cigarette on the beach, where Steve Dugan joined me. "How's about that story you promised, Janice?" she said.

I sat with her and told it, and when I finished she said, "Another one we won't print. I had figured out a lot of it, and you filled the gaps. What did you think of my report of the 'accident'?"

It had been a good one, very convincingly written, that news account of the double tragedy which occurred when Luther Avery, prominent Honolulu resident, lost his life in a heroic attempt to save that of his neighbor. Faye Clarke, the story said, was known as an expert swimmer but had succumbed to a sudden cramp, and Luther had gone gallantly to her rescue. The rest of it was the usual blah, an obituary of Luther and of Faye. Other versions might leak out, but no one would ever be certain. Those of us who knew the truth had our own reasons for silence.

"So the Bensons are back on Maui," Steve said. "How's the romance progressing?"

"Ellen writes that Fred Coffee is planning to open a law office at Wailuku. It sounds promising, and she is quite happy."

"Do you think Julia Avery will ever come back?"

"I don't know. She's in Santa Barbara now, and her house is leased for three years."

"John Atherton sailed for California last week."

"Is that so?" It didn't matter.

"And Glamour Boy went to New York. Heard from him recently?" Steve pursued.

"Tony? Not yet. But I expect to! My story of the village will appear in the November issue; his was scheduled for December." I was looking forward to that communication from Tony.

"What did you do about water for this place? Julia's tenants don't pay the bill, do they?"'

"David Kimu took care of that. There's a line direct from the city supply now. The Hawaiians will pay for their own water."

"Can I do a feature on it?" Steve sounded pleased.

"Certainly. Do another eulogy on Avery generosity." I wasn't successful in keeping bitterness out of my voice. After what had happened, I couldn't stop worrying over the security of the village.

"Yes, by all means do a story," Lily Wu said. We turned and saw her standing behind us. Lily's black hair hung to her shoulders; there was a gardenia pinned over one ear. She wore a green *pareu* which wrapped her slim body like the sheath of a flower. There was little of the Oriental sibyl in Lily that day. Except for her oblique eyes, she looked completely Polynesian.

She dropped to her bare knees in the sand and reached inside the bosom of her *pareu* for a folded paper. "John Atherton sent this, Janice. He asked me to give it to you and say that Julia cannot bring herself to write but that she wants you to have it."

As I opened the crackling paper I heard Lily say to Steve, "Now you can do a really big story about Wainiha."

I read with a feeling of bewilderment at first, then with steadily rising joy as I understood its meaning. It was a deed to the land, to be held by David Kimu, Lydia Brent, and Grace Hamilton in trust for the Hawaiians as long as they or any of their descendants wished to live there. Provision about the number of houses, the number of families to occupy the village, etcetera, etcetera, I couldn't read because I began to cry. I brushed hastily at my eyes and rose, looking for Makaleha. I saw David instead and ran to him with the document.

"Yes," he said, laughing, "I know about it—my signature is on there." He took it from me and laid it on the *heiau*, with a rock over it and a *lei* on top.

"We'll tell the others after we finish eating. Right now there's work to be done."

David strode toward Steve and Lily, who were brushing sand from themselves. "The net is ready. Are you?"

He lifted one of Lily Wu's slim arms and said, "Think a doll like you can be of any help? We need somebody out there who can really *huki.*"

Lily said, "I've got all the Chuns to help. And Kapsung's family. Besides—there's Dynamite."

Dynamite indeed was at the water's edge, snapping enthusiastically at bits of foam. He was going to lose all the lacquer from his red toenails.

David wasn't looking at Dynamite. He was looking down at Lily. She dimpled at him.

"Try me. "

"Me too," Steve interrupted. "What I lack in brains I can make up in weight."

"Speaking of weight," I said, "look at that!"

Makaleha was wading majestically into the ocean with both hands firm on the net, while the pink *mumu* ballooned around her like a vast bright tent. She turned and called:

"You, Kulolo! Come, bring dose *wahines* and tellem *wikiwiki!* Evabody *hukilau* now, so we have one fine *luau!*"

We walked into the water and took hold of the net. The wind blew our hair into our faces, the Pacific lapped around us, and as we began to *huki,* our laughter mingled with the laughter of Wainiha's people.

THE END

About The Rue Morgue Press

The Rue Morgue vintage mystery line is designed to bring back into print those books that were favorites of readers between the turn of the century and the 1960s. The editors welcome suggests for reprints. To receive our catalog or make suggestions, write The Rue Morgue Press, P.O. Box 4119, Boulder, Colorado (1-800-699-6214). The Rue Morgue Press tries to keep all of its titles in print, though some books may go temporarily out of print for up to six months. The following list details the titles available as of September 2001.

Catalog of Rue Morgue Press titles May 2002

Titles are listed by author. All books are quality trade paperbacks measuring 9 by 6 inches, usually with full-color covers and printed on paper designed not to yellow or deteriorate. These are permanent books.

Joanna Cannan. The books by this English writer are among our most popular titles. Modern reviewers favorably compared our two Cannan reprints with the best books of the Golden Age of detective fiction. "Worthy of being discussed in the same breath with an Agatha Christie or a Josephine Tey."— Sally Fellows, Mystery News. "First-rate Golden Age detection with a likeable detective, a complex and believable murderer, and a level of style and craft that bears comparison with Sayers, Allingham, and Marsh."—Jon L. Breen, *Ellery Queen's Mystery Magazine*. Set in the late 1930s in a village that was a fictionalized version of Oxfordshire, both titles feature young Scotland Yard inspector Guy Northeast. *They Rang Up the Police* (0-915230-27-5, 156 pages, $14.00) and *Death at The Dog* (0-915230-23-2, 156 pages, $14.00).

Glyn Carr. The author is really Showell Styles, one of the foremost English mountain climbers of his era as well as one of that sport's most celebrated historians. Carr turned to crime fiction when he realized that mountains provided a ideal setting for committing murders. The 15 books featuring Shakespearean actor Abercrombie "Filthy" Lewker are set on peaks scattered around the globe, although the author returned again and again to his favorite climbs in Wales, where his first mystery, published in 1951, *Death on Milestone Buttress* (0-915230-29-1, 187 pages, $14.00), is set. Lewker is a marvelous Falstaffian character whose exploits have been praised by such discerning critics as Jacques Barzun and Wendell Hertig Taylor in *A Catalogue of Crime*. Other critics have been just as kind: "You'll get a taste of the Welsh countryside, will encounter names replete with consonants, will be exposed to numerous snippets from Shakespeare and will find Carr's novel a worthy representative of the cozies of two generations ago."—*I Love a Mystery*.

Clyde B. Clason. Clason has been praised not only for his elaborate plots and skillful use of the locked room gambit but also for his scholarship. He may be one of the few mystery authors—and no doubt the first—to provide a full bibliography of his sources. *The Man from Tibet* (0-915230-17-8, 220 pages, $14.00) is one of his best (selected in 2001 in *The History of Mystery* as one of the 25 great amateur detective novels of all time) and highly recommended by the dean of locked room mystery scholars, Robert Adey, as "highly original." It's also one of the first popular novels to make use of Tibetan culture. Locked inside the Tibetan room of his Chicago apartment, the rich antiquarian was overheard repeating a forbidden occult chant under the watchful eyes of Buddhist gods. When the doors were opened, it appeared that he had succumbed to a heart attack. But the elderly Roman historian and sometime amateur sleuth Theocritus Lucius Westborough is convinced that Adam Merriweather's death was anything but natural and that the weapon was an eight century Tibetan manuscript.

Joan Coggin. *Who Killed the Curate?* Meet Lady Lupin Lorrimer Hastings, the young, lovely, scatterbrained and kindhearted newlywed wife to the vicar of St. Marks Parish in Glanville, Sussex. When it comes to matters clerical, she literally doesn't know Jews from Jesuits and she's hopelessly at sea at the meetings of the Mothers' Union, Girl Guides, or Temperance Society but she's determined to make husband Andrew proud of her—or, at least, not to embarass him too badly. So when Andrew's curate is poisoned, Lady Lupin enlists the help of her old society pals, Duds and Tommy Lethbridge, as well as Andrew's nephew, a British secret service agent, to get at the truth. Lupin refuses to believe Diane Lloyd, the 38-year-old author of children's and detective stories could have done the deed, and casts her net out over the other parishioners. All the suspects seem so nice, much more so than the victim, and Lupin announces she'll help the killer escape if only he or she confesses. Imagine Billie Burke, Gracie Allen of Burns and Allen or Pauline Collins of *No, Honestly* as a sleuth and you might get a tiny idea of what Lupin is like. Set at Christmas 1937 and first published in England in 1944, this is the first American appearance of *Who Killed the Curate?* "Coggin writes in the spirit of Nancy Mitford and E.M. Delafield. But the books are mysteries, so that makes them perfect."—Katherine Hall Page. "Marvelous."—*Deadly Pleasures* (0-915230-44-5, $14.00).

Manning Coles. The two English writers who collaborated as Coles are best known for those witty spy novels featuring Tommy Hambledon, but they also wrote four delightful—and funny—ghost novels. *The Far Traveller* (0-915230-35-6, 154 pages, $14.00) is a stand-alone novel in which a film company unknowingly hires the ghost of a long-dead German graf to play himself in a movie. "I laughed until I hurt. I liked it so much, I went back to page 1 and read it a second time."—Peggy Itzen, *Cozies, Capers & Crimes*. The other three books feature two cousins, one English, one American, and their spectral pet monkey who got a little drunk and tried to stop—futilely and fatally—a German advance outside a small French village during the 1870 Franco-Prussian War. Flash forward to the 1950s where this comic trio of friendly ghosts rematerialize to aid relatives in danger in *Brief Candles* (0-915230-24-0, 156 pages, $14.00), *Happy Returns* (0-915230-31-3, 156 pages, $14.00) and *Come and Go* (0-915230-34-8, 155 pages, $14.00).

Norbert Davis. There have been a lot of dogs in mystery fiction, from Baynard Kendrick's guide dog to Virginia Lanier's bloodhounds, but there's never been one quite like Carstairs. Doan, a short, chubby Los Angeles private eye, won Carstairs in a crap game, but there never is any question as to who the boss is in this relationship. Carstairs isn't just any Great Dane. He is so big that Doan figures he really ought to be considered another species. He scorns baby talk and belly rubs—unless administered by a pretty girl—and growls whenever Doan has a drink. His full name is Dougal's Laird Carstairs and as a sleuth he rarely barks up the wrong tree. He's down in Mexico with Doan, ostensibly to convince a missing fugitive that he would do well to stay put. The case is complicated by three murders, assorted villains, and a horrific earthquake that cuts the mountainous little village of Los Altos off from the rest of Mexico. Doan and Carstairs aren't the only unusual visitors to Los Altos. There's Patricia Van Osdel, a ravishing blonde whose father made millions from flypaper, and Captain Emile Perona, a Mexican policeman whose long-ago Spanish ancestor helped establish Los Altos. It's that ancestor who brings teacher Janet Martin to Mexico along with a stolen book that may contain the key to a secret hidden for hundreds of years in the village church. Written in the snappy hardboiled style of the day, *The Mouse in the Mountain* (0-915230-41-0, 151 pages, $14.00) was first published in 1943 and followed by two other Doan and Carstairs novels. "Each of these is fast-paced, occasionally lyrical in a hard-edged way, and often quite funny. Davis, in fact, was one of the few writers to successfully blend the so-called hardboiled story with farcical humor."—Bill Pronzini, *1001 Midnights*. Staff pick at The Sleuth of Baker Street in Toronto, Murder by the Book in Houston and The Poisoned Pen in Scotsdale. Four star review in *Romantic Times*. "A laugh a minute romp...hilarious dialogue and descriptions...utterly engaging, downright fun read...fetch this one! Highly recommended."—Michele A. Reed, *I Love a Mystery*. "Deft, charming...unique...one of my top ten all time favorite novels."—Ed Gorman, *Mystery Scene*. The second book, *Sally's in the Alley* (0-915230-46-1, $14.00), was equally well-received. *Publishers Weekly*: "Norbert Davis committed suicide in 1949, but his incomparable crime-fighting duo, Doan, the tippling private eye, and Carstairs, the huge and preternaturally clever Great Dane, march on in a re-release of the 1943 *Sally's in the Alley*, the second book in the dog-detective trilogy. Doan's on a government-sponsored mission to find an ore deposit in the Mojave Desert, but he's got to manage an odd (and oddly named) bunch of characters—Dust-Mouth Haggerty knows where the mine is but isn't telling; Doc Gravelmeyer's learning how undertaking can be a 'growth industry;' and film star Susan Sally's days are numbered—in an old-fashioned romp that matches its bloody crimes with belly laughs." The editor of *Mystery Scene* chimed in: "Enid and Tom Schantz, bless 'em, have just published the second novel by Norbert Davis, one of the most overlooked of all great pulp writers. This one is a comic look at the effects of WWII on the homefront. If you write fiction, or are thinking of writing fiction, or know someone who is writing fiction or is at least thinking of writing fiction, Davis is worth studying. John D. MacDonald always put him up, even admitted to imitating him upon occasion. I love Craig Rice. Davis is her equal."

Elizabeth Dean. Dean wrote only three mysteries, but in Emma Marsh she created one of the first independent female sleuths in the genre. Written in the screwball style of the 1930s, *Murder is a Collector's Item* (0-915230-19-4, $14.00) is described in a review in *Deadly Pleasures* by award-winning mystery writer Sujata Massey as a story that "froths over with the same effervescent humor as the best Hepburn-Grant films." Like the second book in the trilogy, *Murder is a Serious Business* (0-915230-28-3, 254 pages, $14.95), it's set in a Boston antique store just as the Great Depression is drawing to a close. *Murder a Mile High* (0-915230-39-9, 188 pages, $14.00), moves to the Central City Opera House in the Colorado mountains, where Emma has been summoned by am old chum, the opera's reigning diva. Emma not only has to find a murderer, she may also have to catch a Nazi spy. A reviewer for a Central City area newspaper warmly greeted this reprint: "An endearing glimpse of Central City and Denver during World War II. . . . the dialogue twists and turns. . . . reads like a Nick and Nora movie. . . . charming."—*The Mountain-Ear.* "Fascinating."—*Romantic Times.*

Constance & Gwenyth Little. These two Australian-born sisters from New Jersey have developed almost a cult following among mystery readers. Critic Diane Plumley, writing in *Dastardly Deeds*, called their 21 mysteries "celluloid comedy written on paper." Each book, published between 1938 and 1953, was a stand-alone, but there was no mistaking a Little heroine. She hated housework, wasn't averse to a little gold-digging (so long as she called the shots), and couldn't help antagonizing cops and potential beaux. The Rue Morgue Press intends to reprint all of their books. Currently available: *The Black Coat* (0-915230-40-2, 155 pages, $14.00), *Black Corridors* (0-915230-33-X, 155 pages, $14.00), *The Black Gloves* (0-915230-20-8, 185 pages,

$14.00), *Black-Headed Pins* (0-915230-25-9, 155 pages, $14.00), *The Black Honeymoon* (0-915230-21-6, 187 pages, $14.00), *The Black Paw* (0-915230-37-2, 156 pages, $14.00), *The Black Stocking* (0-915230-30-5, 154 pages, $14.00), *Great Black Kanba* (0-915230-22-4, 156 pages, $14.00), and *The Grey Mist Murders* (0-915230-26-7, 153 pages, $14.00), and *The Black Eye* (0-915230-45-3, 154 pages, $14.00).

Marlys Millhiser. Our only non-vintage mystery, *The Mirror* (0-915230-15-1, 303 pages, $17.95) is our all-time bestselling book, now in a sixth printing. How could you not be intrigued by a novel in which "you find the main character marrying her own grandfather and giving birth to her own mother," as one reviewer put it of this supernatural, time-travel (sort-of) piece of wonderful make-believe set both in the mountains above Boulder, Colorado, at the turn of the century and in the city itself in 1978. Internet book services list scores of rave reviews from readers who often call it the "best book I've ever read."

James Norman. The marvelously titled *Murder, Chop Chop* (0-915230-16-X, 189 pages, $13.00) is a wonderful example of the eccentric detective novel. "The book has the butter-wouldn't-melt-in-his-mouth cool of Rick in *Casablanca.*"—*The Rocky Mountain News.* "Amuses the reader no end."—*Mystery News.* "This long out-of-print masterpiece is intricately plotted, full of eccentric characters and very humorous indeed. Highly recommended."—*Mysteries by Mail.* Meet Gimiendo Hernandez Quinto, a gigantic Mexican who once rode with Pancho Villa and who now trains *guerrilleros* for the Nationalist Chinese government when he isn't solving murders. At his side is a beautiful Eurasian known as Mountain of Virtue, a woman as dangerous to men as she is irresistible. Together they look into the murder of Abe Harrow, an ambulance driver who appears to have died at three different times. First published in 1942.

Sheila Pim. *Ellery Queen's Mystery Magazine* said of these wonderful Irish village mysteries that Pim "depicts with style and humor everyday life." *Booklist* said they were in "the best tradition of Agatha Christie." *Common or Garden Crime* (0-915230-36-4, 157 pages, $14.00) is set in neutral Ireland during World War II when Lucy Bex must use her knowledge of gardening to keep the wrong person from going to the gallows. Beekeeper Edward Gildea uses his knowledge of bees and plants to do the same thing in *A Hive of Suspects* (0-915230-38-0, 155 pages, $14.00). *Creeping Venom* (0-915230-42-9, 155 pages, $14.00) mixes politics and religion into a deadly mixture.

Charlotte Murray Russell. Spinster sleuth Jane Amanda Edwards tangles with a murderer and Nazi spies in *The Message of the Mute Dog* (0-915230-

43-7, 156 pages, $14.00), a culinary cozy set just before Pearl Harbor. Our earlier title, *Cook Up a Crime*, is currently out of print.

Juanita Sheridan. Sheridan was one of the most colorful figures in the history of detective fiction, as you can see from Tom and Enid Schantz's introduction to *The Chinese Chop* (0-915230-32-1, 155 pages, $14.00). Her books are equally colorful, as well as showing how mysteries with female protagonists began changing after World War II. The postwar housing crunch finds Janice Cameron, newly arrived in New York City from Hawaii, without a place to live until she answers an ad for a roommate. It turns out the advertiser is an acquaintance from Hawaii, Lily Wu, whom critic Anthony Boucher (for whom Bouchercon, the World Mystery Convention, is named) described as an "exquisitely blended product of Eastern and Western cultures" and the only female sleuth that he "was devotedly in love with," citing "that odd mixture of respect for her professional skills and delight in her personal charms." First published in 1949, this ground-breaking book was the first of four to feature Lily and be told by her Watson, Janice, a first-time novelist. No sooner do Lily and Janice move into a rooming house in Washington Square than a corpse is found in the basement. In Lily Wu, Sheridan created one of the most believable—and memorable—female sleuths of her day. "Highly recommended."—*I Love a Mystery*. "This well-written. . .enjoyable variant of the boarding house whodunit and a vivid portrait of the post WWII New York City housing shortage, puts to lie the common misconception that strong, self-reliant, non-spinster-or-comic sleuths didn't appear on the scene until the 1970s. Chinese-American Lily Wu and her novelist Watson, Janice Cameron, are young and feminine but not dependent on men."—*Ellery Queen's Mystery Magazine*. Look for more books in this series in 2002.